Diamonds in the Rough

Vogue

Crown Jewelz Publishing

Diamonds In The Rough
Part One of The Diamond Collection
Second Edition
Copyright © 2013 Vogue

Cover Design by Vogue

ISBN: 978-0-9888004-2-7

Author Blog: www.simplyvogue.net
Email: blaq_pearls@yahoo.com

Acknowledgements

Dreams do come true. I give praise and glory to your name dear Lord for blessing me with this indescribable talent and answering my prayers.

I dedicate this book to the memory of Eldric and Geraldine Blanding. You taught me at an early age to reach for the stars and I did! I live to make you proud.

To Eldrena, you are a diamond that the world is waiting to see shine. The world is filled with endless possibilities. If one of us makes it, then we both make it! Don't ever give up on your dreams!

To Priscilla Murray, James Simpson, Thomas and Vernice Yates, Joel Blanding, Herbert and Delores C. McDowell, Alonzo and Shelldria Collins, LaBrenda Blanding, James and Corinne Trapp, Michael Blanding, Sharon Sutton, Seldrika Teamer, and Shalonda Blanding, thank you for continuously supporting me and being positive role models in my life. Much love to the Blanding and Simpson families. I love you all.

This book would not have been possible without the encouragement and guidance of the following people: Alisha Kennedy, Ashley Gary-Roper, Crystal Starkes, Ashley Grimball, Pauline McCollough, Sherise Jones, Rachelle Orange, Michael Kirk, Ursa Hawkins, Michael Burris, Angela Holland, Jose White, Scott Jackson, Barry Thompson, Cristina d'Erizans, Jamie Steele, Willie Graham, and Gwendolyn Spurlock. Thank you for always having a listening ear.

In addition, I must express sincere gratitude to the following individuals who have impacted my life in more ways than one: Shandy Manigault, Sharon Wallace, Miranda Williams, Kyvia Crisco, Michele Brock, Jessica Banks, Kelly Stratoti, Terrence Thompson, Patricia Kelsaw, Gregory and Angela Manigault, Carolyn Sawyer, William and Mary Bolden, Kristen Anderson, and Erin Byrnes-Green.

To Ramona Kennedy and family, thank you for always being my home away from home!

Act I:
The Good Girl

Chapter One

February

Carmen listened intently as her father read from the newspaper.

"Harold Davenport's company has grossed over four hundred million dollars in revenue this year, making the real estate company one of the biggest Brookstone has ever seen." Carmen's father looked at her, hoping to catch his daughter's reaction to the news. A smile flew across his face when he saw she was pleased. "This is why I've been working so hard lately," he said, picking up the paper.

Carmen smiled at her father's success and took the newspaper out his hands. His picture was on the front, shaking hands with no one other than the famous Donald Trump. "Well, if it isn't Mr. Harold Davenport, big time real estate agent," she said, picking at him.

Her father chuckled at her response and grabbed the paper from her. "Your mother cannot argue with me about those late night meetings anymore. According to this article, I'm on my way to becoming a billionaire," he said, holding the newspaper up.

Carmen displayed a small grin simply because she knew her father wasn't going to brag about his most recent payday without throwing some sort of life lesson in the mix.

"I mean, money isn't everything. It does pay the bills, and it's paying my daughter's tuition to Brookstone University. Money doesn't compare to family or love."

Carmen took a deep breath as her father mentioned college. His words reminded her she had class at one o'clock. She would have much preferred going in a few hours early to her mother's clothing store, Flame, than sitting in another lecture. However, her father was paying her tuition, which meant she had to be in attendance for *all* her classes. "Isn't that the truth," she replied, thinking out loud.

"I think your mother should plan a party in my honor. Invite a few of my co-workers, some of the church members. We can have it in the pool house. You can even invite some of your college friends. Do you think she'd do it?"

Carmen shrugged her shoulders. For the past two years, her mother, Patricia, had been complaining that her father wasn't ever around. She felt he was too wrapped up in his business. The party didn't seem to be a good idea to pitch.

"Don't tell me you're taking her side," her father said, jokingly.

"I haven't said anything," Carmen replied with a laugh. Her father chuckled, but Carmen could see he was worried about her mother's take on the praise he was getting.

"Do you want to get some lunch?" he asked, changing the subject. Harold didn't like pondering on the arguments he shared with his wife especially when the quarrels were tied to his business. Since they were both entrepreneurs, he figured his wife would understand his career before anyone else. However, he spent many nights, lying in bed next to her, often heated, because she claimed he spent too much time away from home. Now, it was obvious his hard work had paid off.

"I don't know. I was kind of planning on going to campus early. Tiara has a class that gets out at 12:15," she told him, mentioning her best friend.

"Oh, Lord," her father said, rolling his eyes. Tiara had been Carmen's best friend since they were in middle school. Even then, the girl had issues. She was always the fast one, trying to get with any and every guy. Her clothes were always risqué and showed off her lithe frame. Harold knew from the first time he saw Tiara she was trouble. It was no surprise when his wife informed him that Carmen had started coming home with stories about her.

"Daddy, don't," Carmen said, jumping to her friend's defense.

"Hey, you were the one who came home when you were in the sixth grade saying you saw her go in the boy's bathroom, only to come out with her skirt half up." Her father shook his head at the thought. He remembered how he prayed every night, since he'd heard the story, that his daughter wouldn't become loose. He was glad to know Carmen was a junior in college and still a virgin. He knew he couldn't protect her forever, but he had protected her for a very long time.

"She's still my best friend, though," Carmen reminded him.

"So you're going to skip out on lunch with me? I'll take you to Cipriani's," he said, begging for her company.

Carmen shook her head and hopped off the stool. Cipriani's was one of the most expensive Italian eateries in Brookstone. Although she was happy about her father's success, she didn't feel like listening to him rant and rave about his article in the paper. Besides, this wasn't the first time he made headlines. The article was only the first to name him as a multi-millionaire. "I'm not feeling it today," she announced, grabbing her tote from beside the refrigerator. She glanced at her father only to see the look of disappointment in his face. Instead of apologizing for skipping out on him, she pretended as if she hadn't noticed the expression.

"Okay, well, I'm going to go ahead and head to the office then," he said, getting off his stool as well.

Carmen watched as her father folded the paper in half, leaving it on the counter. He then left the kitchen without another word. Automatically, the room became filled with an eerie silence. Carmen knew her father was happy about the praise he was getting; however, he didn't know the effect his success had on her. Every day, she had to walk around the city being known as, "the rich man's daughter." It was bad enough in high school when her friends discovered her mother owned Flame, a clothing boutique, where they frequently shopped. Carmen always got teased for being conceited, despite the fact she never exhibited it. It was Tiara who did, and her parents barely made ends meet.

Carmen shrugged her shoulders at the thought and grabbed her keys off the counter. The second she left the kitchen; she could hear her father coming down the steps in the foyer.

"Have a good day, Peaches," he said, opening the door.

"You, too, Daddy," Carmen replied, walking in front of him. A daddy's girl at heart, a part of her felt guilty for declining his offer. The guilt alone made her watch him as he got in his Mercedes Benz. Already, she was having second thoughts. When he pulled out the driveway, she knew the chance was lost. Instead of telling him she changed her mind, she slid in her Lexus and closed the door. She would make it up to him, but she didn't know how quite yet.

***

Carmen stood in the foyer of Gardner Hall waiting for Tiara's class to end. The foyer was somewhat empty with only three or four other students in the area. With fifteen minutes till the end of the current lecture, Carmen appreciated the silence though it was short-lived. Time flew by and the hallway soon became filled with chit, chatter, and warm bodies. Only a few doors down from Tiara's classroom, Carmen looked through the mobs of people for her friend. When she spotted her, she couldn't help to notice her attire for the day. Tiara wore a white button-up, dark denim boot-cut jeans, and a pair of Steve Madden Spikley red pumps. Always one for flair, Carmen broadened her smile once Tiara took notice of her.

"If it isn't Miss Rich Girl," Tiara said, jokingly, shoving a copy of *The Brookstone Times* in Carmen's hands. "Your last name is being spread like wildfire all over this damn town. I know you're proud of your papa, selling one of his high-priced buildings to Mr. Donald Trump."

"Hey, that's my daddy's success, not mine," Carmen said, laughing.

"Yeah, yeah, yeah, my teacher couldn't stop talking about your damn daddy. The good thing is that the article got us out of listening to another lecture. What are you up to?"

"I wanted to hang for a minute before my class. Have you eaten?"

"Nah, I woke up late. I didn't have time to grab anything. Why don't we go to the diner on the Westside?"

Carmen wrinkled her face in disgust at the idea of going to the slums of West Brookstone. The Westside was known for its high crime rate and gang-related activity. While it was Tiara's stomping grounds, Carmen preferred not to frequent the area. On the other hand, Tiara couldn't stomach East Brookstone. *The land of the ritzy and boogie,* Tiara would say. Carmen would always debate the issue while reminding Tiara of their latest fiascos. In fact, she was doing it now. "There are drug dealers all up and through that place. Do you remember the crackhead who pissed behind my car at the house party we went to? What about the gunshot we heard?"

"Carm, nobody's going to hurt you. Now, I'm hungry. We're either going to head to this diner, or you're going to have to treat me to lunch. I don't have any extra cash to be eating at one of those ritzy places you're always going to." Tiara placed her hand on her hip, eyeing her friend quizzically.

"Alright, but I only have like forty minutes. We're going to have to be quick about it. Shoot, I don't mind treating you, but if I do it once then you'll be expecting it every time we're together," Carmen joked.

"Carm, it takes twenty minutes to get there. We might as well go to the cafeteria."

"I'll skip then. We're not doing anything important," Carmen said, making the decision quickly. In less than thirty minutes, she had completely forgotten about how much money her father was paying out of pocket for her education.

"Girl, they are looking for you to be in class. Everyone is talking about your rich daddy," Tiara replied, thinking Carmen was stupid for skipping. If it was her, she would've gone to class to get the praise. She loved attention and craved every second of it.

"Please, it's not that serious. They've known about my father's business since he started it. He takes a picture with a rich white man and now everyone wants to go crazy." Carmen placed the newspaper on top of Tiara's binder.

"It was Donald Trump."

Carmen rolled her eyes, wanting to forget about the issue. "Let's go," she said, turning to walk out the building.

Carmen heard Tiara sigh behind her, but she ignored her. She had to constantly remind her that they both cared about two different things. She could care less about fame, while Tiara hung onto every bit of it. She thought that was one of the reasons Tiara had decided to pledge Delta Sigma Theta in the fall. Her friend wanted attention and wanted everyone to know her name.

"Have you checked out that club, Sapphire?" Tiara asked as they reached Carmen's car. "Everyone has been talking about it lately. I don't know why. It's been open for a while."

Carmen shrugged her shoulders. "We can go tomorrow if you want. I know you party hard." Carmen waited for her friend's response, but Tiara remained quiet. It wasn't until they were inside the car she finally spoke.

"You know me," she said, facing Carmen. "I'm always down for a good party. Besides, I want to meet someone new. These two days without sex is killing me. I can't be like you, saving myself for Boris Kodjoe."

Carmen laughed at her comment as she pulled out the parking lot. She wasn't saving herself for Boris Kodjoe, though she was saving herself.

"You need to get with one of these Brookstone boys. They are all up on you, Carm. You don't want to give them a chance."

"No, I simply haven't found someone I really like."

Carmen's mind wandered to memories of the last few guys she had been out with. None of them had the complete package. In fact, most of them were only checking for the money they heard she had. What they didn't realize is that she didn't have any. The only money in her bank account was from the checks she received from working at her mother's store. While her parents were her providers, she didn't have access to any of their money. It didn't take long for a guy to realize that and soon lose interest. For that reason, Carmen remained single, abstinent, and hardly looking for love at all. She figured it would be the same for today when she pulled in front of the diner. Rather packed, she was lucky to find a park near the front of the restaurant so she could keep a lookout on her car.

When she walked inside, she made sure to stay close to Tiara, noticing that one booth in the diner was packed with a group of guys. The diner was known to be a hot spot for a lot of drug deals. It explained why the restaurant was always crowded and a police officer was on duty in the evenings.

"Let's sit here," Tiara said, choosing the booth across from the guys.

Carmen knew she had chosen the seat on purpose when she saw Tiara's gaze go right to the guys' booth. She was maintaining eye contact with them while at the same time shooting them a smile that clearly expressed her interest. Carmen didn't bother to look their way. Instead, she sat in the booth without even a glance in their direction. She kept her eyes planted on her menu until the waitress came and took their drink orders.

"What's your name?" she heard one of the guys ask. Since she wasn't looking in his direction, she knew the question was directed at Tiara.

"It's Tiara Smith, and yours?"

"Carlos Rodriguez," the guy replied. "Why don't y'all come join us?"

Carmen looked at Tiara, giving her a look that said no. Then, without thinking, she glanced at the guys in the booth opposite of them. It took only a split second for her to notice a caramel-complexioned guy looking her way. They met eyes for a quick moment, but it was all Carmen needed. For the one second she stared at him, Carmen was certain she could draw a picture of his face. His hair was closely shaven, and he bore a beautiful set of hazel eyes that reminded her of a summer sunset. She wanted to look again yet her nerves kept her face towards Tiara's.

"I think we're fine right here," Tiara said, pleasing Carmen with her response.

"We ain't gonna bite; we wanna get to know you. If you ask me, I think my boy wants to get to know your friend, too. He can't take his eyes off her."

The comment made Carmen turn her head in the direction of the guy. Like his friend stated, he was staring directly at her. That is, until she looked at him. His gaze was now on his food as if he hadn't been looking at her at all.

"You want to go?" Tiara asked, breaking her gaze.

Carmen shook her head and listened as Tiara told Carlos no once again. He looked disappointed and immediately started whispering a few words under his breath. Before she knew it, Carlos was sliding out the booth. She figured since Tiara wouldn't come to his booth, his next move was to join them. Carlos sat next to Tiara and immediately stroked her jet black hair with his fingers. While Tiara smiled at the affection, Carmen became somewhat uncomfortable. To add to her nervousness, she listened as Carlos invited the rest of his friends to their table.

"Jay, Malik, Rakim," he called out, waving to the other guys in the booth. "There's plenty of room. Bring your asses over here."

Carlos' antics were unwanted by Carmen and Jay. Matter of fact, Jay turned away from his friend, ignoring the request. Nevertheless, he couldn't stay turned away for long. The girl in the booth had captivated him and he was searching his mind for why. There was something different about her, yet he couldn't quite put his finger on it. She was pleasing to the eye, bearing a blemish-free chestnut brown complexion that matched perfectly with her beautiful, bouncy hair that stopped at the base of her neck. Her curvy figure was perfectly proportionate, and he could see she had expensive taste. Most girls weren't driving a Lexus in West Brookstone, at least not the model she was in. It raised a red flag in Jay's mind as he tried to figure out who she was. West Brookstone was home to a rival drug dealer, Pierre, who was known to keep only top notch chicks around him. She could've belonged to him, or she could've been the daughter of a judge or doctor in East Brookstone who simply wanted to get a taste of the Westside.

"Damn, Jay, you've been staring long enough," Carlos said, slamming his hand on the table. "Bring your ass over here."

"Y'all go ahead," Jay said to Malik and Rakim, eyeing the girl once more. He was still apprehensive about approaching her. When he didn't get a response from his friends, he turned to look at them.

Malik and Rakim Washington were two twins originally from Virginia who he put on his team when they were in high school. They were much younger than him and Carlos and looked to be the same age as the girls in the booth. Too busy eating to pay the girls any mind, Jay could tell they weren't interested.

"You don't want to go over there?" Malik questioned, sliding a French fry in his mouth.

Jay shook his head as he continued listening to Carlos' conversation.

"Are you in college?" Carlos asked one of the girls.

"Yeah, we go to Brookstone," Tiara replied. "We're both majoring in Business."

Carlos noticed they were on the wrong side of town.

"I live on the Westside. I'm over on Rochester," Tiara continued, seeing the waitress returning with their drinks.

"You're from the same hood as Malik and Rakim," Carlos said, turning to look at his friends. He planted his eyes on Jay because he knew his friend was trying to act hard. He wanted to pretend like he didn't want to talk to Tiara's friend when it was obvious she caught his eye. If it wasn't the girl then Carlos knew it was the Lexus. Jay was probably wondering if she was a girl Pierre had scooped up. A known enemy of Jay's, his friend probably wanted to know if she was claimed by his rival before he spit game.

"Would you like to order now?" the waitress asked.

Her presence interrupted Carlos' thoughts while it gave Carmen the opportunity to look over at the booth. The guy, who she assumed was Jay, was busy eating his food, which meant his eyes weren't focused on her. It gave her the opportunity to study him even more. From what she could see this time around, he was extremely tall, way over six feet and appeared to be biracial. In addition, he had a set of keys lying next to his plate. The Rolls Royce keychain automatically made her shift her focus from him to the parking lot. A Rolls Royce was parked outside, which told her he was the one driving it. She looked at him, giving them both the opportunity to lock eyes again. This time, he didn't turn away until after a few seconds.

Carmen became lost in her thoughts as she started to wonder what the guy did to be driving a Rolls Royce. She hated to judge him, but the only thing she could think of was that he was a hustler. *Shoot, it doesn't help we're on the Westside. This is where drugs reign supreme*, she thought. Carmen sighed and glanced at Tiara, who was giggling away at a joke. Unsure of what she and Carlos were discussing, she knew she wouldn't get a chance to find out when she heard one of the guys in the booth ask, "Is that your car?"

Carmen turned to face the parking lot and uttered a sigh of agitation. A man dressed rather ruggedly was knocking on the front driver's side window of her car. The sight of him made her look at Tiara as a wave of déjà vu came over her. "I guess I'll handle this one," she told her, recalling the last incident she had with a drug addict. Tiara only shrugged her shoulders as she stood up. Carmen told the waitress to give her a second, however, she didn't expect for Jay to block her path.

"I got it," he said, holding his hand up to her, "order your food."

Carmen parted her lips to respond yet Jay was walking out the diner. If he thought she was going to stay inside and let him handle the situation, he was mistaken. It was her car, and she was going to deal with the addict who mistook it for a drug dealer's.

"Get the fuck off that car," Jay was saying once she got outside.

She watched him as he pulled the man away, pushing him in the opposite direction of the restaurant. Obviously homeless, his clothes were torn, his salt and pepper hair bushy and he stunk of urine and last month's trash.

"You got something for me, man? I know you do."

Jay gave the man another hard shove towards the street, trying his best to direct him away from the restaurant. "I don't have shit for you. You can't be rolling up on people's cars like that. Do you know what I would do if you rolled up on my car?" Jay lifted his shirt, revealing the nine millimeter that was tucked perfectly in his waistband. It didn't scare the man off, only intensifying his need for a quick high.

"I need a hit, man. You got something for me?"

"Get your ass out of here."

"You always got something, man. I know about you. I know what you do. You got something, man." The crackhead started pacing the parking lot and before long, he was scratching at his left arm.

"Look, man, don't roll up on this Lexus again. I'll smoke you for that shit, real talk." Jay knew he had scared the man because he started walking away from the diner. He didn't mind missing the sale when he knew his biggest customers were on the corporate level. CEOs and stockbrokers were his main customers and how he made his real money. Crackhead money was only chump change. The high school boys Carlos put on dealt with them. He would only sit back and collect his paper.

Jay pushed the thought of crackheads and drug dealing out his mind when he remembered the girl was still standing there. "You should've stayed inside. I had this," he said, leading the way inside the diner.

"It's my car," she replied with an attitude. "I had this."

Jay took a long look at her, stunned almost in a way at how she responded. She was innocent while at the same time, she was feeding him attitude that surprisingly turned him on. He gave her a closer look. She was built to perfection with a full bosom and hips that were accentuated nicely in her Roberto Cavalli jeans. Her beauty alone made him forget about her snide remark. In fact, he followed her to her table and even motioned for Malik and Rakim to join him in the booth. Though he had warned himself of her, his dick was now talking for him.

"I knew you were going to come over," Carlos admitted as he made room for the twins.

"Nah, you had a lucky hunch," Jay said, digging in his coleslaw. He put some of it in his mouth and looked at the girl, watching her sip on her drink. He swallowed and then proceeded to pursue her. "What's your name?"

"Carmen," she answered after taking the straw out her mouth.

"I'm Jay," he said, looking at her nails. Nicely manicured, he took a closer look at her appearance. Her teeth were blindingly white and straight while her shoes appeared to have been worn for the first time. Her jewelry appeared to be of the upmost quality and not one single strand of hair was out of place. When he saw her lips move again, he gave her his full attention.

"I know," she muttered. "Your friend introduced you."

Jay narrowed his eyes as he caught another whiff of her sarcasm. This time, it wasn't a turn on. If that was how she normally was, Jay knew he would be turned off quick.

"Carmen doesn't frequent this area much," Tiara explained, trying to take the tension off the table. "She lives on the Eastside. You know how those Eastside people are."

"How are they?" Jay asked, eyeing Tiara. "I live on the Eastside."

Tiara straightened her grin as she realized she backed herself in a corner. Nonetheless, as quickly as she had gotten there, Carlos swooped in and saved the day.

"Y'all party?" Carlos asked, thinking of Jay's club, Sapphire. He felt Jay's eyes burning on his, but he didn't care. He wanted to see Tiara again and he knew Jay already had his eye on Carmen. Sapphire was the perfect place for their second meeting to be.

"The party doesn't start until we get there," Tiara exclaimed.

"Then y'all need to come by Jay's spot," Carlos said, sneaking one of Malik's fries. "He owns Sapphire; it's over there on the Eastside. Y'all probably have already been there."

Jay tensed up, not wanting Carmen to know he owned a club. If he was honest then he would admit he didn't want her to know anything about him. He only wanted to know about her. Nevertheless, he had already given her a clear indication of his business endeavors when he ran off the crackhead. For all he knew, he could've scared her off before he had the chance to pursue her.

"You own the club?" Carmen asked, wondering how old Jay was. He looked to be in his twenties, but now she was guessing he was probably in his early thirties. He gave her a look as his response, allowing Carlos to answer for him. When his friend said yes, Carmen inquired some more, "How did you get a club?"

"A lot of people can get a club," he responded, dryly. He gave Carlos a mean glare to let him know he spilled the beans too soon. Carlos didn't seem to care because he only went back to talking to Tiara.

Still, Jay knew Carmen was going to continue to question him. Eventually, he would have to give her answers, which meant digging up his past.

"The reason I asked is because my mother owns Flame downtown. She has been talking about expanding and I might be managing my own store one day. We're not in the same industry, but you never know, maybe, we can network or something." Carmen waited for his response, yet she only received another glance. This time, her stomach twisted as their eyes met as she was reminded of the nine millimeter in his waistband. It instantly made her want to retract her statement. Though she couldn't deny her attraction, the gun was a clear reminder Jay wasn't what she wanted or needed.

Chapter Two

The reservations Carmen had about Jay remained on her mind well into the evening. Neither class nor her father's continuous display of excitement over his company's sale could keep his image out her mind. Even as she lay sprawled out on her parents' bed, she was barely listening to their conversation about the article. It wasn't until her father left the room she came back to reality.

"If I hear Donald Trump one more time," Patricia fussed. "I swear, Carmen, I'm going to scream."

Carmen peered at her mother, watching her as she placed several blouses in a drawer.

"Just think, I still have to go to dinner with the man," her mother said, loudly. "He's going to be bragging the entire time."

Carmen knew it had been a while since Flame had been acknowledged in any form of media. It was only natural for her mother to be annoyed or to exhibit some form of jealousy. "You would be the same way if they had written about Flame in the paper," Carmen replied, sharing her thoughts.

"No, I would act civilize. Your father wants me to throw a party in the pool house in his honor. It's not that serious."

Speaking of party, Carmen thought as her mind wandered to the guy she met at the diner. *This might be the best time to talk about Jay.* "Have you ever been with a thug?" Carmen blurted.

Disapproval formed on her mother's face as she stared blankly in her eyes. "Carmen Denise Davenport, do I look like the kind of woman who wants to get caught up in a case? I hope you're not trying to bring home a hoodlum."

Carmen twisted her mouth, remembering how her mother felt about the people who lived in West Brookstone. She had warned her of them ever since she was a little girl. Her mother played a huge role in what she thought of the Westside. Still, Carmen knew she couldn't stereotype everyone who lived in West Brookstone. Matter of fact, it was Jay, a resident of East Brookstone, who pulled out a gun at the diner.

"See, I met this guy today," Carmen started to explain. "He kind of has an edge."

"Is he a thug, Carm? He wears baggy jeans, big t-shirts, and big ass chains?"

"I mean, he's got an edge."

"He's a man who hustles, bustles, all for the cash?"

Carmen laughed so hard at her mother's antics; she almost didn't take her seriously. However, she had to remember the question was serious to her. From what she had seen at the diner, Jay was obviously a drug dealer. She wanted to tell her mother he was a hustler, yet she didn't want to ruin the chance of her mother fully accepting him—if she decided to pursue him. "I don't know," she finally replied. "He drives a Rolls Royce. I met him in West Brookstone."

"Thug," her mother quickly responded, heading to her closet.

"That's a stereotype."

"Yeah, but that's where the hoodlums are," Patricia replied. She stared in her walk-in closet, forgetting about the conversation as she debated over which dress to wear that night. Though her husband was still on his Donald Trump high, it would be in her best interest to go out to dinner with him. She needed to be seen on his arm in one of her latest designs. Just her luck, her newest piece would catch the eye of the public and instantly boost sales.

For the last two years, Patricia had been hiding from her family that sales had plummeted. While she did want to breakdown and ask for help, she didn't want to appear weak beside a man whose success was the hot topic of the city. Patricia believed once she kicked off a new marketing campaign, she could bring more revenue to her store.

Meanwhile, Carmen's mind was far from anything involving Flame. She was still focused on Jay and was even starting to feel as if she had wasted her time. Her mother was convinced that West Brookstone only bred hoodlums, which meant she would never accept him. It was best for her to simply end the conversation, which she did when she left her parents' room. She walked inside her own right when her cell phone started ringing. When she saw Tiara's name flash on the screen, she knew her best friend was ready for a night on the town.

"Guess who called me," Tiara yelled when Carmen picked up.

"This isn't a hard one, it's Carlos."

"You're right on the money. There's a block party going down over here on the Westside tonight. It's hosted by some guy named Pierre. Carlos invited me to come and word on the block is that Jay put in a special request for you to be there, too."

"I don't believe you," Carmen snapped. "Admit it. You don't want to go by yourself."

"Okay, I lied. The truth is, I don't want to go by myself," Tiara shot back. "I even called Monifah to see if she wanted to come. When was the last time we all hung out?"

"It has been awhile," Carmen admitted, thinking about the mutual friend they shared. She wrinkled her face as she thought about whether to go or not. Her mother wouldn't be pleased to know she was heading to the Westside, which meant she had to keep it a secret. If her mother was still home when she left, she would have to tell her they were going to a comedy show.

"Great, then get dressed and meet me at my place at like ten. I'll drive us there since I know where it is."

Carmen agreed to the plan and hung up the phone. Tiara hadn't left her much time to get ready, which meant she had to find something quick. If Jay was at the block party, she did want him to notice her. Whether a second conversation would occur, she didn't know, but she could at least wear something to catch his eye.

The second she opened her closet, her eyes landed on a pair of white gauchos and a royal blue and white striped tube top. The outfit exhibited sex appeal while at the same time maintained her classiness. Carmen pulled the items from her closet along with a pair of gold thong sandals since it was rather warm outside.

"Peaches," her father called, knocking on the door.

Carmen turned around having forgotten she had left her door ajar. Her father was dressed in an all-black suit, which had been accentuated with a maize pocket square and tie. From the way he was dressed, Carmen knew he was taking her mother to a five star restaurant.

"You're going out?" he asked, gazing at the clothes in her arms. "I thought you were in for the night."

"We're going to a comedy show," Carmen lied. She gave her father an innocent smile, which she could see he bought. He was easy to fib to because he wouldn't prod in her business like her mother.

"Well, your mother and I are going to be out for a while. I got a few things planned she doesn't know about," he announced.

His eyes were still on her clothes as if he was debating about commenting. When his lips moved again, Carmen knew what to expect. "Is that what you're wearing tonight?" he asked.

Carmen held up the tube top so he could see the length. "It's appropriate. I'm not showing anything."

"How about you put on a little more fabric? A jacket would be nice," he suggested, winking at her.

Carmen nodded her head as if she was going to take his advice. The gesture seemed good enough for him because he walked out the room, heading to his bedroom. When she heard him ask her mother how she was coming along, Carmen knew they wouldn't be in her hair for long. Whether she wore a jacket or not, her father would never know. Besides, she had to leave something to the imagination and the tube top did just that.

***

Since Carmen had picked out her outfit in a short amount of time, she didn't consider how she would look up against her friends. Now that they were stepping in the vicinity of the block party, she was starting to feel like the oddball. Tiara, who was rather model-esque, wore a black tube dress that stopped mid-thigh while Monifah showed off her six-pack abs in a hot pink bra and black mesh top. Though her friends complimented her attire, Carmen debated about changing. When she was about to share her thoughts to Tiara, her friend cut her off.

"I don't even see them," she heard Tiara say as they walked past several parked cars. "Carlos said they were here."

"Who are they, anyway?" Monifah asked with an attitude.

Carmen watched as Tiara turned towards Monifah as if she should've already known who they were.

"Come on, Tee, you didn't tell me much about them and you know how I roll," Monifah continued. "I want a man with some benefits, 401K, an annuity, and some dividends."

"They do have money, lots of it," Tiara responded, stretching her eyes. "I don't think it's the kind you can put in a 401K, though."

Carmen frowned at Tiara's reply because her friend had admitted that Jay and his friends were involved in something illegal. While she had suspected it, Tiara's words made everything certain. It also made her feel as if she had wasted her time even coming to the block party. She could never bring anyone home to her parents who potentially had a record.

Carmen's thought left her mind when her eyes met with the bearer of the hazel eyes. Jay was staring directly at her, causing a knot to form in her stomach. Nevertheless, it wasn't because they were staring at each other. It was because he wasn't alone. A light-skinned girl dressed in a pair of white shorts and a tight black tank top had her arms around his neck while his arms were around her waist.

"There they are," Tiara announced, spotting Carlos and the rest of the guys they met at the diner. She headed over to them while Carmen's eyes focused in on Jay and his girlfriend.

"He's cute, but she isn't," Monifah said in her ear.

Carmen looked at her friend as she realized she been caught. Her disappointment had to be written on her face. It made her wonder if Jay could see it, too. When she looked at him, she noticed he was still staring at her. Not only noticeable to her, the girl he was with, grabbed his chin, and brought his face towards hers.

"Are you okay, Carm?" Monifah asked, seeing her friend almost in a trance.

"Yeah," Carmen muttered, trying to ease out a smile. "I'm a little thirsty. Do you want something to drink?"

"Nah, I'm good. I'm gonna go catch up with Tiara."

Carmen gave her friend another smile to ease her worries before heading in the direction of the refreshments. When she came to a table filled with drinks, she picked up one of the cups and took a quick sniff. Almost instantly, she smelled the alcohol and immediately set the cup back on the table.

"How about a soda then?" a guy asked her.

Carmen turned to her left to see a dark-skinned guy with cornrows offering her a can of Pepsi. She hadn't noticed him before and kindly took him up on his offer.

"Thanks," Carmen replied, taking the soda out his hand. She opened the can as her eyes went back on Jay. This time, she noticed he was standing in front of his Rolls Royce. The girl was still all over him, which gave Carmen the opportunity to dissect her. Obviously Latina, she had long silky black hair that had been flat-ironed bone straight and a large set of hips that were proportionate to her small waist. In Carmen's opinion, the two looked like the ideal couple with their matching complexions.

"Are you going to stand here all night?" a voice asked, interrupting her thoughts. Carmen turned to find the dark-skinned guy still standing beside her. This time, he had a Corona in his hand. She also could smell the hard stench of liquor on his breath.

"For the moment," she told him with a slight attitude. *Who is he?*, Carmen questioned. *I can stand wherever the hell I want.*

"You want to come chill in my Benz?"

Carmen glanced at him before replying with a quick no. The block party may have been filled with easy women, but she wasn't one of them.

"I'm messing with you, beautiful. I'm Pierre. This is my block party."

"Nice to meet you, I'm Carmen," she said, extending her hand. She remembered the name because Tiara had mentioned him on the phone. Pierre accepted the gesture, taking her hand in his and unexpectedly brought it to his lips. Carmen instantly felt chills when his lips touched her skin.

"As the host, it's my job to make sure you're having a good time. I want to see a smile on your face. If you aren't having a good time, then that's a problem I need to fix. Who did you come with?"

"I'm here with two of my friends."

"Ahh, they left you hanging?"

"Something kind of like that," Carmen joked. *That isn't the case. It's more like, I left them hanging. I couldn't stomach being over there with Jay and his girlfriend.*

"Oh, well, I got the nicest DJ here. Do you dance?"

"I dance," Carmen admitted, putting the Pepsi to her lips.

"Will you dance with me then?" he asked, setting the Corona on the table.

Carmen looked at Jay before she gave her response. The girl was now kissing his neck. Immediately when she noticed, she turned her head. There was obviously no way she and Jay were going to be able to talk. "Sure," she replied. She threw the rest of her Pepsi in a trash can and extended her hand once again to Pierre. While he wasn't Jay, he would at least keep her mind off him for the time being.

Pierre pulled her into the crowd and without hesitation, pressed his body up against hers. Closer than what Carmen intended, she decided to go with the flow. It seemed to work because she spent most of the evening dancing with him. Every now and then she would try and catch a peek of Jay, but towards the end of the night, she had forgotten all about him. She figured Pierre had felt a connection with her as well when he placed his mouth right beside her left ear.

"I want you to come chill with me tonight," he whispered.

Carmen narrowed her eyes at the offer. The last thing she wanted to do was lead Pierre on. She had no intention of sleeping with him and she knew that was what he wanted. She had to let him know it wasn't going to happen. "I can't," she told him, breaking away from him. He nodded his head, understandingly.

"I'm not going to hurt you, ma. I'll be straight up with my shit," he said, tightening his grip on her waist. "I got a baby mama. I also got about five different dudes who want to pop a bullet in my ass. I'm single, though. I fuck around a little bit, but I'm looking to settle down. I felt something tonight. Maybe, I could eventually settle down with you."

Carmen let out a deep sigh at how open and honest he was. "Well, that's all nice to know and what not. Still, I don't get down on the first night," she replied.

"That's cool, too. I only want to see what you're about."

"I don't get down on the second night either," she told him, hoping he caught the hint.

"I get it," Pierre said, pulling her close. "I can get you out those panties, ma. All I need is time." He brushed his lips against her cheek before planting a small peck on her lips.

Carmen wasn't one to move fast, however, she did like the affection. She only wanted him to be aware it wasn't going any further than that. When he asked for her number, she was quick to comply, yet she couldn't get the first digit out before they were interrupted.

"Do you see Carlos over there?" a brown-skinned guy asked who had come up beside them.

"I saw him. I'm going to get at him in a minute. I'm busy right now."

"Nah, we need to get at him now."

Carmen looked in the direction of Jay's Rolls Royce. She noticed that the Carlos they were discussing was the same Carlos she knew. That very same Carlos was also friends with Jay.

"He crossed you again. Word is that he's back working with Jay. He still hasn't paid you but took work from the next man."

"I'll take care of him in a minute, Shakeem."

"Nah, you need to get at him now. He's taking your shit, but you haven't seen any of the profits. I say we smoke him now."

Pierre looked at Carmen, knowing their conversation was over. He then looked at his right-hand who was pressuring him into dealing with an issue he wanted to see about after hours. Too many witnesses were around for what he really wanted to do. "You want to get him?"

Carmen stared at them and then looked at Carlos. She didn't know whether to warn him or stay put. She knew snitching was against the code of the streets, but she felt obligated to say something since Carlos was Jay's friend.

"Nah, we're a team when it comes to this shit. Jay is probably locked and loaded. Why did his ass show up here in the first place? Is he trying to extend an olive branch?"

Although Carmen had listened to their whole conversation, the only thing she could focus on was the word Jay that had come out Shakeem's mouth. If he was thinking of going at him, she was going to say something.

"Alright then," Pierre said, realizing he wasn't going to get a chance to chill. He looked at Carmen, somewhat upset, since he had to go see about business earlier than expected. Apparently, Carlos hadn't taken him seriously when he signed him on to his team. "Don't leave until I get back," he told her. "I want to spend the rest of the evening with you."

Carmen didn't have the intention of spending the rest of the evening with anyone. If anything, she was getting the hell out of dodge before anything popped off. All she needed to do was find her girls and they would be far away from the Westside in a few short minutes. In addition, she needed to find Jay.

The second Pierre let her out his grasp; she grabbed another Pepsi and headed in the direction of Jay's Rolls Royce. She figured Monifah and Tiara were still over there although she didn't necessarily see them at the car.

"So you're rolling with rapists now?"

Carmen felt someone's hand on her elbow, which made her stop in her tracks. The grip was tighter than she would have liked, and she was surprised when she looked up to see Jay. He was completely alone, which meant the opportunity was there for them to talk. She wasn't quite sure what he meant by his comment. Therefore, she hesitated in answering. To buy herself some time, she opened her soda can and took a long sip.

"Maybe you need to ask someone what you're getting yourself into. Why did you let him kiss you?"

"Maybe, you should mind your business," was her reply. She didn't really mean it, but she wanted to get back at him for not being available. To put even more gas on the flame, she walked away from him. He only followed her, keeping up with her every step.

"Hold on," he barked, grabbing her arm.

Carmen was startled and accidentally dropped the open soda can on the ground. The soda splashed everywhere, catching the attention of everyone around them and prompting a few others to move away.

"Sorry," Jay mumbled, not expecting for her to be caught off guard. While it wasn't his intention to make a mess, he now had her attention. "How do you know Pierre?"

"What does it matter to you? Where's your girlfriend, anyway?"

"Is that what this is about?"

Carmen was shocked at how he tried to flip the script on her. She hadn't made a single comment about the girl until he brought up Pierre. It was obvious he was bothered by her dancing with him. "Look, Jay, you're the one who approached me about Pierre. I'm trying to figure out why you care so much. Your mind should've been elsewhere."

"Pierre is not someone you want to get involved with."

"Thanks for the memo." Carmen turned away from him but felt him grab her arm once more.

"I'm serious, Carmen. You're not from the Westside. You don't know how these dudes roll. You're a rich chick from East Brookstone who is trying to hang in the hood. You're walking in this whole situation blind."

Carmen folded her arms across her chest. "You're right; I'm not from the Westside. I don't know Pierre and I don't know you. What I do know, however, is that Pierre doesn't play when it comes to his money. You might want to share that word of advice with Carlos."

"Does he have a hit out for Carlos?"

"Maybe," Carmen replied, moving her hands to her hips.

"Don't play with me. Does he have a hit out for Carlos?"

Carmen could see a sense of urgency in his face. She decided to take the matter serious as well. "Apparently, Carlos has been working for him, but not giving Pierre his cut," she told him. "Pierre left with a guy named Shakeem. I guess he went to get something to mess Carlos up. Right now, I'm looking for my girls. We need to get out of here before the bullets start spraying."

Jay mouthed the word *fuck*. "I knew Carlos was lying when he said he didn't sell for that motherfucker." Jay looked in the direction of his car and remembered Carmen's friends were inside. "Monifah and Tee are in my car," he told her, "y'all need to go ahead and go. No telling what is about to pop off."

"Great," Carmen told him, heading in that direction. She wanted to hurry up and find her friends. Hopefully, they wouldn't hear anything about the block party on the news that night.

"Carmen?" Jay grabbed her arm again, causing Carmen to pause in her tracks. "Good looking out." Jay watched as Carmen gave him a wink. When she started to walk off for the second time, he called her name again. She turned around to face him, giving him another chance to stare at her. "Tricia isn't my girlfriend," he continued. Jay made sure he cleared that up although he was lying through gritted teeth. He might've been taken, and Pierre might have pounced on her, but he was the one who had seen her first. He didn't have a hidden agenda while he knew Pierre simply wanted to break Carmen down until he had her opening her legs for anyone with a dollar. One thing was for sure, he would go head to head with Pierre over her.

"It doesn't matter," Carmen said with a chuckle. She pretended she never was interested and walked away from him. He didn't try and stop her, which meant she could finally get out the Westside.

In the meantime, Jay watched her as she left, wishing he didn't have to deal with the situation between Pierre and Carlos. If Carmen hadn't of dropped the dime that Pierre was looking to attack then he would've made sure they had more than a five minute conversation. Now, he had to find Carlos and possibly pull out some heat. He had allowed her to slip through his fingers, but he promised himself he was going to have her. *Good girls like bad guys*, he reminded himself. If Carmen was getting ready to get down with Pierre, then she could get down with him.

Chapter Three

The following afternoon, Carmen stood in the foyer of the Mulberry Building where her Finance class was held. This time, she wasn't waiting on Tiara, but simply passing the time. She figured if she stayed around campus, her peers and the scenery would help keep her mind off the situation between Pierre and Carlos. She learned quickly that the idea was farfetched. If she wasn't seeing Pierre in her mind then she was seeing Carlos and when they weren't there, which was most of the time, she saw Jay. She wondered if she would ever lay eyes on him again. If she really wanted to, Carmen knew where she could find him. Carlos had already told her that Jay owned Sapphire, which meant she could find him at the club.

"Carmen," a voice said, quietly.

Loud enough to catch her attention, Carmen turned to her left to see one of the twins she met at the diner. She didn't talk to him at the block party, but there he was, at Brookstone University, with a book bag on his back.

"Hi," she stuttered, not being able to tell which one it was.

"Rakim," he said, extending his hand. He waited until Carmen had shaken it before he pointed to the mole on his left cheek. It was the only blemish that would help her tell him and his brother, Malik, apart.

"Got it," she said with a giggle.

"I'm a student here," Rakim explained, knowing she was shocked at his presence. "I wanted to mention that at the diner, but there was a lot going on. I saw you at the block party, too, but we didn't get a chance to speak. I'm majoring in Biology."

"You have a tough major. Does Malik go here, too?"

"Nah, you know Malik rolls with Carlos and Jay all day, every day. He isn't about the books. I can't complain, though. If it wasn't for him and the two scholarships I have, I wouldn't be able to stay enrolled."

Carmen gave Rakim a big smile since she had finally found someone from West Brookstone to refute her mother's stereotype.

"Where are you headed?" he asked, looking around the hallway.

"I really didn't have a place in mind. I was just chilling out here to pass the time. What about you?"

"Jay is about to scoop me up. We're going to his club to get it ready for tonight. You want to come?"

Carmen shrugged her shoulders only because she didn't want to seem too excited over the opportunity to see Jay. In addition, she wasn't quite sure if the drama was over between his crew and Pierre's. "I don't know. Last night, at the block party, things were kind of heated."

Rakim smirked as he thought about the dime Carmen had dropped. Though she had snitched on Pierre, it showed she didn't have any loyalty to him. Rakim hoped it stayed that way since he knew of Pierre's history with women. The last thing he wanted was for a sheltered rich girl from East Brookstone to get caught in his web. "Things didn't go anywhere last night. Pierre didn't pop off at all. That shouldn't be your concern, though. What you need to be worried about is keeping yourself away from him. He's a pimp and he uses sweet talk to lure girls into his sex ring. You're not anything, but dollar signs to him."

"So I've heard," Carmen replied, recalling her conversation with Jay.

"Then, take heed to the warning."

Carmen raised her brow at him before facing the front entrance of the Mulberry Building. She was hoping to catch a glimpse of Jay's Rolls Royce, but only students were passing by. Rakim seemed to know what she was looking for and asked her again if she wanted to come to Sapphire. When she obliged, they made their way out the building and waited on the steps for Jay to arrive. For the fifteen minutes they waited, they made small talk until a black Rolls Royce pulled up in front of them.

"Let me make sure it's cool with Jay first," Rakim said, running down the steps.

Carmen remained where she was standing until Rakim motioned to her that it was okay. When she started to come down the steps, she saw Carlos as he moved out the front seat. When he slammed the door closed, she knew he disapproved of her joining them.

"Hey," Jay greeted as soon as she sat in the passenger seat.

"Hi," she replied, turning to look at him. They met eyes for a brief second before she stole away to look at Carlos in the rearview mirror. "Hi," she repeated, trying to settle the tension. His disgruntled expression didn't change so Carmen tried to compromise. "If you want the front seat, you can have it," she told him with a smile.

"I don't give a fuck about that," he blurted.

Carmen looked at Jay, somewhat confused about why Carlos was upset. Jay's eyes were already on hers as if he was merely waiting to give an explanation.

"He had a run-in earlier today with some of Pierre's goons. Give him a few minutes to calm down and he'll stop bitchin'."

Carmen bit her lip as she thought to the night before. Pierre had already been planning to go after Carlos and had sent his goons to do the job. It made her wonder if Jay had even told Carlos that Pierre was coming for him.

"They tried to run up on me like I was pussy or something. I left one of them bitches bleeding like a spilled drink. I could've done more damage if I knew someone was gunning after me. You like to run your mouth, but you didn't run it to the right person. I fucked up my jeans trying to kill those motherfuckers," Carlos yelled.

"Damn, Carlos," Rakim said, taking his book bag off his back. "They are going to be on your ass tonight."

"You don't think I know that shit? There needs to be topflight security if Jay doesn't want bullet holes in his walls."

Carmen tried her best to swallow her nervousness. If Carlos had goons after him, the last place she needed to be was in a car with him. Unfortunately, it was too late for her to get out. Jay had already pulled away from campus and was headed towards downtown Brookstone.

"I don't need topflight security," Jay shot back. "Pierre knows how I get down. Your concern should be the money you owe him."

"Pierre isn't losing any sleep over that money. He only cares about this bitch you got in the car. You know he got a hard-on for her."

Carmen turned around, facing Carlos. "What did you call me?"

"Everyone saw you and Pierre last night," Carlos ranted. "Most of the chicks at the party know to stay clear of him. Don't believe any of that bullshit he told you. He only wants to make money off you. He's a pimp, dope dealer, and a straight con artist. Once Pierre gets his eyes on a bitch, he doesn't want anyone else touching her unless they're paying the price. He would flip a bitch if he saw you in Jay's car."

"Shut the fuck up," Jay growled, looking at Carlos through the rearview mirror. He knew his friend was only trying to look out for Carmen but calling her out her name was about to get him put out the car. Besides, he had already talked to Carmen about Pierre. If she listened to him like he thought, she would never cross paths with him again.

"Shit, I'm telling her the truth. Pierre doesn't care about anything except a hard-on and a dollar."

Carmen turned around in her seat once more so she could clear the air on her and Pierre. "We don't have anything going on. I danced with him, talked to him for a bit, and that was it. We didn't even exchange numbers."

"You don't have to explain yourself, Carm."

Carmen parted her lips to respond to Rakim, yet Jay interrupted her. "Pierre isn't going to try anything."

Jay was being reassuring only because he knew something the others didn't. He had heard through the grapevine that Pierre was somewhat serious about Carmen. From a mutual friend of theirs, Jay had learned that Pierre had been asking any and everybody about the mystery girl at his block party. Just like him, Pierre had picked up on her innocence and had discovered he had found an untarnished jewel. The thought of Pierre's eyes on her warranted a phone call. Later that night, Pierre was scheduled to make an appearance and Jay's plan was to steer him away from all things Carmen. If things worked in his favor, Pierre would forget about her and in no time, he would make his move to win her heart.

***

Sapphire was less than ten minutes away from Brookstone University. While Carlos and Rakim had immediately went to one of the club's bars in VIP, Jay had directed Carmen upstairs to his office. Carmen assumed he wanted to talk to her in private; however, he wasn't saying one single word to her. He was too busy sifting through the stacks of papers on his desk to even hold a conversation. After five minutes of silence, Carmen started to question why she was there. "So, did you want to talk about us working together?"

Jay looked at Carmen and quickly shook his head. "You're not ready," he told her, looking through some more papers on his desk. He was busy trying to find a contract for a special guest DJ, who was supposed to be coming through to fill out the paperwork.

"I'm not ready," Carmen questioned. "My mother has been grooming me since I was old enough to work. My father owns his own business, too. I've been watching them for years. On top of that, I'm majoring in Business. I think I'm ready. Did your parents own their own business? I know they're proud of you. You're young, Black; you're doing well for yourself."

Jay dropped the papers that were in his hands at the sound of the word parents. He peered at Carmen with a blank expression and had to remind himself the comment was innocent. Carmen didn't know anything about his past and he wasn't ready to tell it. He did, however, want to respond. "My parents are from Puerto Rico. My father was full-blooded Taíno, and my mother was black."

"Was?" Carmen asked, seeking clarification.

Jay caught his mistake. He had used the word, "was," correctly; however, it had cost him an explanation. "They're dead," he quickly said, "my father owned this club. I inherited it from him." Jay looked at his desk and almost magically, the contract appeared. He grabbed the three-page document and placed it on top of the other papers so it would be easily accessible when he returned later that evening.

"Sorry to hear that," Carmen replied. "How did they—"

Jay cut her off before she could finish the question. "I don't want to talk about it. Look, I have a few errands to run. Do you want to come with me, or do you want me to take you back to campus? It's your call. You can even stay here."

Carmen narrowed her eyes at the thought of being in the club with Carlos. Rakim may have been there as well, but his presence alone wouldn't help her forget that Carlos had called her a bitch. "I'm not staying here," she blurted. "Not with Carlos, no sir."

"I figured that." Jay gave her a slight smile as he remembered her question about them working together. "Do you really want to work with me?" Jay didn't give her a chance to answer, continuing to speak as if he hadn't asked a question. "You keep asking yet I know you're not ready. You're a sheltered little girl who somehow became linked up with a very dangerous man. How did you manage that?"

Carmen shrugged her shoulders as she glanced around the room. "If that's who you are," she told him, her eyes on the mini-bar, "then it's because you seem harmless. You're like a gentle giant."

"Looks can be deceiving," Jay shot back.

Carmen stared him in his eyes until he held up his keys. Then, her eyes focused on the cold hard steel in his hands. Without saying a single word, he was asking her once again if she wanted to come with him. While her answer should've been no, Carmen obliged. Jay was about to show her a whole new world and she was ready for the tour.

Chapter Four

For the first fifteen minutes of the ride, Jay took her on a tour of their city's financial district. He pointed out several points of interest, stopping at a few of them to handle his business. Though it was never his intention to show Carmen as much as he did, he wanted her to see that her world was one big pot of deception. He showed her stockbrokers who were using petty cash to feed their crack habit and three CEOs who were stashing drugs inside their basements in exchange for a quick high.

His intention was to show her that East Brookstone was just as grimy as the Westside. She was so easily trusting and eager to work with him; she didn't even know he was showing her his stomping grounds. The CEOs who were stashing drugs in their basements were hoarding his product. The stockbroker who was stealing petty cash out of his company's account was using the money to pay him.

Then, there she was, an innocent college student, who had caught the eye of a pimp (Pierre) and one of America's biggest drug lords (Jay). Carmen represented everything he was not. From the physical to the spiritual, she was the exact opposite of him. Carmen seemed to be the girl who would give him balance. He only had to make her believe it. So far, he seemed to be doing a good job.

After a little coaxing, she agreed to meet up with him later that night at Sapphire. Jay planned on using the time to delve more into her background and to feel her out. Of course, it would be right after he took her off Pierre's radar and Carlos settled his business with him.

When the club finally opened, both Jay and Carlos were busy studying the security cameras. Carlos was waiting for the exact moment when Pierre or one of his goons stepped in Sapphire. "Do you have everything in place?" he asked, looking at Jay. He noticed his best friend's eyes stayed locked on one specific camera. Jay was looking for Carmen and every second she wasn't there, his agitation increased.

"I got this," Jay snapped, "Do you have his money?"

Jay eyed his friend angrily only because Carlos was still displaying the same selfish demeanor he always had. His friend was more concerned about a potential shootout then paying Pierre what he rightfully owed him. From the beginning, Jay had warned Carlos of Pierre. They were on the same page once upon a time until Carlos requested a ton of work that Jay refused to give him. Upset by the decision, Carlos went behind his back and acquired a ton of bricks from Pierre. In the end, Jay was forced to watch his friend struggle to pay the debt.

"I got his shit." Carlos picked up a black briefcase, which had been set at his feet and placed it on Jay's desk. He opened it and showed his friend the large amount of dead presidents.

"Then everything's in place," Jay replied, not looking at the money. His eyes went to the cameras that faced the parking lot of Sapphire. Not seeing one single image of Carmen, he scanned the rest of the screens until he noticed her in VIP. She was there with Tiara, and they looked to be in heavy conversation. She was dressed in a bright pink peplum dress that fit her frame perfectly. Aside from the physical, she still had the look of innocence that had attracted him in the beginning.

"You're really feeling her, aren't you?"

Jay parted his lips, yet he didn't answer Carlos' question. His eyes were still focused on Carmen as he watched her and Tiara converse.

"The party is downstairs," a loud voice barked, coming in the room. "Y'all two are stuck up here like y'all don't need a drink."

Jay took his eyes off the screen long enough to see Malik sit a bottle of Belvedere on his desk. It was about three-fourths full, which meant Malik had already gotten started on his first drink of the night. Jay wasn't much of a drinker though he downed plenty whenever he was stressed.

"I think Jay might need one," Carlos suggested, pointing at an image on the camera. He watched as Jay's eyes followed his finger. His friend's expression didn't change although Carlos expected for it to. Jay had been too busy looking at Carmen to even notice Pierre had entered the club. Two men were with him and instead of climbing the steps to Jay's office, he was headed to VIP.

"He went straight for Carmen," Malik noticed, pointing his glass at the camera. "What is it with you two and her? Does she really have as much loot as Rakim says she does?"

"I think Jay is trying to put her on," Carlos whispered.

Jay heard both comments, yet he didn't reply. Instead, he pulled a silver pistol from his drawer and stuck it inside his waistband. He then poured himself a glass of Belvedere, taking the drink down in one quick gulp. Once the drink was gone, he told them only five short words, "We have business to handle."

***

Carmen wasn't the least bit surprised to see Pierre standing over her. She had already suspected he was coming to the club after hearing about the altercation between Carlos and his goons. She figured he remembered her from the block party and was going to try to run his game on her again. This time, she planned on taking Jay's advice.

Pierre was eyeing her suspiciously and Carmen wondered what he was thinking. *Can I help you?*, was at the tip of her tongue, but she didn't dare ask the question. She simply waited for him to speak.

"Do you know Jay Santiago?" he asked her.

Carmen looked at Tiara who was steadily sipping on her mixed drink. Her friend was trying to stay clear of the conversation, which Carmen wished she could do. "He owns this place," she answered, looking at Pierre. "I met him at your block party." Carmen told a small white lie only because she wasn't sure where Pierre was leading the conversation.

"He does own this place," Pierre reiterated. "He also thinks he owns you." Pierre paused for a second or two as he tried to take note of Carmen's reaction. Her face was still rather blank. "I want to apologize for what happened yesterday at my block party. Shakeem has some real animosity towards one of Jay's workers. We had to handle some business."

"Okay," was the only word Carmen muttered.

Pierre took offense to her response only because he knew Carmen was hiding something. She tried to downplay her relationship with Jay when he knew there was something going on between them. Jay had made a personal phone call to him, inviting him to the club to discuss her. "Why are you shittin' on me?"

Carmen raised her brow unsure of what Pierre was getting at. "I'm not shittin' on you. What are you talking about?"

"I know you roll with Jay. Word on the street is that he's real nice on you. I got a verbal warning to keep my distance."

"I met Jay at your–" Pierre cut her off, dropping knowledge about Jay's past.

"That dude is fucked up in the head. You can't trust him. You saw what he did with Carlos. He wouldn't even put his own friend on. Carlos had to come to me to get work. Jay may seem like he's straight, but he has a few loose screws. He saw his pops die right in front of him."

Carmen rubbed her lips together and glanced at Tiara. Her friend was looking in the opposite direction to ensure she wasn't forced to comment. To make matters worse, Tiara stood up and quickly left VIP. Carmen followed Tiara with her eyes until she blended in with the rest of the crowd. Now forced to deal with Pierre alone, she quickly whispered, "I barely know him."

Pierre leaned down so his lips were right next to her ear. He spoke in a murmur, which made it hard for her to hear him. Carmen barely made out his words, yet she did feel his lips caress her right cheek. The kiss made her pull away and she looked in the crowd for any sign of Tiara. She didn't see her friend, yet she did see Jay approaching. She then noticed Carlos and Malik behind him. Carlos had a briefcase in his hand and Malik was holding a bottle of vodka. She wasn't quite sure what was about to happen until she saw a girl step in front of Jay. She blocked her view, which made Carmen look at Pierre.

"You didn't answer my question," he said, finally speaking at a volume where she could hear him. "Are you rolling with me or what?"

Carmen knew the answer was no. She was getting ready to say it until her eyes found their way to Jay and she saw the girl wrap her arms around him. She recognized the girl as the same chick who was all over him at the block party.

Carmen instantly felt her heart sank. She thought Jay was coming to tell Pierre off, but he had made a U-turn. The girl, obviously his girlfriend, had snagged his attention once again. Overtly disappointed, Carmen turned towards Pierre. "I am rolling with you," she told him. "Where do you want to go?"

Pierre's mouth formed a large grin. He didn't know what had caused Carmen's change of heart and frankly, he didn't care. All he knew is that she had chosen him. "I know the perfect place," he told her. "Come with me."

***

Jay's jaw tightened at the sight of Carmen leaving the VIP room with Pierre. Though Tricia was blocking most of his view, he had seen enough to know Carmen hadn't taken him seriously. There she was, walking hand in hand with Pierre, giving him the ultimate disrespect.

"Fuck that bitch," Carlos muttered behind him.

Jay wanted to repeat the words, but he couldn't. Something told him Carmen had seen him with Tricia and wanted revenge. If that was the case, she was playing a game she didn't know the rules to. Carmen wasn't street smart neither did she know how to handle a guy like Pierre. In knowing that, Jay knew he had to reel her back in. The protector in him wouldn't allow her to leave the club. Therefore, he broke Tricia's hold, which prompted her to grab his arm. "I can't talk right now."

"What's going on?" Tricia yelled; making sure he heard her above the music. "Every time I'm around you, something is catching your attention."

"I can't talk right now," Jay repeated, loosening his arm out her grasp. He signaled to Malik and Carlos to follow him as he started walking through the crowd. In the process, he spotted Rakim and Tiara who were standing near the DJ booth. When he raised his arm to motion for them to come with him, Tricia grabbed it.

"What's going on?" she yelled again, this time much louder. "You've been pushing me away since the block party. What happened?"

Jay's agitation grew at each question Tricia threw at him. He wanted her to accept that he didn't have time to talk instead of blocking his path. The further she pushed him, the closer he got to telling her it was over. Carmen had caught his eye and he wanted to put his energy into her. "Look, give me some time," he yelled at Tricia. "I have business to handle."

Tricia let out a deep sigh, which Jay could've cared less about hearing. He turned his attention to Rakim and Tiara, motioning once again for them to follow him. When they were halfway to him, he started the trek once again to the club's entrance. This time, Tricia took the hint and stayed put. When he reached the front door, he saw Carmen as she got inside of Pierre's black Mercedes Benz. Automatically, his hand became draped over the pistol in his waistband.

Meanwhile, Rakim eyed Jay closely. He could already see the look of a predator in his friend's eyes. He had seen it once before when he witnessed Jay murder a guy who he discovered was stealing money from him. The look was back, which meant Jay was going to kill someone. "Where do you think he's taking her?"

Jay looked at Rakim as he pulled his keys from his pocket. He wasn't quite sure where Pierre was headed. He only knew he had to move fast to keep up with him. Pierre knew he was coming for him and would hurt Carmen only because he knew he wanted her. The strife between them had officially put Carmen in the middle and it was up to him to ensure she didn't get hurt. "Doesn't matter," he muttered, starting to head towards his car, "I'm still going to follow him. I want to kill that motherfucker."

Rakim turned to his brother and Carlos, almost begging them to step in. From the way Carlos was looking, he seemed to be relieved he didn't have to give up the briefcase. Malik, on the other hand, was downing the bottle of Belvedere even faster than before. When it came to Tiara, she was on her cell phone, and he knew she was trying to reach Carmen. From the looks of things, none of them were focused on what Jay was about to do. Rakim felt as if he was left alone to coax him out of committing a crime. However, his chance became lost when he saw Jay pull out the parking lot. In a flash, Jay's Rolls Royce disappeared into the New York street, and he was left standing outside of Sapphire.

Chapter Five

Carmen knew something was wrong when Pierre pulled into an abandoned field a few miles north of West Brookstone. He had told her they were going for a bite to eat; however, he had driven passed several restaurants without stopping at one. She questioned him about it, yet he would never respond. At the same time, her phone constantly vibrated and when she tried to answer, Pierre pulled the phone from her hand. Then, once he parked the car, he did the inevitable.

Before she knew it, he was pulling her from the car like he was about to walk a dog. Too much in shock to fight back, Carmen's body landed with a loud thud as Pierre dropped her down on the cold, wet grass. She screamed for him to let her go until both of his hands gripped her neck, pulling her towards him. Unable to breathe, tears streamed down her face, forcing her eyelids closed. Unexpectedly, Pierre loosened his grip, allowing her body to fall on the ground. With every slow breath she took in, Carmen felt her strength returning. Before she knew it, she was charging full throttle at him. He fell to the ground, taking hold of her until he finally got the upper hand. He used his body weight to restrain her, smacking her around with an open palm.

"So you thought you were going to play me, huh?"

Pierre punched her in the face repeatedly, sending her mind into a million different places.

"Bitch," he screamed in her ear. "You thought I wasn't going to find out about you snitchin'? You were at my joint," he yelled. "My people always report to me. You warned Santiago of our hit."

Pierre muffled her screams with the bandana that had been holding down his braids. While trying to spit it out, she heard him unzip his pants. She tried to move away, but to no avail. Then, she took another blow to the face as the cool night air brushed up against her skin.

"I told you I was gonna get you out these panties."

Immediately, Carmen's world went dark. *You're not going to let this happen. You're not going to let this happen,* a voice chanted. Carmen couldn't respond. She didn't know who was speaking and she couldn't see the face.

Everything was completely black around her. She tried listening for the voice again, but she couldn't hear anything. Then, she heard the explosions.

Carmen opened her eyes to see a blurred vision of Jay standing over her. When she looked down at her body, she saw Pierre lying on top of her, rather complacent. Slowly, her senses returned, and she started to feel the warm blood gushing out Pierre's chest.

With limited time to spare, Jay didn't let Carmen's current state faze him. He pushed Pierre's body to the side before placing a silver bullet in the center of his forehead. At the sound of the gunshot, Carmen moaned, reminding Jay to pull the bandana from her mouth. Her dress was covered in Pierre's blood while bruises were starting to form on her face.

Jay could hear cars approaching in the distance. He picked up Carmen just in time to see Carlos' car driving into Allen's Field. Tiara was in the passenger seat while Malik followed behind him with Rakim. By the time he was at his vehicle, Carlos and Rakim both were at his side. "Get the door," he ordered Rakim. He then turned to Carlos, instructing for him to call Jimenez Funeral Home. Owned by one of his partners, Jay paid the undertaker a pretty penny to cover up any body that didn't need to be on the police's radar.

"Let me look at her," Rakim demanded, opening the passenger side door. He tried to reach for Carmen, yet Jay pushed him away using Carmen's body as a shield.

"Open the back door. I need you to drive."

"She needs a hospital," Rakim argued.

Jay gave Rakim a single glance, which told him to follow his orders. Rakim did as he requested then he took the driver's seat. When he looked in the rearview mirror at Jay and Carmen, he noticed the way Jay had his hand draped around her face. He was trying to calm her while Carlos was outside doing the same with Tiara. Rakim shook his head at the images of the two as he started up the car. He wasn't sure where he was headed, but he knew Jay would direct him in due time. For now, he made sure to get as far away from Pierre's body as possible. Police would be scouring the area and the only thing he wanted them to find was an empty lot.

Carmen grimaced as Tiara stroked the powder brush up against her cheek. She wanted to tell her friend to be easy on her, yet it still hurt for her to speak. She also felt as if her jaw was sitting in the back of her throat. Although she knew that wasn't the case, the pain told her otherwise. The pain was probably just as bad as the bruises on her face. She didn't see what she looked like until she passed a mirror in Carlos' apartment. The last place she wanted to be, Jay had insisted Rakim drive them there versus his place, which was on the outskirts of East Brookstone.

"I should've never left you," Tiara cried, feeling partly to blame. "I didn't think it was going to go that far. I thought—" Tiara's voice trailed off as she thought back to the events, which led to Carmen's attack. "I should've never made you come to that block party." Tiara placed the powder brush in her makeup bag and examined Carmen's face. With the extra layers of concealer and the caked on foundation, Carmen looked like a model whose makeup needed to endure a set of heavy lights.

"My parents are going to crack," Carmen mumbled

"It's almost six in the morning," Tiara replied, looking at the alarm clock on Carlos' bedside table. "I don't even know if this makeup is going to help. It might make things worse. You look like you had a botched cosmetic job. I agree with Rakim. We should've taken you to a hospital."

"Then we might as well file a police report."

Tiara looked at the doorway of Carlos' bedroom and wasn't surprised to see him standing there. She figured he had come to see what was keeping them and had caught the tail-end of the conversation. She knew firsthand he didn't care for Carmen, but he had to admit she needed to be looked at by a professional.

"How's your head?" Jay asked, joining Carlos in the doorway.

Tiara looked at Carmen as she waited for her response. When her friend's lips started to move, she could tell she was still in a lot of pain. Thankfully, her friend was able to answer the question.

"My head is fine," she stuttered. "It's my jaw that hurts."

Jay moved further in the room and placed his hand on the top of Carmen's forehead. "I'm talking mentally," he explained. "I know you're still shook up."

Carlos followed in behind Jay, standing next to him. "Right now, we need to think about retaliation. Shakeem is going to be on our ass because you killed Pierre. You also made his body disappear while his car was left in Allen's Field. Someone is going to ask questions."

"My workers took care of the car," Jay told him, not looking in Carlos' direction. "You don't have anything to worry about. I have something for Shakeem, too. He'll get the same treatment as Pierre."

"Man, we need to institute something with these murders. I'm not trying to feel a cell. Shit, this money that I was going to pay Pierre, I'm going to take and invest in a laundromat or something. Maybe, I'll get a club."

Jay kept his eyes planted on Carmen on purpose. He rolled his eyes at Carlos' comment only wanting her to see. When a smile spread across her face, he knew it was safe for her to go home. If she was still antsy, he would've suggested for her to spend the night at Tiara's. "You need to take it easy tomorrow," he told her, moving his hand off her forehead. "If you don't work, I suggest you stay in bed."

Carmen nodded her head and attempted to stand up. She fumbled for a second or two before finding her balance. Jay grabbed her arm to help, and she noticed Carlos when he sucked his teeth because of it. Ever since she told Jay about Pierre's hit, she had been on his bad side. Whether they would make amends, she didn't know nor did she care. Based off what had happened that night, she wasn't coming anywhere near them. She would forever be indebted to Jay for saving her life, but she didn't want to see him again. She wanted to forget the night had happened and go back to her life before she met them.

Now, for the first time in her life, she understood her mother's thoughts regarding people from the Westside. It was a world of its own and a population she didn't need to mix with.

Chapter Six

Most of the day was gone when Carmen finally woke up. The house was dead silent, except for the sound of a radio, which had been left on in her parents' bedroom. Nearly four o'clock, Carmen knew she needed to be getting to her mother's store. By the time five o'clock rolled around, Carmen was busy stretching her legs. When she finally left the bed, the first thing she did was look at her reflection in the mirror. The size of the bruises had gone down only slightly, and it appeared as if she had small birthmarks on her face. Certain she could cover it with concealer and foundation; she prepared for work and headed to her mother's store.

Once she was there, she could tell business had slowed down drastically. Saturday was usually their busiest, but the store appeared somewhat dead. Due to the lack of customers, she was able to spot Monifah who was browsing through the store's accessories. Carmen approached her, tapping her friend on the shoulder.

"Girl, you almost scared me," Monifah said, dropping one of the necklaces she was holding. "What's good with you?" Monifah did a double take, noticing the amount of makeup Carmen was wearing. She had already heard about the incident at the club but wasn't going to press Carmen to discuss it. She would have much preferred for her friend to tell her on her own.

"Just trying to make it," Carmen replied. "What's good with you?"

Monifah held up the necklace she was holding. "You know me; I always have to have a little retail therapy."

"At least someone does, it's dead in here." Carmen took another long stare around the store and shook her head. "It'll be a surprise if we've made two thousand dollars today."

"Well, you know I'm not spending that," Monifah joked. "So," she said, not being able to fight the urge, "do you want to talk about it?"

Carmen let out a deep sigh. Her brush with death wasn't a subject she wanted to speak about. She was already trying to get the night out her mind and speaking of it would only make matters worse. Still, she knew from

Monifah's question that Tiara had spilled the beans. About to reply, she was interrupted by a familiar voice.

"Can you please tell that guy to move his car? He's in a no parking zone. I would do it but I'm working on a layaway."

Carmen turned to see her mother with a sales slip in her hand. Her eyes then darted towards the registers where a customer was waiting. Carmen knew her conversation with Monifah had to be put on hold. Not the least bit upset, she quickly excused herself and headed outside where she found a black Ferrari parked. The top was down, which allowed her to get a good look at the driver. Somewhat shocked to see Jay, she knew he had come to check on her. While it was her intention to stay away from him, she had to speak to him to deliver her mother's message. "You can't park there, sir," she greeted.

Jay's mouth grew to a large grin when he noticed Carmen. She was wearing less makeup than before, which meant the bruises were starting to fade. With the way she greeted him, he decided to play along. "I'm sorry, ma'am. I figured it was okay since I was only going to be here for five minutes."

"Oh, well don't let me hold you up," Carmen joked. She gave him a small smile before reminding herself she was supposed to be staying away from him. Nevertheless, every time he flashed his pearly whites, he made it harder for her. Too add on to the pressure, he was now moving closer to her.

"Today's a beautiful day," he added, looking at the sky. "It is a beautiful brand new day." Jay paused in his step once he stood in front of Carmen. "My name is Jay Santiago. It's a pleasure to meet you." He held out his hand to her as if they were meeting for the first time.

Carmen didn't shake it although she responded with, "Carmen Davenport."

Jay caught the snub and placed his hand at his side. "The store isn't busy," he began, "maybe, we could take a ride through downtown for a few minutes."

Carmen shook her head before peeking inside the store. Her mother wasn't at the register and Monifah was now looking through a rack of baby tees. She was hoping one of them was about to come out and demand her attention. From what she was seeing, she was stuck with Jay unless she got rid of him.

"We need to talk Carmen," Jay stressed. "Last night—" Carmen cut him off.

"Last night is a night I want to forget. It's no secret I'm indebted to you. Still, I would prefer it if you didn't come around. You can go back to running your club and I'll go back to my classes and my mother's store. You were right. I'm not ready for this and this life isn't for me. Let's go our separate ways. Is that a plan?"

Jay stuffed his hands in his pockets. Carmen's words were a complete surprise, yet he tried to hide his shock. He had saved her life and although she had told him thank you, she was acting as if it didn't mean anything. Aside from keeping her from death, he had gone the extra mile and came by her mother's store to see if she was making progress. It was obvious that like most rich girls, she was a spoiled brat.

Not yet ready to give up, he peeked inside Flame to see what he could use to get her number. "Is that your mom?" he asked, pointing at a lady who was on her way out.

Before Carmen could respond, she watched as Jay approached her mother. Carmen instantly went on pins and needles since she was unsure of what he was going to say.

"Hello, ma'am, I'm Jay Santiago," he stated, holding out his hand. "I own the club, Sapphire, down the street. I was wondering if I could take your daughter out tonight."

"No," Carmen yelled, not giving her mother the chance to respond.

"Well, I guess you got your answer then," Patricia replied with a laugh. "Carm, I was going to ask you to look at this design, but I see your hands are full. By the way, you didn't tell that guy to move his car?"

Carmen bit her lip before looking at Jay. She narrowed her eyes so he would catch the hint that he had outstayed his welcome. He took note of it and held up his keys as a sign he was leaving. Not out the clear yet, Carmen wasn't able to let out a sigh until his car disappeared from Flame.

Chapter Seven

Carmen was certain she had gotten through to Jay. Once he left her mother's store, she returned inside, helping her mother straighten several of the racks and complete the markdowns. By the time they were finished, and the store was closed for the night, Jay was nowhere near her mind. She didn't think of him again until Sunday morning when she was sitting beside her mother in worship service. Their minister's sermon was focused on starting over, which hit close to home since Carmen was trying to put her life back on track. So far, it seemed to be working until Brother Peters finished the benediction.

Tears were flowing from her eyes and her mother was questioning what had brought on the waterworks. While she hadn't shared what she had been through with her parents, she was surprised they hadn't asked her why she came home late. Carmen was starting to believe she would take the attack to the grave.

Her mother offered her a Kleenex, which she kindly took, wiping the rest of the tears from her face. Once she had herself together, she searched the church for any sign of Tiara. Her friend normally came with her stepfather while her mother opted to worship at Bedside Baptist. This time, she didn't find Tiara with her stepfather, but standing next to Carlos, followed by the twins and Jay.

Carmen swallowed at the sight of them, and she knew she wasn't getting away easily. It was obvious Jay had only given her a pass at her mother's store. He was back for round two and this time, she knew he wasn't going to let up.

"Wait a minute, Carmen, isn't that the guy from my store yesterday? I didn't know he worshipped here."

Carmen didn't utter a response. Her eyes were more focused on Jay, who was walking towards her, then what her mother was saying. To make matters worse, he completely ignored her, heading straight for her mother.

"Good afternoon, Mrs. Davenport," he greeted, holding out his hand. "I didn't know you were a member here. How long have you been worshipping with us?"

Carmen let out a slight grunt at the words that poured out his mouth. *He knows this is the first time his ass has ever been inside this building. We've been attending this church since I was a baby. I've never seen him, Carlos, or the twins in any one of these pews.*

"Oh, we've been here for years," Patricia exclaimed. "You must sit up in the balcony. I've never seen you here before. You do look nice today. I love the suit," her mother said with a giggle.

"William Stacey and Henry Adams knew a thing or two about dressing a man."

Carmen raised her eyebrow at Jay all while giving him the once-over. Navy accentuated his skin tone well and she had to commend his effort. It was the first time she had seen him in a two-piece suit and without a doubt; she had to admit his style was fresh. *Don't get sucked in*, she reminded herself. *Don't let those hazel eyes and designer clothes fool you. Remember, he is only a figment of your past.*

Carmen met eyes with Jay only to see him turn his attention to her mother. At this point, the others had gathered around them.

"I'm treating everyone for lunch over at Cipriani's," Jay announced. "You and Carmen should join us."

Patricia grabbed her chest, playfully. "Well, this is a pleasant surprise. I will have to take you up on the offer. I'm certain, though, that you only want to get in my good graces so you can date my daughter. Is that so?"

Jay shifted his attention to Carmen. He gave her a devious smile because he knew he was getting under her skin. Carmen may have warned him to stay away, but he couldn't. Once he saw something he wanted, he had to have it. "I would have to agree," he answered, turning to Patricia. "Is it working?"

"It sure is," Patricia yelled. "Carmen, what do you say? Do you want to take Mr. Santiago up on his offer?"

Carmen shot her mother a fake smile. In her head, the words, *hell no*, were ringing loud and clear. However, the word, *yes*, was the one that sounded out her mouth.

"Great, then it's settled," Jay replied. "You two can ride with me. I have plenty of room in my new Benz."

Carmen exhaled as she watched Jay grab her mother's hand. He led her out the auditorium while Tiara made her way towards her. Carmen gave her friend an expression that said she was fed up.

"He's working hard to get you," Tiara whispered in her ear.

Those weren't the words Carmen wanted to hear. She wanted someone to tell Jay to leave her alone. To add on to her fury, he was dragging her mother into the situation. She was the innocent party and not the least bit aware she was about to be sitting at a table with a bunch of guys from the Westside. Whether they would change her mother's mindset, she didn't know. With the way her mother was carrying on, she didn't care where anyone was from. She was too busy conversing with Jay about their businesses. Carmen had followed behind them with Tiara until her friend snuck off to ride with Carlos.

When Jay opened the back door for her, Carmen got ready to get inside until she gave the car a closer look. She hadn't thought twice about his comment regarding a new Benz until now. The car was new; however, it wasn't his. The car belonged to Pierre. It was the same car she was dragged out of Friday night. When he saw her hesitation, he gave her a slight push towards the car.

"You're safe with me, remember?"

Carmen eyed him in disbelief. She didn't know what he was trying to do or insinuate. *Does he think I owe him something? I know I do but showing me this car as a reminder he saved my life is not going to make me date him. If anything, it makes me want to run away from him.*

"Get inside, Carmen, I'm hungry," her mother urged.

Carmen stared at her mother who was already putting on her seatbelt. Aware she couldn't stall any longer, she got inside the car. She held her breath every two minutes she was inside until they reached Cipriani's. The sight of the restaurant calmed her nerves and things only got better once she was seated inside.

***

Once everyone's order had been taken, Carmen could tell her mother had the itch to start questioning Jay about his businesses and background.

Everyone else seemed to be miniscule to her because she made sure to sit next to Jay and look him in his eyes with every question she asked.

"So you said your name was Jay Santiago?" Patricia asked. "Hmm...that name sounds familiar. Was your mother Puerto Rican?"

Carmen tapped her mother's leg underneath the table. It only resulted in a quick exchange of glances before her mother turned her focus back to Jay for her answer.

"My mother was a black Puerto Rican," Jay replied, picking up his iced tea. "Her ancestors are originally from Africa. Back in slavery times, they were brought to Puerto Rico and sold. My mother's parents were born in Puerto Rico and likewise. She even spoke Spanish fluently."

"Your father is—" Patricia's voice trailed off on purpose. She wanted Jay to finish her sentence so she could get more information about the man who was trying to court her daughter.

"My father is Puerto Rican as well. Both my parents are." Jay took a quick sip of his tea before switching the topic of conversation. "Tell me about your husband, Mrs. Davenport."

Patricia laughed at how proper he was being. "Please call me, Patricia. I'm not that old. Now, what is it exactly that you want to know about my husband? You probably know who he is. He recently made headlines because he sold one of his buildings to Mr. Trump. He owns Davenport Realty. He would've been here with us, but he had to take a quick trip out of town. Now, on to more important things, do you like my daughter?"

"Mama," Carmen blurted. She covered her face at how brash her mother was being. She knew her mother was curious, but to come right out and ask in front of everyone was embarrassing. When it came to Jay, he seemed to be comfortable answering the question.

"I do like your daughter, Mrs. Patricia. She has a sort of innocence about her that I'm drawn to. I also like her aspirations. She told me she is supposed to be inheriting your store. Is that true?"

Patricia turned towards Carmen and let out a deep sigh. While it had been discussed, nothing was official. "Well," she began, stressing the word.

Carmen stood up from the table not quite ready to hear her mother's response. She hadn't lied to Jay about inheriting the store; she simply hadn't told him it was only an idea. "I'm going to the bathroom," she said, quickly, excusing herself. She dropped her cloth napkin on her empty plate and headed for the restroom. She saw Tiara following behind her, giving her the opportunity to vent about the afternoon. Once she was inside the bathroom, the word, "shit," was muttered constantly out her mouth. Tiara only laughed in response until Carmen appeared to be on the verge of tears.

"What is he doing?" Carmen cried. "He surprises me by coming to my church. He's driving Pierre's car and then he drags us to Cipriani's? He knows what Pierre did to me. He was there. Why would he put me through this?"

Tiara shrugged her shoulders. "I don't know, Carm. He pulled a fast one on everybody. Carlos was really upset about it when we got to church this morning. That car is hot. Once someone files a missing person's report on Pierre, everything he owns is going to be under a microscope." Tiara stared at her shoes as she thought the matter over. "Maybe, he wants to keep his respect. You know how these street guys are."

"No, I don't know," Carmen reminded her. "I don't know at all."

"You also don't know that Carlos and Shakeem had a run-in last night."

Carmen immediately went in one of the stalls and closed the door. She didn't bother to lock it so Tiara followed behind her, opening the door so she could see Carmen's face. Her friend was sitting on the toilet with her head in her hands. Tiara didn't know whether to continue the story or let her be. Since she had already started, she decided to finish.

"It was pretty bad, Carm. Carlos was throwing bottles and busted up Shakeem's face bad. He's in a coma. No telling what kind of retaliation is going to happen now."

Carmen grabbed several sheets of toilet paper and wiped her face. Her bruises had faded traumatically so she wasn't concerned about wiping some of her makeup off. "Why did this have to happen to me? Why won't he take his friends and go back wherever he came from?"

"He likes you. You're like the yin to his yang. You're the good girl, he's the bad guy. You know, now that Carlos and I are getting closer, I would like to see you give Jay a chance. I mean, he did save your life."

Carmen nodded her head in agreement. The fact that Jay saved her life made her feel like she owed something to him. She simply didn't know if it meant she had to give him a chance.

"Minister Hawthorne said this morning, 'God has already seen you through plenty of storms and will most definitely help you get through your current one. Don't let the rain and the hail stop you. Grab an umbrella and get out the house'. You need to take his words to heart."

Carmen gave Tiara a slight smile. "You're right, Tee."

"I know I am," Tiara sighed. "Now I'm hungry so let's hope the waitress has brought our food. I can't be cooped up in this stall for another second."

Carmen let out a chuckle as she stood up. Not quite sure what she was going to do with Jay, she knew once the way was clear, he was going to be all hers. A one on one conversation was desperately needed.

***

It was Carmen's intention to speak with Jay once they were back at church. Her plan was for them to simply drop her mother off before taking a quick ride around the city. What ended up happening was totally different than what she planned. Jay was standing at her mother's car still in heavy conversation while Carmen was standing at his. The twins had returned as well for a reason Carmen was unsure of until she felt Rakim poke her in the shoulder.

"Do you have class tomorrow?" he asked, displaying a large smile.

"I sure do, bright and early at eight o'clock. Do you?"

"Mine is a little later, but I was thinking that maybe we could meet at IHOP for breakfast. Do you eat there?"

Carmen let out a slight giggle. She may have been the daughter of a millionaire, but that didn't mean she only ate at ritzy places. "Of course I do. What time do you want to meet?" She took a quick peek at her mother's car seeing Jay and her mother conversing heavily.

"Let's meet at seven," Rakim suggested. He followed Carmen's gaze and noticed she was staring at Jay. "They're getting along good," he noticed. "I can't really say the same for you and him."

Carmen turned towards Rakim and narrowed her eyes. Her relationship with Jay was supposed to be nonexistent. Every day since the day she met him, he had been in her presence. Sometimes it was for the good, sometimes for the bad. Nevertheless, he was there. About to express this to Rakim, she wasn't given the chance when she saw Jay walk up to them. Rakim excused himself, leaving her alone with Jay while her mother waited in the car.

"So," he said with a grin, "can we schedule a date?"

Carmen bypassed his question and went straight for the gusto. "I was serious about what I said yesterday. I really don't want anything to do with you or your friends. Now, I am very grateful for what you did on Friday night. I will forever be indebted to you, but I'm not about this life. I don't want to lead you on or make you think we have a chance when we don't. I'm sorry." Carmen let out a deep breath, hoping Jay would catch the hint. His expression changed yet he hadn't responded. Since he hadn't, Carmen continued. "I made the final decision when you showed up at church in Pierre's car. You should've known I wouldn't want to be anywhere near that Benz. You forced me inside."

"The car is a material object that I drove around to give his workers a reminder. It has nothing to do with you. It was a sign to anyone else that wants to come at me what I'm capable of. If you're really concerned, just know I'm getting it painted tomorrow and the inside redone. No one will even know its Pierre's car after today."

"It has nothing to do with me?" Carmen yelled. "You killed him because of me," she whispered through gritted teeth. "That has something majorly to do with me."

"I was going to kill him, anyway. It was only a matter of time."

Carmen could tell by his response that the façade was over. The real Jay, the one who murdered Pierre, the one who revealed the secrets of their city's financial district, was starting to make himself known once again. "Did you really think I wasn't going to see through your act? You show up at my church, pretending to be a member, wining and dining my mother and me, and for what? To prove to me that you're nothing, but a fake. I can see the real you, Jay. You are the dangerous man you told me you were. In the end, you're just like Pierre. You only have a little more heart."

Jay tried his best to keep his cool. His hands became stuffed in his pockets, and he controlled his volume so he wouldn't attract attention. His tone, on the other hand, was still as harsh as he wanted it to be. "You're an ungrateful bitch. You say thank you and fuck you at the same time. I saved your life, and you want to push me to the side?" Jay huffed before continuing. "I knew I should've let him rape you."

Carmen slapped Jay hard across the face before she knew she had. It prompted her mother who was watching their convo to come screaming from her car.

"What is going on?" Patricia asked, running up to them.

Jay spat on the ground his eyes still frozen on Carmen's. "We were having a disagreement, Mrs. Patricia. I guess I said the wrong thing."

"He definitely said the wrong thing," Carmen murmured.

"Maybe we should go," Patricia urged, grabbing Carmen's arm. "This argument has turned violent, and we don't need any fighting in front of the Lord's house."

"One minute, Mama, we're not finished talking."

"Go with your mother," Jay ordered, staring Carmen in the face.

The word no was stern and fierce out Carmen's mouth. She turned to her mother so she could see her facial expression. "We're actually going to cruise around downtown for a little bit. We'll be fine, I promise." That really wasn't her plan, but she said it to get her mother away from them. Carmen watched as her mother looked back and forth between her and Jay. She then stumbled a bit over her words as if she was debating about whether to leave her in the church parking lot or not. When she finally said she would be on her way, Carmen waited until she left before she spoke. Unfortunately, the words never came as Jay snatched her up by the shoulders.

"Bitch, I will kill you if you ever put your fuckin' hands on me again."

Carmen pulled herself from his grasp, taking a step away from him. She knew his words were more of a promise than a threat. He had already dropped one body and she knew he would do it again.

"I can't explain it, Carm," he told her, calming down. "You're not like any other girl out here. You don't need me for anything. You have everything already in your hands. Every other girl out here wants to take. All I asked you for is a chance." His voice trailed off for a bit. "I'm sorry," he continued. "I shouldn't have called you a bitch. I also should've never said anything about letting him rape you. You know I didn't want that to happen."

Carmen stared at him in disbelief. One second, he was putting hands on her, and the next, he was sentimental. *Perhaps, he wanted to right his wrong.* She swallowed as she felt herself giving in. *This was not the plan,* she reminded herself. *You were supposed to let him have it. You were supposed to make it clear that y'all weren't going to be anything more than two people who had met randomly. Now, you're falling deeper in his game.* Carmen shook her head back and forth at the final decision she was making. "Okay, Jay, one date, we'll see how it goes."

Jay's face broke into a large smile. "Can I also have a kiss? You can put it right here, right where you smacked me. It still stings a little bit," he joked, pointing at his right cheek.

"Absolutely not," Carmen replied with a chuckle.

"Please," he begged. "Right here, it's a little sore."

Carmen rolled her eyes before grabbing his face. When she leaned up to kiss his cheek, his chin immediately shifted in her hands. Unsure of what he was doing, Carmen was shocked when his lips smashed up against hers. In an instant, both their mouths were opening, allowing their tongues to dance. Once they were finished, Carmen had to exhale. She had never shared a kiss with anyone as passionately as she had with Jay. While it wasn't her first kiss, it felt like it on so many levels. In addition, it made her feel like they had sealed the deal. She may have started the day thinking they were parting ways, but the day had ended with them becoming joined. Now, she had the pleasure of sitting back and watching how far they went.

Chapter Eight

For the second time, Carmen spent her afternoon being led on a tour of the city. This time, Jay pointed out several businesses he had invested money into. His name wasn't necessarily listed as an owner or partner, but he bragged that he saved a lot of business owners from going under. Most of the places were restaurants and bodegas that Carmen didn't even know were in danger of foreclosure. It surprised her that Jay had his money wrapped up in so many endeavors when he only owned a club. Though things had been rocky when they were at church, the drive made Carmen a little more confident in starting a potential relationship with him.

They didn't part ways until later that evening when he dropped her off at home. The plan was to meet up the next day, but he left without her ever giving him her phone number. She figured he would stop by her mother's store or show up on campus to see her. Before she could meet with him, she first had to meet with Rakim.

Bright and early at seven in the morning, she strolled into IHOP to find him already seated at a booth. She quickly joined him, and they made small talk until both their meals hit the table. Carmen was busy digging in her Colorado Omelette when Rakim struck up a conversation.

"I'm thinking of joining a fraternity," he announced.

Carmen put her fork down for a quick second. "This semester?" she asked him, knowing she had seen a few postings for membership intake. "That is big," she told him, "and expensive." Carmen thought for an instant to retract her statement. Rakim could easily toss aside the dough since he probably racked in thousands hustling.

"Do you think it's a good idea? I think it will help me network with other people in the medical profession and it'll look good on my resume. Not to mention, I want to go to John Hopkins for graduate school. The only issue is I need another good reference for my membership application. I figured since your mother is a Delta she could help me."

"How did you know my mother was a Delta?" Carmen frowned at the thought because she hardly ever saw her mother in her paraphernalia. If anything, her mother only discussed her organization when there was a gala or community service event.

"She had on her pin at church yesterday. I wanted to talk to her about it, but Jay had her attention most of the time. Maybe you could talk to her about being a reference for me. I know we don't know each other that well, but maybe, I can tell you about a few things I've done, and she can write something for me. I already have a professor and a dean submitting, but I would like someone outside of the university."

"I understand. I'll mention it to her when I go to work tonight. I'll see what she says and let you know."

"I appreciate it," Rakim replied. He went back to eating his food before placing his eyes on Carmen. "I guess we can say we're friends. Do you consider me a friend?"

Carmen swallowed some of her omelette so she could answer his question without a full mouth. "I think we're friends," she told him, agreeing. "I like you."

"Can I ask you a question?"

Carmen nodded her head while still scooping more of her omelette on her fork. She became sort of apprehensive, thinking Rakim was going to lead the discussion to Pierre.

"When we first met at the diner, I noticed you. Sometimes, I'm shy. I don't always voice my thoughts. If Jay hadn't of hollered at you, would you have given me a chance?"

Carmen dropped her fork on her plate. "I wasn't looking for anybody that day. I would have to say no. Right now, Jay is forcing me to be exclusive with him. He won't take no for an answer."

"It's cool, at least you were honest." Rakim looked away, somewhat disappointed. He knew Jay had more money than him and their looks were incomparable. Most girls naturally gravitated towards Jay and Carlos while he and Malik were always the second pick. He figured it was the light skin that attracted them versus the dark skin he and his brother possessed. "So, you're with Jay and Tiara is with Carlos."

Carmen shrugged her shoulders. She didn't know what Tiara and Carlos were doing. She knew Tiara was hanging with him, but her friend hadn't confirmed if they were in a relationship. She thought Rakim was going to ask about it some more, but he only went back to eating. When she looked at him, she had to admit he was easy to talk to. He wasn't as aggressive as Jay and was friendlier than Carlos. She figured he had become wrapped up in Jay's criminal enterprise through his brother.

Throughout the rest of the meal, Rakim didn't expound much on anything. He was rather quiet and eventually, they parted ways. Carmen headed to campus while Rakim stated he was going to make a stop at a local convenience store. With four classes to attend that day, Carmen struggled to keep her mind centered on her studies. Her much needed break didn't come until she walked inside her mother's store at four o'clock. Her mother was working the register and immediately started up a conversation the second she saw her.

"Your father got back in this afternoon."

Carmen shot her mother a smile only because her mother didn't sound happy at his return. Carmen had missed her father over the weekend and was glad he was home.

"He bought me tickets to an opera that's going to be in Pennsylvania. He found out about it when he was up there on his business trip. So, we're going back this weekend. You'll have the house to yourself for a few days. We're leaving on Friday and won't be back until Sunday evening."

"Cool," Carmen replied, starting to sign in on one of the registers. She figured her mother had the front controlled, so Carmen decided to take it upon herself to work some of the racks. Business hadn't been booming, but they needed to always keep the store presentable.

"You know, your guy friend really inspired me on Sunday. I know you've been asking for me to let you design some things for the store and I'm thinking about taking you up on the offer. I know I can't afford to put out an entire men's line unless we find some funding or take a loan from your father. Still, I would like to see what you come up with. Are you ready for the challenge?"

"I was born ready. I guess Jay made quite the impression."

Patricia stopped what she was doing to look at Carmen. "Is that the guy with the edge you were talking about? If so, he looks good for a hoodlum."

"Mama, Jay lives in East Brookstone. That is where he's from. Now, my friend, Rakim, is from West Brookstone, but he has a lot going for him. He's a Biology major, has plans to go to John Hopkins, and wants to pledge a fraternity this semester. He doesn't fit your idea of people from West Brookstone."

"Oh wow," her mother said, sarcastically. "You find one random guy to prove me wrong. Do better next time."

Carmen glared at her mother in disgust. "What is it that you have against people from West Brookstone? Why are you trippin' and shit?"

"Did you curse at me?"

Carmen felt her face tighten. She stormed out from behind the clothes rack and ignored her mother as she called her name. She headed straight to the store's break room where her mother followed her.

Patricia found her daughter sitting at one of the tables with her arms folded across her chest. "Carmen Denise Davenport, have you lost your damn mind? There are customers in the store, and you are walking around with a temper tantrum." Patricia slammed the door closed to the break room. "Let me tell you one thing, Miss I'm-Twenty-One–Now-And-I-Can-Do-What-I-Want. You have no idea the type of mess, and people, West Brookstone produces. I have my beliefs about them because of the things I've seen. I wasn't forty-five all my life. I partied, I drank, and I even sowed my wild oats for a bit until I settled down with your father. That was all because I hung out with those hoodlums. I was a good girl just like you. I got wrapped up and almost lost my life trying to get out some bullshit. I'm not saying Jay is a bad guy. I'm not saying Rakim is, but I am warning you. If Jay has an edge, then guess what, he probably has a whole mountain to go with that edge."

"I'm mad at how you dissed Rakim not Jay."

"I didn't diss him, but if you felt like I did, I apologize. You must understand. I only want the best for you. I don't want you to get caught up and make the same mistakes I did." Patricia paused for a few seconds so she could catch her breath. "Now, since Rakim seems to be a good friend of yours, should I invite him to dinner, too, tomorrow night?"

Carmen peered at her mother unaware that a special dinner had been scheduled at their house. "Did I miss something?" she asked.

"Jay didn't tell you. He is supposed to be coming over for dinner so he can meet your father. That isn't going to happen, though. Your father claims to have a very important business meeting tomorrow night."

"He didn't tell me. I'll let Rakim know, though. Thanks for the heads up with Daddy. He has been super busy since selling that building to Trump."

"Yeah, he has. Well, I'm going on the floor. Don't stay back here too long, those shelves aren't going to straighten themselves."

Carmen narrowed her eyes playfully as her mother walked out the break room. She sat there for a few more minutes and then proceeded to the floor to start straightening some of the racks. It took her only an hour or two and then she started working on counting down one of the registers. By the time she was finished, the store had closed, leaving her and her mother alone. Carmen had started vacuuming while her mother was updating sales and expense reports. With the only noise in the store being the sound of the vacuum, it took Carmen a second or two to notice that Jay was standing outside. Immediately when she noticed him, she turned the vacuum off, running to unlock the front door for him.

"Mr. Santiago," she greeted. "This is a pleasant surprise."

Jay didn't hesitate to grab Carmen into a hug. He even placed a slight peck on her lips. "You knew I was going to come by and see you. I got here a little later than I wanted, but I'm here."

"I'm glad you could stop by."

Carmen was about to say more until she realized they were no longer alone. When she looked behind her, she saw her mother standing there with a questionable expression on her face. "We have a visitor," she exclaimed.

"Well, isn't it a pleasant surprise," Patricia gushed. "I'm glad you're here. I told Carmen about our dinner tomorrow. I also told her to invite your friend, Rakim. Make sure he gets the message. I'm already working on the menu."

Jay responded with, "Sounds good." He didn't necessarily understand why Rakim had been invited, but the issue was minimal.

"If you don't mind me asking," Patricia began. "How old are you, Jay?" He appeared to be around the same age as Carmen, but she couldn't be so sure. He was already established with a club under his belt and fancy cars to his name. In her opinion, he had to be closer to his thirties than she originally thought. When he told her he was twenty-seven, she became slightly more content with the idea of him and Carmen dating. In response, she merely nodded her head at him before returning to her office.

Meanwhile, Carmen playfully pushed him. "Are we going on another tour?" Carmen was looking forward to another long drive. She always learned the most about Jay from the tours he would give her. He never delved too much into his personal life, but it was enough to keep her hungry for more.

"I can't tonight. Some business needs to be handled. I did want to see you, though." Jay grabbed her in his arms, wrapping his arms tightly around her waist. He could tell Carmen was feeling him more than before because of the amount of affection she was giving him. When she grabbed his face for a kiss, he didn't stop her. They stood there for a few seconds simply taking each other in until they broke apart to catch their breath. "So, it's official then?"

Carmen backed away only because she knew she was going to say no. While they had made out on two separate occasions, she wasn't yet comfortable with the idea of Jay becoming her boyfriend. In addition, he had never explained his situation with Tricia. Carmen assumed they weren't together, but she didn't know for sure. "Why rush?" she asked him. "Let's take our time."

Jay wrinkled his face though he knew he shouldn't have. He was still very much Tricia's boyfriend although he was parading around with Carmen. He planned on breaking things off with her as soon as time permitted. For now, he was dodging her.

"What are you thinking about?"

Jay had been silent for a few seconds too long, yet his thoughts weren't anything he needed to share. To ease her worries, he placed another long kiss on her lips before telling her he had to go. After a quick peck on the cheek, he left the store and the vacuum roared back to life.

Chapter Nine

Tuesday afternoon, Carmen made sure to arrive on campus a few minutes before her one o'clock class so she could talk with Tiara. Rakim had confirmed she had a relationship on the rise with Carlos and Carmen felt the same when it came to Jay. She figured it was time for them to be open with each other regarding their new relationships. Though her time with Jay had been cut short at Flame, Carmen was looking forward to spending some quality time with him after dinner.

The thought hadn't even left her mind when she spotted Rakim on the steps of Gardner Hall. Unsure if Jay had told him about dinner, Carmen rushed to him.

Rakim watched as Carmen ran up the steps to meet him. "You know, in the past I would walk past you and wouldn't even get noticed. Now, you recognize me out a crowd of millions."

Carmen playfully hit him on the shoulder. "I didn't know you then. Shoot, it's not like you spoke to me." Carmen took a second to catch her breath before she told him about dinner. "I told my mother about you. She is cooking dinner tonight for Jay and thought it would be good if you came over, too. It starts at seven. Can you make it?"

"I'll be there. I'll ride with Jay. He is actually on his way here now."

Carmen's mouth made a small O. She would've known Jay was coming on campus if they had exchanged numbers. For some reason, they always forgot when they were in each other's company. About to comment, she heard Tiara's loud voice before she saw her.

"Carmen Davenport."

Carmen looked past Rakim and spotted Tiara coming out Gardner Hall. Her friend's smile was almost as large as the color of her coral platform pumps. There was obviously news to share, which Carmen soon learned when Tiara grabbed her hand and led her down the steps. When they arrived in front of a burgundy Bentley Brooklands, Carmen's mouth dropped wide open. She stared at the car in amazement. The Bentley had a peanut butter-colored interior that had been paired with a spacious backseat. There were also TVs on the back of the driver and passenger side headrests. Carmen knew without Tiara even telling her that Carlos had shelved out the dough for the car.

"Carlos surprised me with it this morning. He said he couldn't be with a girl who was riding around in a jalopy."

Carmen was speechless. She knew Carlos had money, but not the kind that allowed him to buy a whole Bentley for a girl he hadn't even known a week. Carmen couldn't help but to think about the kind of sex moves Tiara had to be putting on him. She obviously had Carlos whipped. "It's nice," she finally said, walking around the vehicle. "It's really nice."

"I'm glad you approve. While I would love to stay and chat, your mother was nice enough to give me an afternoon position at Flame. I need some cash to help me keep up the maintenance on the car." Tiara held up the car keys in her hand, then quickly unlocked the doors.

If she wasn't moving so fast, Carmen would have questioned her new position. In her opinion, her mother didn't need to be hiring anyone. In fact, she needed to do some firing. The store's revenue was barely covering salaries, insurance, or utilities. With Tiara added to the roster, someone's hours were going to be cut. That someone would be her. She would complain about it because her paycheck from Flame was the only way she had her own money.

If she lost half of her hours then she would be forced to depend on her father. He would give it, but she would never learn to be independent. Carmen wanted to call her mother about the decision; however, Jay's black Ferrari was pulling up in front of Gardner Hall.

"Stay here," Rakim ordered, walking down the steps.

Carmen eyed him carefully unsure of why he told her to stay put. When he got inside of Jay's car and closed the door, Carmen crossed her arms over her chest. He wasn't in the car for long and once he emerged, he told Carmen that Jay was all hers. He didn't say much else, leaving Carmen suspicious. Somewhat concerned, she walked down the steps and got inside the car.

"Well, hello," she greeted, sneaking a quick peek at the time. There was about fifteen minutes before her class started. "I wish I had of known you were coming."

Jay eased out a slight smile as he pressed his foot on the gas. When he started to speed through the campus, Carmen reminded him she had class at one.

Jay heard her yet his mind was focused on a new deal he was working on. It was one that didn't have anything to do with drugs that he thought she could possibly handle. She had asked to work with him in the past and he had told her she wasn't ready. Now, she seemed like she may be the missing link he needed.

"Do you like diamonds?" he asked, putting the car in park.

"Do I like diamonds? Why are you asking me that? Does this have something to do with Rakim? Y'all only spoke for like a second."

"I want to know if you like diamonds."

"Diamonds are a girl's best friend."

Jay glanced at her to see if she was serious. "I got a lead on some diamonds. I figured we could get a small crew together, me and you in the lead, and make some serious money. If this works, I could possibly leave all this drug shit behind. What do you think? No one would expect a girl like you to be Catwoman."

"I think you're out your damn mind. Are you talking about stealing diamonds? Why would you think I would even want to be a part of something like that? I told you, I'm not about this illegal stuff. If you want to do that, fine, I'll visit you in a prison cell."

Jay's face was blank at first only because he should've remembered how Carmen was. She wasn't going to sign on to his team even if her life depended on it. She was more concerned with maintaining her wholesome image than stealing some stones. "I was fuckin' with you," he lied. "We obviously aren't on some Bonnie and Clyde shit." He let out a nervous chuckle so she would know he was only playing around. Unsure if she believed him, he remembered he had a small gift for her in the backseat.

"Actually, I asked you if you liked diamonds because I got you this."

Jay showed her a white box, which he opened to display a pair of oval-cut white diamond drop earrings. Carmen gasped in response, and he picked up one of the earrings so she could get a closer look. She looked at the earring, yet she didn't take it.

"I don't know what you and Carlos are doing," she finally said. "Carlos surprised Tiara with a car this morning and now you're surprising me with diamond earrings? What do y'all want?"

Jay's forehead furrowed. "What do we want? What kind of question is that?"

"I can't take these earrings. We're not official. You're not my boyfriend or my husband. I haven't even known you for a week and you're giving me diamond earrings?"

Jay was extremely confused. If he was handing the earrings to Tricia, she wouldn't have questioned anything. Carmen, on the other hand, acted as if she didn't want the gift. "This is some bullshit." Jay dropped the earring back in the box. "You know what I do, Carm. You know I have money. Those earrings didn't hurt my bank account. That was my lunch money. I bought the earrings so you would know I was serious about you."

"I'm appreciative, but you are moving too fast. Carlos is moving too fast. He shouldn't have bought Tiara a car."

"When you have money, you can make moves the average person can't make. Carlos didn't buy her a car because he was madly in love with her. He needed to move some things and Tiara had great credit. He bought her a car so he could use her name and control the vehicle. It's a game, Carmen, it's all a game."

"I don't want to learn the game."

Jay turned the key inside of the ignition switch and listened as his car roared to life. The innocence he loved about Carmen was also one of the things that irked him. It stopped her from accepting his gift while at the same time; it reassured him she would never cross him. She wasn't with him for his money.

"What part of the game is this?" Carmen asked as he drove back to campus.

Jay didn't answer. Deep down, he didn't want to. If she wasn't getting the earrings, he didn't need to respond. The earrings would soon fall in the hands of a person he knew wouldn't turn down the gift. Tricia looked forward to material things, which was the reason she was dating him. Though her feelings for him were sincere, she loved everything that glittered and shined.

Carmen stared at Jay until his car stopped in front of Gardner Hall. She knew he was upset with her, and their encounter would only make dinner awkward. The more she thought things over; she realized she was being hard on him for no reason at all. She mistook his sincerity and if she continued to do so, her actions would drive him away. "I'm not good with this stuff, Jay. I haven't been in a relationship in a long time. Add that to the fact you're a drug dealer, which I'm trying to hide from my parents, all of this is new. I can see the earrings came from a sincere place from how quiet you're being. This obviously has made you upset."

Jay remained quiet until he felt Carmen's hand slide the box out from underneath his fingertips. When he looked at the clock on his dashboard, he saw it was five minutes till one. Carmen wasn't going to skip, which meant he had to ease the tension between them before she went to class. "Do you really not like the earrings?"

"I never said I didn't like 'em," Carmen said with a grin. "I love the earrings." Carmen truly was appreciative and wanted to show him she was. With little to no hesitation, she leaned in closer to him and pressed her lips against his. The kiss only lasted about a minute before she pulled away. "Are we good?" she asked him.

"We're good," Jay replied. "Make sure you wear my earrings tonight."

"I will." Carmen snuck him another kiss before sliding the earrings in her tote bag. Since she was pressed for time, she quickly told him goodbye and got out the car. *Now*, Carmen thought, *how am I going to explain these earrings to my mother?*

***

Patricia stood at the far end of the dining room, admiring a vase full of white and gold flowers. Six small white candles had been set around the vase, which was centered in the middle of the dining room table. She wasn't much of an interior designer, but Patricia had to admit she had done the job well in a short amount of time. "This is beautiful," she bragged.

Carmen came out the kitchen just in time to hear her mother's comment. From where she was standing, she had to admit her mother had decorated the table nicely. "It is. You may have found a new hobby."

Patricia let out a small chuckle. "Maybe, who knows? What time are they getting here?" When Carmen told her seven, Patricia knew she had timed everything perfectly. "Good, really good," she continued, still admiring the table. "I wish your father was here to see this. Well, I want him to see the decorations. I don't want him here for dinner. He started on that Donald Trump high again. He got on my nerves so bad; I definitely was going to send him to the pool house to sleep."

Carmen smiled and sniffed the aroma coming from the kitchen. "I'm glad you made your famous sweet potato soufflé," she said, smelling the potatoes from the dining room.

"Yeah, so you can eat it all up. That's what you and your father do," her mother joked. "Your father doesn't even need to be having all that sugar. If he doesn't—" Patricia was interrupted by the sound of the doorbell.

"It's them," Carmen yelled, running to the door. She looked through the peephole to see Rakim and Jay standing outside. When she opened the door for them, she could hear her mother approaching from behind.

"Well, good evening, gentlemen," Patricia greeted. "Ahh, Rakim, it's nice to see your handsome face again," her mother said, grabbing his arm. "You, too, Jay, y'all boys come on in."

Carmen watched as her mother pulled Rakim into the dining room, already starting up a conversation on Greek life. She smiled and looked at Jay as he stepped in the house. She shut the door, locking it, and saw him glancing around the foyer. "Are you impressed?"

"A little," he said, honestly. "You don't have shit on my house, though." Jay looked around some more until he smelt the aroma floating around the foyer. "Can you cook, Carm?"

"Don't worry, papi, you won't ever go hungry."

"I smell a carrot cake. Is there a carrot cake in the kitchen?"

Carmen raised her brow only because the carrot cake wasn't something she smelt. While there was a carrot cake in the kitchen, her mother hadn't fixed it. It had been purchased from a bakery. "Yes," she told him, slowly. "You smell that?"

Jay nodded his head. He knew there was a carrot cake in the kitchen because he was the one who purchased it and dropped it off at Flame. It was all a part of his plan for their mini-date after dinner. "I do," he lied. "There's a spot I want to take you to. We can take a few slices of cake with us." A flirtatious grin flew across his face as he pulled her closer to him. Jay knew he couldn't keep his hands off her and the longer she was in his presence, the further he wanted them to go. When he was getting ready to kiss her, he heard her mother and Rakim returning to the foyer.

"Um, you two can join the rest of us," Patricia stated. "This isn't a dinner date. If I wanted that, I would've taken Rakim to Cipriani's."

Carmen rolled her eyes, yet she only allowed Jay to see it. Instead of voicing her true thoughts to her mother, she grabbed Jay's hand in hers and led him to the dining room. She knew she would have to help her mother bring the food out, so she directed Jay to his seat before disappearing in the kitchen. She grabbed the pan of baked macaroni and cheese while her mother carried out a tray of baked chicken. It took about three trips before the entire spread was on the table.

The first five minutes were spent in silence as they fixed their plates until Patricia started a conversation with Rakim. "So, Carmen tells me you want to join a fraternity this year. What made you decide that?"

"A fraternity is good for networking. I want to become a doctor and it'll be good to have some brothers who can help me along the way. Not financially, because I have that part taken care of, but when it comes to references and things of the like."

"How are you going to pledge and work?" Jay wondered if Rakim was aware of how much time was going to be devoted to the pledge process. He was already coming up short on his paper because of school.

"Oh, where do you work?" Patricia asked, realizing she never asked him. She waited for an answer as Rakim stumbled over his words. In the meantime, she watched as Carmen stood up, pouring everyone a glass of iced tea. By the time she was finished, Rakim still hadn't responded. Somewhat puzzled, she listened as he started to form an answer.

"I work at a pharmacy, I'm just an assistant though, in training, assistant in training," Rakim lied. He looked at Carmen to see if she thought her mother had bought the story. She only shrugged her shoulders at him before going back to her food. He wished he could've done the same, but her mother only probed him more about his decision to pledge. After a good ten minutes of giving her a verbal resume, he was finally able to eat. When his plate was clear, he helped Carmen gather the dishes while Jay and Patricia struck up a conversation on Flame.

It took about twenty minutes to clean up the kitchen and once they were finished, they returned to an empty dining room. Patricia and Jay were both standing in the foyer as if they were saying their goodbyes. Carmen and Rakim quickly joined them since dinner was over. Carmen wasn't quite sure what had been accomplished aside from the fact her mother had offered to write Rakim a letter of reference.

"I'm going to be back in about thirty minutes," Jay told her, knowing it was going to take that long to get Rakim home.

"Cool, I'll be here." Carmen gave him a quick peck on the cheek as she walked him and Rakim outside. She stood in her driveway until Jay's Ferrari disappeared down the end of her street. Only then, did she return inside to see her mother headed up the steps with a bowl of ice cream. "Mama," Carmen called out. She locked the front door as her mother became frozen on the stairwell. "Do you approve of Jay?"

Patricia knew the question was coming. She was simply waiting for it. "I've been very observant when it comes to Mr. Santiago. I know he's the one with the edge. Now, Carmen, I don't want to judge anybody, but I'm suspicious of him. Today, I noticed he was driving a black Ferrari." Patricia paused for a second so Carmen could have time to see where she was going. "He was driving that same car on Saturday. On Sunday, at church, he was in a Mercedes Benz. Then, when he came by the store on Monday, he was driving a Rolls Royce."

"He has three cars, Mama."

"He has that on a club owner's salary?"

Carmen heard the suspicion in her mother's voice. She wasn't buying the story. Though it was true Jay owned a club, she wouldn't dare tell her mother he was a drug dealer. "I guess," she replied. Carmen listened as her mother sighed. She knew she didn't believe her. *If she doesn't press the issue, I'll be fine. Once she does, I can kiss Jay and all things regarding our relationship goodbye.*

Thankfully, Patricia dropped the issue. She continued up the steps, still eating her ice cream. As for Carmen, she waited downstairs for Jay to come back. When he finally returned, he took her to a dead end street in her neighborhood. Carmen had piled several slices of carrot cake on a paper plate, which she had now divided between them. Now, they were doing more eating than talking, which seemed to satisfy them.

"This is good," Jay moaned, biting into another slice of cake. Most of his slices were gone while he noticed Carmen still had half of hers. He figured that once he ran out, he would sneak some of hers if he wanted more. He quickly learned the thought was mutual when Carmen grabbed one of his slices. She bit into it all while giggling at the robbery.

"I know you didn't do that shit," he fussed. "That was my slice. You had your own. Look at how much you have compared to me."

In a jokingly fashion, Carmen held up the slice she had stolen. When he gave her a sinister expression, Carmen calmed him down by placing a kiss on his cheek. Instead of leaving lipstick, she left an imprint of icing.

"I can feel that shit, Carm. You're going to be licking that off." Jay shook his head as he proceeded to look for a napkin.

Before he could wipe his cheek, he felt Carmen's tongue as it slid up against the side of his face. She had done it only once, but it was enough to make his manhood stiffen. The affection caught him off guard. "You're starting to open up a little more," he expressed. "I can see you coming around."

Carmen sat back in her seat, shyly. The move was so spontaneous; she was still trying to grasp what she'd done. While her tongue had been inside his mouth on several occasions, she had never actually licked him.

"It's a good thing," Jay explained, hearing her silence. "I like it."

"Good," Carmen muttered. She slid another piece of cake in her mouth to keep from having to say more. The lick made her remember that she had never told Jay she was a virgin. If he asked, she knew she would have to tell him. How he would feel afterwards, she didn't know. She would also have to tell him she wasn't going to sleep with him. She could tell he was someone who was used to getting his on the regular, which meant celibacy might be a problem.

"I had fun tonight, Carm."

"Me, too," Carmen replied. She set the rest of the cake on the plate and watched as Jay did the same. Once all the slices were on there, she wrapped it up in plastic wrap and slid it in a bag for Jay to keep. There were many more slices at home, which she figured her parents would finish.

"I need to get you home. You know I'm trying to impress your mother by getting you in at a decent hour."

Carmen agreed with him. It was nearing midnight and she had classes and work the next day. Throughout it all, she would have to find some time for him.

When he started up the car, she knew their time was dwindling. In less than three minutes, he was back in her driveway and Carmen was scribbling her phone number on a napkin. He did the same before walking her to the door. Jay didn't allow her to say goodbye to him. Instead, he grabbed her face and kissed her lips softly so she could tell from his touch how deep his feelings were becoming. Usually, his kisses were rough, but the one he gave her now was filled with passion and sensuality. After a few moments of taking her in, he broke away and whispered goodnight.

Carmen replied the same before going inside the house. Once the door was closed behind her, she exhaled. In such a short amount of time, Jay had made her fall for him. She had tried to hold back, but she no longer could. She liked him and it was something she no longer could hide. In fact, she didn't want to. Right then and there, Carmen made the decision she wanted Jay to be her boyfriend. The next time they talked, she would demand they become official. He had saved her life and from the looks of things, he was going to save her from ever living life alone.

Chapter Ten

Carmen had been dreaming of her and Jay's first sexual encounter when a loud, thunderous voice sounded inside her dream. Slowly coming to, she awoke Wednesday morning to learn her parents were engaged in a full blown argument.

"You promised me this weekend, Harold," her mother was saying.

"I know I did, but something came up. I gotta cut it short. I'm not saying we can't go, but I have to be back by Saturday night."

"I'm sick and tired of this. We need this vacation, that's why we're going," her mother yelled. "We need this time together."

"Baby, I'm sorry. I told you things were going to be getting really hectic around here."

Carmen opened her eyes, realizing her parents were right outside her door. She grunted at the sound of them before climbing out of bed to see if she could calm the argument. Since she was an only child, she sometimes had to be the mediator between them. Though her father never wanted her involved, he started to listen to her opinion once she turned eighteen. By the time she was twenty, he was taking her advice.

When she opened her door, the first thing her father said to her was an apology. He was standing in the doorway of their bedroom while her mother was seated on the bed with a planner and cell phone in her hands. She didn't stay there for long, getting up and slamming her bedroom door closed. Harold appeared to be shocked while Carmen knew it was coming. Her mother was fed up and had every reason to be. Carmen had barely seen her father in the last couple of days. Even Sunday morning, he wasn't at worship service with them.

"Daddy, for one day, can you cancel whatever it is you need to do? You and Mama need this time. As you can see, this is really bothering her. If you give her this one weekend, she may be able to handle the rest."

Her father parted his lips as if he was going to debate the issue with her as well. Carmen was certain he was, but she didn't give him the chance. She simply went in her room and closed her door. With two doors closed in his face, Carmen knew her father was going to knock on one of them. As expected, he ended up knocking on hers.

"It is so hard to be the only man in this house. You women love to stick together," he joked.

Carmen gave him a shy smile as she moved away from the door. She knew he wanted to tell her what was going on so she could be in his corner.

"Now, Carmen, I know you think I'm coming in here to talk about the problems your mother and I are going through, but I'm not. What I want to discuss with you is the rules of the house. Now, I know you're twenty-one, but we will not have another night like last Friday. You didn't come home until Saturday morning. I let it slide—" Carmen interrupted her father.

"It won't happen again," she told him, quickly. "I promise."

Harold was taken aback. He didn't know what kind of response Carmen was going to give, but he knew he didn't expect that. "Um, well, okay," he stammered. "Your mother says you have a little guy friend now. I knew it was bound to happen. I figured I needed to come in and have this discussion again. If you ever get in that spot when you feel like you can no longer control your—"

"Stop," Carmen yelled, covering her ears. She had spent the last seven minutes fantasizing about sexing Jay and now her father was warning her of the dangers of it. "Please, let's not discuss this right now. Can I at least have breakfast and a cup of coffee first?"

Harold held up his hands in defense. "Okay, we won't discuss it. You know about the birds and the bees. You also know your mother and I will not be cradling any babies before you're married. So, since you know, I'll let you be."

Carmen breathed a sigh of relief when her father walked out her room. He closed the door behind him, and she immediately grabbed her cell phone. Though it was still early, not even eight o'clock, she called Jay to tell him about her father's attempt to talk to her about sex. When he didn't answer, Carmen didn't think anything of it. She figured he was still asleep and made plans to call him later around lunchtime. She simply left him a message before getting in the shower. With less than an hour to get ready for her first class, she needed to move quickly. The day had already started with a bang, and she could only imagine what was to come.

Like she had planned, Carmen called Jay in between her morning and afternoon classes. She got his voicemail again, which she found unusual. Once again, she left a message for him to call her. By Friday, she was on pins and needles. She hadn't heard from him or seen him. At this point, multiple voicemails had been left and she had even stopped by Sapphire only to receive the message he wasn't there. Even his friends gave her the same story, neither of them had heard from him. Carmen was nervous, scared, and angry all at the same time. On Tuesday, they had shared something special and now he had disappeared into thin air. Carmen didn't know what to think or make of their relationship now.

To get some advice, she called Rakim up, who agreed to meet with her that afternoon at his house in the Westside. He shared the two-story home with Malik, who wasn't there when she arrived. Immediately when she walked inside, she noticed five guys who looked disheveled, sitting in his living room. She recognized them from school and Rakim quickly pulled her away, saying they were going to his room.

"Rakim, what is going on?" she asked as they climbed the steps. Earlier that week, he needed a reference letter, and now, it appeared as if he was already pledging. It didn't make sense to her, but Greek life didn't either. She was Greek illiterate despite her mother's membership in one of the largest female organizations.

"Don't say anything, Carm. You're not supposed to be here," he said, leading her up the steps. "Don't tell anyone who you saw here."

Carmen agreed to keep the secret as Rakim opened the door to his room. When she walked inside, she noticed it was decorated like most guys his age. There was a large sound system, a king-sized bed, posters of half-naked women, and a desk, which held a laptop and textbooks. She sat on his bed while Rakim remained standing. "You can't sit down with me?" she questioned. "I don't bite."

"Shut up, Carm," Rakim muttered, rolling his eyes. "I need to stand."

Carmen looked at him quizzically until she remembered a scene from the movie, *School Daze*. "Oh," she mouthed, seeing an image of Spike Lee's character being hit with a wooden paddle. She shook the image from her mind so she could get started on what she really came over to talk about. "I don't know where Jay is," she told him. "I've been calling him, going by Sapphire, talking to you and Carlos, but no one knows anything. I'm worried about him. Where could he be?"

Rakim shrugged his shoulders. Since he had begun his pledge process, he hadn't been around much. What he did know was that Jay's disappearing act wasn't anything new. A couple days out the month, Jay would take off and no one would know anything until he popped back up. They never questioned him, and he never volunteered the information. "Look, Jay can be a mystery sometimes. If he isn't trying to contact you then don't worry about him. He'll come around when he's ready."

"I can't accept that, Rakim. I care about him. He made me care about him. How can he do this to me? He comes in with a bang and then disappears?"

"Damn, Carmen, play the same game he's playing. If he's not calling you, don't call him. You barely even know him. It's been like a week since we met y'all at the diner. You don't even know his middle name."

"He doesn't have one," Carmen answered.

Rakim threw his hands up. "Okay, he doesn't, but you get my drift, right? Leave him alone. You need to make him chase you."

Carmen knew Rakim was right. Jay's disappearance could be another game he was playing with her. She was falling in his trap, and she didn't even know it. 'I guess that's what I'm going to do," she finally decided, standing up. "I miss him, though." Carmen watched as Rakim playfully rolled his eyes. She laughed in response as Carlos and Malik came up the steps. They both stopped at the door as if they couldn't believe she was there. When Carlos gave her the finger, Carmen knew it was time to make her exit. She gathered her things and allowed Rakim to walk her to the door. She didn't wave goodbye to the guys in the living room since she wasn't supposed to know they were there. She did, however, hug Rakim goodbye before driving over to her mother's store.

***

"I've already went through the shipment in the back," Tiara announced, sliding a few hundred dollar bills into an envelope. "I changed the display in front as well. It should last for a month or two before we go with a different theme." Tiara looked at Carmen, not hearing a response and realized her friend wasn't paying her any attention. "Um, Miss Davenport, can you do some work today?"

"Yeah," Carmen stammered, not able to take her eyes off the girl who walked in the store. Carmen didn't expect to ever lay eyes on Tricia again. If she was honest, Carmen had to admit the girl's name was almost as nonexistent as Jay. Tricia was outfitted in a pair of tight straight-legged jeans and a black top that showed off her ample cleavage. On her feet was a pair of gold ALDO platform heels, which Carmen had in her closet as well. A cell phone was glued to the girl's ear and Carmen desperately wanted to know who she was talking to.

Since Jay had disappeared on her, Carmen took it upon herself to see if she could get information from Tricia. She wasn't necessarily going to talk to her, but she was going to listen to her conversation. Carmen moved closer to her, pretending she was straightening one of the clothes' racks.

"There is a cute dress in here I know you'll like," she heard Tricia say. "I have some money left so I can get it for you. I know you want to see me in it."

Carmen narrowed her eyes at the girl's words. Tricia was obviously talking to a guy, but she didn't know if it was *her* guy. Automatically, Carmen started to compare herself to the girl. Physically, she knew she didn't stand a chance. Tricia was a bad bitch if Carmen had to say so herself. The girl's ass alone could grab a man's attention.

"Carmen, stop staring, ask her if she's with Jay."

Carmen jerked her head to find Tiara and Monifah standing beside her. "Will y'all go somewhere? Y'all are going to ruin my detective work."

"Shit, I'll go talk to her," Tiara mumbled, walking in Tricia's direction.

Carmen tried to grab her friend's arm, but Tiara was already at Tricia's side, asking her if she needed any assistance. Carmen turned away only because she didn't want Tricia to see her. If she did, the girl would know she was up to something. When Tiara finally came back, she gave her the signal that they needed to cut the girl's head off.

"I'm not going to beat around the bush with you, Carm. She's with Jay. He gave her some money to spend, and she is up here shopping with it. She didn't have to tell me because I heard Jay's voice on the phone. He's still banging that chick."

Carmen balled her hand into a fist. If Jay was still messing with Tricia then it explained why she couldn't get in touch with him. He couldn't talk to her because he was too busy trying to hide her from his girlfriend. What Jay didn't know was that she wasn't anyone's side chick. She had too much going for herself to even stoop to that level. "I want to confirm that information. I need to talk to her."

"Oh, no, you're not," Tiara yelled, grabbing Carmen's arm. "I'm not going to have you bitch slapping anyone in your mother's store."

"I don't care. I want to know if she's fuckin' my man," Carmen spat. She felt her anger elevate to the point that she wanted to confront Tricia. However, she knew she was the one in the wrong. Tricia was with Jay way before they had even met. If anything, Carmen needed to be apologizing to her.

"Carmen cursed? Oh, damn," Monifah said, grabbing Carmen's other arm. She had never heard her friend utter a four-letter word unless she was rapping along to a track. She knew now that Carmen was heated.

Tiara took it upon herself to calm her friend down. "Carmen, this isn't anything new. Do you know how many girls have stepped to me, saying they're still fuckin' Carlos? I even had a girl approach me at the mall saying she has a baby by him. Can you believe that? She didn't have the child with her so maybe she does, maybe, she doesn't. Who knows? If you ask me, they don't like me because he bought me a car. If Carlos is the father of her baby then she needs to put him on child support because he sure as hell claims—wait a minute, enough about me. Carmen, this shit isn't anything new. These girls are trifling out here."

"I don't care about that shit, Tee. I want to talk to her."

Carmen stared in anger as Tricia took a few dresses to the counter. Another associate, Tammy, rushed to help her since she and Tiara were on the floor. Her friends held her in place until Tricia's items were bagged, and she walked out the store. Carmen wanted to follow her, but her friends' grip wouldn't allow her to make a move. Before long, Tricia was gone, and Carmen was forced to accept that Jay had played her.

Chapter Eleven

Carmen was relieved when she returned home that evening to find the driveway empty. It meant her parents had left for their trip and she would have the house to herself. She could mope around the house and even cry if she wanted to. No one would be there to question her or stop her from even sneaking open a bottle of wine. If it was going to be anyone, it would be Tiara, who was on the phone with her.

"Monifah and I are going to Sapphire tonight? You want to come?"

"I'm not giving Jay any of my money or time. I hope he rots in hell."

"I knew you were going to say that," Tiara replied. "I hope he pops up soon. If I see him at the club, I'll curse him out for you. I can't believe his ass, sitting up here, trying to play somebody."

Carmen parted her lips to respond until she saw a set of bright lights behind her. She figured it was one of her neighbors until the sound of the car's motor grew louder. When she turned around, she was shocked to see Jay's Rolls Royce in her driveway. "Tee, let me call you back." Carmen hung up the phone not even letting her friend respond. She stuck her phone in her coat pocket as Jay got out his car.

"Are your parents' home?" he asked her.

Carmen placed both hands on her hips to let him know he started the conversation off wrong. She hadn't seen him in three days, discovered he was in a relationship and all he wanted to know was the whereabouts of her parents. Carmen was ready to unleash her frustration and he gave her the ammunition to do it.

"I know you're mad at me, Carm. You have every reason to be, and I want to clear everything up. Can I come inside?"

Carmen shook her head. Since the weather was starting to feel more like February, she wanted him to stand outside in the cold. If anyone was going inside, it was going to be her.

"I know you saw Tricia at your mother's store. She told me she saw you and that Tiara approached her. I had a lot of questions to answer with her, too. Now, it's my turn to come clean with you."

"Do it then," Carmen snapped.

Jay stuffed his hands in his pockets. "I was still dating Tricia. I hadn't broken up with her yet because I wasn't sure where we were headed. After Tuesday night, I knew we were going to be together. I ended up going out of town to Puerto Rico. I never told anyone, but I feel comfortable telling you. I have a house there. It was left to me by my parents. I have a butler named Silvas who takes care of it for me. Sometimes, I get homesick, and I need to get away. When I'm there, I ignore everything, even you. When I got back in town, Tricia's car broke down and she needed some help. I gave her the money; she got the car fixed and went shopping with the rest, which is why you saw her at Flame. When she approached me about you, I told her the truth. I told her I wanted to be with you. She was hurt, but she understands. Things are over between us. You won't ever have to worry about her again."

"So you think it's that easy?" Carmen yelled. Jay was being calm, but Carmen still wanted her scene. She wanted to embarrass him for the hurt he caused her. "You think you could come up here in your slamming car, talking about your house in Puerto Rico, say you broke up with her and I'm supposed to fall in your arms? Get the fuck out of here."

"I broke up with her, Carm."

"I don't care. I can't trust you. It's over. You can leave now."

Carmen turned away from him and opened the front door. She could hear him coming up behind her and he tried to force his way inside. He was too strong for her and managed to come in. He slammed the door closed behind him and even locked it. Unsure of what was going to happen, Carmen stood there in disbelief. She wanted to scream and cry yet her body wouldn't let her. All she could do was stand there in silence.

"I'm sorry, I was wrong, we can go through the whole spill. All I want you to do is forgive me. I know I hurt you. I apologize. Can we move on and finish where we left off on Tuesday?"

Carmen huffed in reply and marched into the dining room where she dropped her tote bag on the table. Jay followed behind her until they were both standing in the kitchen. She was taking a bottle of wine from the fridge, which she desperately needed to deal with his antics. Apparently, he didn't want her to have the drink because he pulled it from her hands.

"Tell me you forgive me," he demanded.

Carmen didn't say a word. To add to his fury, she opened one of the cabinets, taking out a wine glass. The move was enough to make Jay grab her, yet Carmen didn't expect for him to pin her down on the counter.

"Say it," he yelled. "I'm not fuckin' with her."

Carmen had to admit she was scared out her mind. Jay's behavior was becoming somewhat uncontrollable. For a quick second, she thought to call the police until she remembered he saved her life. If that one major detail wasn't hanging over her head then she would have. Instead, she forgave him and even told him so. The words seemed to calm him because he loosened his grip. He didn't let her go, but Carmen wasn't as scared as she once was. In fact, she had relaxed enough to allow Jay to position his lips on top of hers.

Since she had officially forgiven him, Carmen allowed him to stay in the house. To add even more reassurance, she gave him a tour of the home and the pool house. By the time they reached her bedroom, she had already dispelled that her parents were in Pennsylvania and weren't set to return until Sunday. The news alone was enough reason for Jay to get comfortable. He took off his shoes and laid on her bed where Carmen joined him. Since they had officially made up, Carmen expected for them to start reliving her dream minus the actual sex. However, Jay had other plans.

"You were so upset about Tricia, but Carlos told me he saw you in Rakim's bedroom."

Carmen leaned up so she could make sure she heard him correctly. "He told you what?" she asked him. Carmen knew what he was talking about, however, the story had become twisted. She was in Rakim's bedroom, but there wasn't anything going on. It was completely innocent. Matter of fact, she was there, discussing him.

"I've noticed how close you two have gotten. Rakim is a very loyal person and I trust him, but like me, he still has a dick that needs attention. Has he made a move on you?"

"Hell no," Carmen screamed. "I can't believe you listened to Carlos. We weren't doing anything. We were only talking."

"Why were you talking in his bedroom? Why were you even at his house? You don't even like going to the Westside."

Carmen stood up at the questions Jay was throwing at her. "Why are you questioning me about this? You're trying to flip this whole thing around on me. You were the one who was cheating, not me."

"I never cheated on you. Let's get that clear. I cheated on Tricia."

"Does that make it better? You know what; I don't want to deal with this. Put your shoes on. You need to go."

"I'll leave when I'm got damn ready," Jay yelled back. "I don't give a fuck whose house this is. I want to know what you and Rakim have going on. You feel comfortable enough to go to his house, which means there's a connection there. Now, I'm asking you, did he make a move on you?"

Carmen picked up the phone, preparing to call the cops. Jay didn't want to leave so she had to make him. When he heard her talking to the dispatcher, all hell broke loose. The phone went up in the air and he was pulling her across the bed to make sure she never picked it up again.

Out of nowhere, Carmen's rage reacted. They both began to battle yet Jay only tried to restrain her while Carmen constantly punched him in his face. Her blows weren't doing any harm, which made Carmen question her force. If anything, he was only becoming agitated. Eventually, he let her go and Carmen watched him as he slid his shoes back on. She knew he was getting ready to leave when he left the bedroom. She followed behind him until they were both on the steps. She didn't want to leave without ending things. She grabbed his arm to get his attention. He had to know that things between them were officially over.

Somehow, Carmen managed to get in front of him. He jerked his arm out her grasp, but she only grabbed it again. To free himself, he pushed her, not knowing she was barely on the step. Carmen could feel her feet come up from underneath her. She braced herself for the impact; however, she felt his hands snatch onto hers to hold her in place.

It took a second or two for her to regain composure. As for Jay, he sat on the step, burying his face in his hands. Carmen's nerves didn't allow her to say anything. She simply stood there, trying her best to catch her breath. Ten minutes passed of total silence before Jay gave her a much needed apology.

Too much in shock to respond, not one word was uttered out her mouth, not even when he stood up and went in her bedroom. All Carmen could do was stand there. *This is not what is supposed to be happening. We're supposed to be in each other's arms, sharing kisses, and exploring each other's bodies. That was the vision I had.*

Carmen wiped the tear that had fallen down her face. She joined Jay in her bedroom to see him underneath the covers. His shoes were next to her desk while he had draped his jeans and T-shirt on her chair. She needed to tell him to leave. She needed to make it clear that their relationship was over. She even needed to tell him he was bipolar. Nevertheless, what she needed to do didn't match with what she wanted to do. Only a minute passed before she heard him calling to her. He welcomed her in his arms and like a naïve little girl, she went to him. She became trapped in his arms, allowing his lips to explore the areas she had envisioned him doing. Every kiss ended with an apology and Carmen soaked it all up.

Chapter Twelve

The smell of cinnamon danced around Carmen's nostrils, waking her. When her eyes opened, she was surprised to find herself alone and nearly nude in the bed. Topless and wearing only her underwear, Carmen recalled almost everything that occurred between them. Since Jay wasn't there, she glanced around the room for any sign of his things. His jeans were gone, but his shoes were still beside her desk. Unsure of where he was, she grabbed her bathrobe and slid it on. Since she was smelling food, her first thought was to check the kitchen. When she walked inside, she found him at the stove, shirtless, making French toast.

"Good morning," he greeted, obviously refreshed. "This is the last one, you made it down just in time. I hope you don't mind me cooking."

"No, it's fine," Carmen replied. She spotted slices of bacon and scrambled eggs on the stove. Two glasses were set on the island as well as plates and silverware. Carmen watched him patiently as he finished cooking and then as he fixed her plate.

"I want to talk about last night," he told her, setting the plate in front of her. "I need to talk about last night," he corrected.

"We can let it go," Carmen responded. She picked up a fork, sticking it in her eggs. "You apologized like a thousand times already."

"I know I have a problem."

Carmen paused from eating. She looked at him, knowing he was going to admit to being bipolar. He didn't say those exact words, but he said enough for her to know he was aware he had an issue. He promised to get help and Carmen believed he would. She accepted his apology and went back to eating while he headed to the fridge. She thought he was going to get something out until she saw him pull a piece of paper off the refrigerator. "Oh, I drew that," Carmen told him, realizing he was looking at her family portrait. "That's me with my mom and dad. Do you like it?"

Jay felt a rock sit in the pit of his stomach. The image of Carmen's father made him nervous, and he couldn't explain why. There was something about the man that intimidated him. It even brought an image of his own father into his mind. "Yeah, it's nice," he replied. He put it back on the refrigerator before retrieving the orange juice from the fridge. He poured a glass for them both, continuing to serve her. They ate in silence and once he was finished, he cleared his plate so he could shower. Not quite sure of Carmen's plans for the day, he didn't want to keep her from her homework or Flame.

"I'm going upstairs to shower," he announced. "I'll be back down to clean up the kitchen. Are you enjoying everything?"

Carmen was too busy studying his muscle tone to even answer. His body was free of blemishes except for the numerous tattoos that covered his neck, arms, and chest. The mere sight of his golden skin and six-pack abs made her say something she normally wouldn't have said. "Do you want me to join you?"

A smile rapidly flew across Jay's face. "Most definitely," he replied. "Finish eating and we'll go up."

Carmen parted her lips at what she insinuated. She had spoken too soon and could see the excitement all over his face. She wanted to tell him she changed her mind, yet the words never came out. Unsure of what to do, she decided to go with the flow. She knew she wasn't going to sleep with him. She would have to control her hormones once they both were completely naked. If he hadn't pressured her last night then he wouldn't do it when they were at their most vulnerable.

Jay didn't let her down and never mentioned anything about them going all the way. Still, Carmen experienced more with him in those short ten minutes in the shower than she had in her entire life. She had allowed Jay to touch in her places no one had seen. She hesitated in bathing him until she could no longer stray away from feeling his manhood in her hands. Tiara claimed all men experienced shrinkage in water, but if that was the case then Jay was astronomically big when he was dry. It wasn't long before Carmen had her hands all over him and witnessed her first erection. Jay tried to hide it from her, but Carmen saw him when he came on the shower wall. Aware she had brought him to that point, she received a self-esteem boost.

She quickly finished showering and got out, leaving him to finish. She was already dressed when he emerged from the bathroom with a freshly shaven head. He was dressed in his clothes from the night before, which made Carmen question if she should give him something of her father's.

Certain her dad wouldn't miss it; she thought to suggest it to Jay until he spoke.

"Was I big enough for you? You didn't say anything about it."

Carmen erupted into a series of giggles not expecting his question. After what happened, she thought he knew she was pleased. If anything, she thought he was too big for her. Since she was a virgin, the idea of his penis one day going inside of her was a little frightening. *Hopefully, by that time,* Carmen thought, *I'll be well versed in how this whole sex thing works.*

"Say something; did you like it?" he asked, grabbing himself.

Carmen felt a chill run through her body as he held himself. "I did like it," she told him, moving closer to him. "I even liked the surprise ending." Carmen placed her lips on his while her hands became draped at his groin. Without hesitation, she grabbed his package, massaging him like she had done in the shower. When he pulled away, she thought she had done something wrong.

"I heard a door close."

Carmen took her hands off his manhood to listen for any voices in the house. Not hearing any, she told him her parents weren't coming back until Sunday night. "My father took my mom to an opera. They won't be back until tomorrow."

Jay shook his head. "I heard a door close," he repeated.

"Maybe—" Carmen paused, hearing the voices she had heard for many years. Her parents were home and to top it off, they were arguing.

"This weekend was supposed to be fun. You tricked me into accompanying you on some got damn business trip. I told you, I wasn't going if it wasn't going to be about us."

Her mother yelled the entire time she was climbing the steps. Unsure of what to do, Carmen pushed Jay into her bathroom. If her mother was fussing then her father had to be near.

"Patricia, I said I was sorry. You were the one who demanded I bring you home. We could've stayed for the opera," her father replied.

Carmen knew her parents were now right in front of her door. They could open it at any minute to see if she was there.

"We need to be concentrating on the main issue at hand. I want you to tell me why there's a got damn Rolls Royce parked in my driveway."

Carmen closed her eyes tight, forgetting about Jay's car. It was no use in running now. Her father knew she had someone upstairs.

"I want to know who that car belongs to. If Carmen has gone and bought a car behind my back, oh, I'm going to wear her ass out."

Carmen winced and looked towards the direction of the bathroom where Jay was peeking out. She was waiting for her mother to slam the door, which would usually be followed by her father banging up against it to get her to come out. However, that didn't happen. Carmen looked at Jay and saw him as he walked hurriedly out the bathroom.

"Shit, it's going to have to go down," he said, grabbing his keys from her bedside table. Carmen pushed him back and motioned for him to be quiet. She could almost hear her father breathing right outside her door.

"I heard a voice," her father said.

Carmen knew she was caught. Jay motioned for her to go ahead and open the door, but she was scared. She knew her mother wouldn't be surprised to see Jay, but her father had never met him. Carmen listened as her mother tried to help her by continuing to argue about the trip. It didn't work and in almost slow motion, Carmen watched as her bedroom door flew open.

"What the fuck?"

"Mr. Davenport, I'm sorry we had to meet this way," Jay began.

Carmen looked at her father who had his eyes glued on Jay. He didn't even acknowledge her presence. His eyes went up and down Jay's entire body as if he was dissecting him. His expression, which was one initially of surprise, had now turned to one of almost empathy.

"Harold, I said I was going to deal—" Carmen's father put his hand up, silencing his wife without taking his eyes off Jay. He stared him down for a good solid minute before leaving the room.

Jay had felt the man's eyes burning right through him. The feeling he had when he saw the drawing of Carmen's father came back, but almost tenfold. "Why did he stare at me like that?" he asked, puzzled. No one answered his question and the only response he got was when Patricia told him he was dismissed. Her words were stern, which told Jay he outstayed his welcome.

Carmen knew it was best for him to leave. She grabbed her car keys and walked him to the door. She wasn't ready to deal with the lecture coming from her parents, so she wanted to get out the house as well. She figured she would drive around for a bit to collect her thoughts. "Are you going home?" Carmen asked once they were outside.

Jay told her yes before giving her a quick kiss on her lips. He wanted to do more, but her father was looking down on them from his bedroom window. The sight of the man didn't sit well with him, and Jay no longer wanted to stick around. He wanted to get as far away from the house as possible. With another small kiss, he got in his car, leaving the property.

Carmen watched as he left, wanting to go with him. She then looked at her house. She was in big trouble but going back inside was not an option. The idea came in her mind to follow Jay, which led her to getting inside her car. *I can see where he lives and leave. He will never even know.* She was going to have to speed up to catch up with him, but the idea seemed attainable.

She pressed her foot harder on the gas pedal and sped through the neighborhood until she was a couple of yards away from him. She didn't know if he could see her or not. To make sure he couldn't, she allowed another car to get in front of her. Carmen could tell after a few minutes that Jay lived far out when he hit the interstate. She drove a few minutes longer, before checking the gas gauge to make sure she could make the trip. It wasn't long before Jay took an exit. *Maybe, he's not going home. Maybe, he's going somewhere else. I hope he didn't lie to me. I don't want to catch him in anymore lies.*

Carmen followed him and watched as he turned onto a street that looked almost like a dead end. She looked around the area, seeing a large house sitting on a hill. She realized it was more of an estate than a house. When Jay's brake lights came on, she stared in amazement at a set of steel gates. Carmen's mouth dropped open as the word Santiago separated into two as the gates opened. She quickly pulled over, getting out the car and slipped inside before the gates closed.

Carmen didn't know what to think when Jay got out the car. She wanted to scream his name while at the same time; she didn't want to make her presence known. Things turned around in her favor when Jay looked behind him. He noticed she was there and even motioned for her to come to him.

"I'm sorry," she told him as she neared him.

"I was mad ten minutes ago. I knew you were following me."

Jay was trying to maintain every secret he had, but Carmen wouldn't let him. She was forcing him to become open when he wanted to remain a mystery. Now that she had discovered where he lived, he had to tell her the truth. If she had made it this far then he knew she could handle it. Therefore, he invited her inside and listened as she gawked over the décor.

Carmen let out a slight shrill, looking at the framed paintings on the wall as she walked down the hallway. The first room she came to, the living room, was a big spacious area with loveseats, recliners, and even a leather sofa. "This is beautiful," she admired, looking around. Carmen stared at the fireplace until she noticed an oil painting overhead. It was of a man who looked like Jay except he was a rounder version with curlier hair. He had an olive skin complexion and his stomach protruded outwards.

"I'm gonna change," Jay told her, leaving her alone.

Carmen nodded her head as she continued to give herself a tour. There were other picture frames that lined the walls and Carmen wanted to learn everything she could about Jay's family. Her eyes eventually landed on a picture of a Hispanic man and black woman who she assumed were Jay's parents. She even recognized the man as the person in the oil painting. Jay's father was dressed in a black tuxedo and his left arm was draped over the woman's shoulders. Meanwhile, his mother wore a pale yellow chiffon gown. The woman was extremely curvy with large round hips and thighs. Next to their picture was a small, framed portrait of a baby boy. It didn't take her long to notice the hazel eyes and realize she was staring at Jay.

"Do you like what you see?"

Carmen turned around, seeing Jay in a white T-shirt with grey sweatpants. "Yeah," she told him, sitting on the sofa. "Your parents look happy together," she commented.

"They were happy together."

Jay sat down next to her, and Carmen immediately started to comfort him. "I'm sorry," she murmured, kissing his cheek. "I know losing them hurt." Jay pulled away, whispering, it was a long time ago. Carmen could tell it still bothered him from how he was staring at his father's painting. She studied the portrait as well until his father became recognizable. *No God, it can't be. Is this who I think it is? This man can't be his father.*

"You're Hector Santiago's son?" Carmen asked.

Jay's head dropped to the floor. No one had mentioned his father's name in a long time. It sent chills through his body to even hear the name Hector.

"He was the famous politician from Puerto Rico, who owned all those businesses? Jay, where have you been? I remember reading in a magazine about how people were thinking you had vanished overseas. It was a big spectacle a year back. Someone had bought one of your father's businesses and people were speculating about who the money was going to. One day, the whole thing was over."

Jay's jaw tightened as she spoke of the rumors that were circulating about him. He knew people were looking for him. They wanted to interview him, make him face the rumors of his father's cartel and even steal his fortune. He tried to remain out the public eye so he could live in peace. The only two people who knew his truth were Carlos and Rakim. Carlos had grown up with him while Rakim was smart like Carmen and could put two and two together. Tricia never knew and Malik only accepted what Jay told him.

"Your father did a lot for the Hispanic community. He was a brilliant man, rich, powerful, and very community-oriented. He gave to a lot of—" Carmen stopped, not knowing if she was upsetting him.

"My father was not a hero. You think because he opened some damn companies, turned a dollar into millions, and gave a few Hispanics a job; he was some King of New York? He wasn't," Jay said, turning to face her. "He's the reason I'm fucked up now. Do you think I'm a drug dealer because I can't get a job?"

"I don't know, I never really thought about it."

"My father was a drug dealer in Puerto Rico. He knew he could keep his Puerto Rican connect and make more money in the states. He also knew if he got in good with the government he didn't have to worry about having any heat on his back. Cops were picking up black men off the street, throwing them in jail when they knew they were using their paychecks to buy shit from my father. While everyone was running around, yapping about the heroin epidemic, my father was laughing his way to the bank. He had the rest of his men laughing with him."

"Your father was an icon, Jay. He was like Martin Luther King."

"My father ran drugs in and out his businesses. He was the savior to the Hispanic community. Do you know how many men were able to send their kids to college because of my father? My father was everything in the book, good and bad. He was the best father I could've asked for, but I saw a lot of things I wasn't supposed to see. He put my mother through a ton of shit. Do you think my father hesitated in killing someone? I've seen so many heads shot off in my lifetime. That shit doesn't faze me, Carm. Killing Pierre was minuscule. My mother didn't want me around that shit because she knew it would fuck me up. Look at me," he yelled, holding up his arms. "I can't even control my aggression with my girlfriend."

"Your father, he—" Jay cut her off.

"My father ran a drug cartel. He was a gangster, murderer, and a businessman all rolled into one who had the country fooled. I heard my mother beg my father many nights to come correct, but he was on a high. He had secured this connect in the Bahamas and wasn't about to stop. He already had the US and Colombia on lock. He didn't even know what he was doing to me. I woke up in the middle of the night plenty of times to people arguing and gunshots. To think, they called our house, Casa de Sangre. I was a kid, Carm. I was living in a house called the house of blood."

Carmen felt a tear slide down her face.

"Then, one of those motherfuckers broke in our home, and shot my father point blank in the head. He left me to wake up in the middle of the night and see his fuckin' brains splattered everywhere. I lost my mother nearly a year later because she couldn't deal with the pain. She shot herself. That vision has never left me. I go to sleep seeing my father's head busted open, and I wake up to my mother screaming. She shot herself in her damn heart. I couldn't even move my parents' bedroom suite out the house. Somewhere deep down in those wooden cracks, there's a trace of my parents' blood I might not have cleaned up too well."

Tears streamed down Carmen's face. She watched as Jay turned and faced the painting of his father.

"The next thing I want to do is find the man who killed my father. I could care less about the men who took their money and ran. They didn't even stay around to keep his companies running."

Carmen stood up, walked towards him, and placed her hands on his shoulder. "You don't have to do this," she said, rubbing his shoulders. "You don't have to look for him. You can stop."

"I'm too deep in this to stop. You don't even know who you're dealing with. I'm deeper in this than you think." Jay turned to face her. He saw the tears coming down her face, but he knew she could handle the truth.

"You need some help."

"Give me the name of one person who can help me? I've been doing this shit since I was ten years old. I killed a man at fifteen. Don't feed me any false hope, Carm. Who can help me?"

Carmen backed away, wiping her face. "I can help you," Carmen whispered. "We'll go see someone. You need to get this out."

"The world is ready to devour me. I'm sitting here on all this money. I own all these properties. I own all these companies, yet no one has seen me. I'm a ghost. Tell me what the state of New York is going to do when Jay Santiago reappears?"

"Is this what you want? You want to live up here by yourself?"

"It is what it is."

Jay pushed past her and walked out the living room towards the stairwell. With each step he took, the sound became louder and heavier. He could hear Carmen following behind him as he returned to his room. He allowed her inside, showing her the huge king-sized bed that was covered in cream sheets and pillows. He moved behind her, gripping her waist as his lips nibbled at her right ear. "You've never experienced shit. Now look at you, you've fallen for a fuckin' monster. You're not scared of me, Carm?"

"No," she answered in a low voice.

"Would you move up here with me?"

Carmen took a deep breath, trying to figure out what he was getting at. "I don't know," she said, feeling his lips on her neck. For minutes on end, she started to get lost in his kisses. To make matters worse, Jay's hands were now cupping her breasts, sending tingles throughout her body. Carmen couldn't withstand him any longer. She wanted to feel every part of him and the only way to do it was for their souls to touch. There was no time for second thoughts as they both slid on top of the covers. Things had happened so fast; Carmen didn't even remember her shirt coming off. All she knew was that Jay was unhooking her bra and placing warm kisses in the middle of her chest. She cradled his head in his hands until she felt her panties being slid towards her ankles.

Carmen knew what was coming next. She had never officially disclosed to Jay she was a virgin, but she figured he knew. If he didn't know, it would show in how she performed. For now, Jay was busy digging inside one of his drawers. When he pulled out a condom, Carmen became embarrassed. She had completely forgotten all about protection. Since he had remembered, she watched him as he slid the rubber on. His attention soon went back to her, and Carmen felt his hands as he separated her legs. His fingers slowly slid inside of her and she couldn't help but close her eyes. His fingertips were exploring every inch of her region, forcing her to become wet from his touch.

Jay studied Carmen's face in absolute admiration. Her eyes were closed, her head tilted back at a near perfect angle. He knew she wasn't ready for him so he played around with her some more until she could handle him. Once she became moist, he took his fingers out of her and slowly slid his dick in, whispering he would go slowly. When he saw her wince, he pulled himself back out. He waited until she encouraged him to continue before he tried again. Only the tip was in and when he pushed himself inside even further, he saw the look of pain on her face. Immediately, he pulled himself out. "I'll stop if you want me, too," he said, not wanting to hurt her.

Carmen shook her head. Jay slid himself back inside and gave one small thrust, his body tensing up with pleasure. Unable to control himself, he thrusted inside of her, repeatedly. His hands grabbed her hair as his speed increased and eventually, Carmen wrapped her legs around him. They stayed in that position until Jay felt he was about to cum. He wanted to prolong it so they came together, but he couldn't hold it any longer.

When he felt he was about to release, he stared at her face, seeing she did somewhat resemble her father. It turned him on even more, thinking of how he was fucking Daddy's little princess. He hated to be thinking of her father while he was sexing her, but the man wouldn't leave his mind. Jay knew him from somewhere, but he couldn't put a finger on it.

As he stared at her, he saw she couldn't handle the sensations that were coming. He pumped faster and harder until he felt her legs stretch out underneath him. Jay froze, feeling himself release as they both came. Although he had done most of the work, Carmen had satisfied him more than Tricia ever had. When she smiled at him, he began to smell the scent of their lovemaking. Sweat beads had also formed on his forehead.

Jay was still looking at her when he found the answer he had been searching for. In a split second, he started to see Carmen in a different light. He immediately pulled himself out of her, almost scared to touch her. Automatically, he was ashamed of what he'd done. It wasn't the fact he'd taken her virginity, or that he hadn't taken it as easy with her as he thought he would. It was the fact he had one name running through his mind: Lotus Pagua.

Chapter Thirteen

Carmen was somewhat frightened to walk inside her house. In only one morning, she had been caught with a man in her bedroom and she had lost her virginity. She thought she could sneak through the kitchen to take the back way to her room, but the door was propped open. Orange juice was splattered on the floor and their glass pitcher was now in broken little pieces. Carmen questioned what she had missed since her father was busy cleaning up the mess.

"Your mother missed my head."

Carmen waited for her father to show her a sign he was joking. He never did so she started to clean up the kitchen. So much had transpired; she forgot she had left the kitchen in disarray. Since her father hadn't fussed at her for it, she realized his mind was on his own problems.

"My real estate business is really taking a toll on my marriage. Maybe, I should go back to selling cheap houses, let us get in debt for a while and maybe your mother will appreciate how hard I work. She can't afford to pay a damn bill in this house, but she fusses at me for keeping the lights on."

"There isn't anything wrong with you working, Daddy. You simply need to stop bringing the shit home."

"What did you say to me?"

Carmen hadn't caught the curse word that sounded out her mouth. She looked at her father inquisitively because she knew her words were crystal clear. If he was upset then it was because she was taking her mother's side. "I said don't bring your work home," she repeated.

"No, you said, stop bringing the shit home. I heard you. I get a glass pitcher thrown at my head and cursed at in one day. That's the life of a real estate agent," her father said, chuckling. He finished mopping and opened the backdoor to sit the mop on the patio. He knew he needed to hose it down, but he didn't have the patience to do it. "I'm heading to the office. I'll probably be home in time for dinner. For right now, I'm trying to stay clear of all flying objects."

Carmen rolled her eyes as her father left the kitchen, but he wasn't gone long. In no time, he was peeking back inside, telling her she had a visitor. Carmen instantly thought it was Tiara until she walked in the foyer and saw Jay. She had left his bed only minutes ago, but he had returned to her house.

"I actually came to talk to you, Mr. Da-Davenport," Jay stuttered.

Harold was on his way up the steps to retrieve his briefcase when he heard Jay's request. Quite naturally, he answered with a resounding, "Why?"

"Can we speak in private?"

Carmen held up her hands, showing off the dish towel. She headed back in the kitchen so the two could be. She tried to listen through the door, yet it was of no use. Her father and Jay were obviously whispering. "So much for being nosy," she muttered under her breath. She went back to cleaning and once she had the dishes put away, Jay was joining her in the kitchen. At the sight of him, she inquired about their conversation.

"I was apologizing for being in the house."

"Oh, well, that was very mature of you. I didn't expect to see you this soon. I figured something else had happened." Carmen gave him a hug to further express her approval of the apology. She knew Jay wanted to meet her father at the right time instead of being caught red-handed in her room.

"It's all good. I would stick around, but I gotta meet Carlos at the diner. He's been calling all morning and I keep sending him to voicemail." Jay broke away from her and was about to head out the kitchen before he remembered he was coming back later. "Oh, one more thing," he continued. "Dinner is at six. We both have to make an appearance."

Carmen grimaced because she knew her parents were going to embarrass her in front of Jay. She could feel it coming. When Jay winked at her, he only confirmed her thoughts. She followed him to the door and watched him as he left until his car disappeared out her driveway.

***

The diner was the site of many conversations that took place between Jay and Carlos. When Jay listened to the last voicemail his best friend left, he knew he couldn't ignore him any longer. Carlos claimed there was new drama brewing and Jay needed to know what it was.

Carlos was already sitting in their regular booth when he approached him, but there wasn't any food or drinks on the table. Jay figured their conversation wouldn't last long so he didn't bother to order when the waitress approached him.

"Shakeem is coming out his coma."

Jay knew exactly what those words meant. Once Shakeem woke up and was back on the block, he was going to come for them. "You got word on it?"

"I hired this cat who lives on Dulin to watch him for me. He told me Shakeem was moving his hands and legs. We need to go ahead and set something up. Either we take him out at the hospital, or we wait until he gets out. We can let him see the sun for a few days, let him get some pussy, and then crack on him."

Jay thought long and hard about who he was going to use to drop the body. He knew he could easily do it, but there had been a lot of talk behind his back about Malik being trigger happy. If Malik wanted a body on his hands then he knew he could toss him Shakeem.

"I want to set it up," Carlos continued, "and I'm going to let Malik drop the body. Rakim is on this fraternity shit so he's out the game. To tell you the truth, he still has a lot of weight on him he hasn't even sold. Malik says his brother goes to school, comes home with about five other dudes and they sit there all night repeating shit until like eleven o'clock. Then, they leave and don't come back until five in the morning. Malik says the carpet stay muddy in his crib."

Jay's temper flared. He knew Rakim pledging was a bad idea. "My shit doesn't need to be there. He knows the code and where that shit is supposed to be. If the cops get a lead, their house is gone. I gave him weight to sell, not to store in a damn house."

"I'm trying to help him, but I can't worry about his weight and my weight, too. He knows cuts are about to come up. He knows if he hasn't sold the shit then he owes you big time."

Carlos felt like he didn't have a choice, but to tell Jay what was going on with Rakim. He hoped Jay would take the weight from him, sell it, and let Rakim be until he was done pledging.

"Fuck that Rakim shit, I'll sleep on that. With Shakeem, I say we get him after he gets out. I would hate for Malik to kill him, and he hasn't gotten any pussy yet."

"You didn't say that about Pierre," Carlos responded, jokingly. He stopped laughing when he saw Jay's expression. His friend's face had tensed up and Carlos knew he was liable to get cut. Obviously, things had changed between him and Carmen within the last twenty-four hours.

"Carmen and I are together now. I want you to respect her. Matter of fact, speaking of Carmen, do you remember, Lotus Pagua?"

Carlos wrinkled his face, not remembering the name.

"He was Bahamian," Jay told him. "He was the guy in my father's crew that was handling the properties and shit. I think he was the one who got your parents that house." From what Jay was seeing, Carlos still looked confused. "He was dark-skinned, baldheaded, and had a really rich Bahamian accent. He was the one who…," Jay tried to think of something the man had done. "He built that clubhouse in your parents' backyard for us."

"I remember him, vaguely, what about him?"

Carlos wondered how Jay had managed to get in touch with Lotus Pagua. Although his own father was close to Hector Santiago, it was Lotus who was really his right-hand man. Carlos remembered Lotus being good with houses, but that was pretty much it. "Are you thinking of taking him down?"

"Lotus Pagua is Carmen's father. He changed his name and probably his whole identity to Harold Davenport. He is still into real estate, but he is making big moves, selling buildings to Donald Trump and shit. He even lost his accent."

Carlos continued to shake his head over the issue. He hadn't stumbled across any of the men that used to run the Santiago cartel. His father, Domino, claimed most of them were dead or locked up. He told him no one had any success after Hector's murder.

"I had just finished boning Carmen when I figured that shit out. The minute she came, the name hit me like bricks. I couldn't believe it. Shit, I couldn't believe how tight her pussy was. That was the tightest shit I've ever been inside. It was the best, though, I wouldn't trade that shit for anything." Jay didn't think twice about what he admitted, until he saw Carlos' expression. A devious smile was plastered on his friend's face and Jay wished he hadn't said anything about how good Carmen had been. "That shit stays between me and you. It doesn't go any further than us."

"Man, you know I can keep a secret. I won't tell anyone."

"Cool, you're in charge of staying updated on Shakeem. Keep me posted."

With those words, Jay stood up and left the booth. If he had more time on his hands, he would've stayed longer. However, with dinner being at six, it gave him a time limit on how long he could be out in the streets. So much had to be done. If he was lucky, he would be able to check on all his spots before returning home for a quick nap and shower.

***

Harold was still surprised when he came down the steps to find Jay in his foyer. Since before that morning, he hadn't seen him since the last time he visited Hector. Jay had to have been around six years old. Harold remembered hearing about him when he was a teenager. He heard he was the exact replica of his father, already learning about the cartel, how to import drugs, and was stacking his own money.

He could relate because it used to be his life. For many years, he tried to put his past behind him. He thought changing his identity would help, but everywhere he turned, his past kept jumping in his face. Even now, out of all the men in Brookstone, Carmen had to date Jay Santiago, the sole heir of the Santiago estate. That detail alone made him stare at Jay.

"I'm not a mind reader, Lotus, but I can tell you want to ask me something." Jay gave Carmen's father an evil smirk. Lotus was furious he was dating his daughter and had even demanded that he break things off with her. To remind him he knew his secret, Jay had intentionally called him by his real name.

Harold eased up a bit, hating the fact that Jay was throwing his past in his face. He had done a lot of reconstruction to himself mentally and physically to get rid of Lotus. As a native of Bahamas, he had trained himself to speak English with an American accent. He had gotten rid of all connections to the island by changing his identity and creating a new lifestyle for himself. Under the name Harold Davenport, he had earned a college degree and used his illegal earnings to his advantage. He had begged Hector to do the same, but his friend never listened and was soon found covered in his own blood and brain matter.

"Every time you see me, you call me Harold Davenport."

Jay smirked, knowing he had Lotus where he wanted him. He was getting heated with him, but he knew he wouldn't verbalize his anger. Carmen and her mother were both in the dining room, setting the table. He knew Carmen was eavesdropping even if he didn't directly see her doing it. He made sure to crank up his volume to ease her suspicions. "Tell me, Mr. Davenport, about how you took one dollar and turned it into a million."

"You need determination and a good head on your shoulders," Harold responded, looking in the dining room. When he noticed Carmen staring at him, he continued the façade. "It also helps to have some sort of degree under your belt. Young Puerto Rican men like yourself…" Harold's voice became a whisper, "can't run the streets forever."

"Dinner is ready," Patricia announced. "Why don't y'all come join us?"

Harold extended his hand towards the dining room. "After you," he insisted. He watched as Jay stepped in front of him and sat down. Hector had taught his son well, but Harold knew he had missed a couple of lessons he desperately needed to learn. Once he had sat down as well, he started to become guilty. Jay had witnessed some of his own deeds as a child, too. He walked in on several of their killings when they thought he was asleep.

"Daddy, you're in deep thought," Carmen said, noticing her father's silence.

"I have a lot on my mind, Peaches."

Carmen accepted his answer and nudged Jay with her arm. She knew he had been in heavy conversation with her father when she was preparing the table. Their mutual interest in business was what probably kept the conversation going. When he nudged her back, Carmen asked if he wanted to say grace.

Jay wasn't a very religious person but decided to comply for the hell of it. "Can we bow our heads?" He waited until he saw everyone's head down before he started. "Dear, Lord, we want to come together and say thank you for this meal that has been prepared for us and the hands that prepared it. In Jesus' name we pray, Amen."

"Amen."

"Let's eat," Patricia said, picking up the potato salad. She scooped some on her plate then passed it to her husband. He paused and she looked in the direction of his gaze. "Take some potato salad," she told him, nudging him in the shoulder. She noticed his eyes were on Jay. She wondered what was going on between the two of them. She hoped Harold hadn't given him the third degree. Her husband finally took the bowl from her and scooped some of the dish on his plate before passing it to Carmen.

"Tell me about this club you own, Jay," Harold asked, curious to know about Sapphire. He remembered seeing the spot in passing, but never paid much attention to it. Harold wondered if it was one of the businesses Hector had opened before his death. After he left the cartel, he rarely got updates on the businesses Hector was working on.

"Sapphire is a hip-hop dance club. I got a bar, VIP section, there's an upper level overhead, but that's my office. We're on the main strip here on the Eastside. My father used to own the club. It got sold to another club owner, but I was able to buy it back."

"How are your parents, Jay? We haven't met—" Patricia glared at her husband when she heard him almost spit out his drink. He quickly apologized, allowing Jay to answer.

"They're deceased," Jay told her. He looked at Lotus to see if he was still in shock. When he saw he was busy fixing his plate, he continued speaking. "I would rather not discuss them."

"Well, we don't have to, do we?" Harold took a piece of fried chicken off a platter before handing it to Carmen.

"Did you know Jay was Puerto Rican?" Patricia asked, stuffing her mouth with potato salad. "Carmen is in an interracial relationship."

"Light-skinned men are trying to make a comeback," Harold mumbled.

Jay paid no attention to him and grabbed the platter of chicken out Carmen's hand. He picked up a breast before setting the platter in the middle of the table. He concentrated on his food while Harold started a discussion on good business. It seemed to keep Carmen and her mother entertained because no one noticed he wasn't talking until fifteen minutes later.

"You're quiet," Carmen whispered.

"I got a lot on my mind," he shot back.

Carmen's mouth made an O. About to respond, she listened as her father stood up from the table.

"Excuse me; I have some work I need to tend to." Her father grabbed his plate, which was still somewhat full. In Carmen's opinion, her father was running from something.

"Harold," her mother said, sternly.

Carmen knew it was coming. She looked at Jay's plate seeing he had eaten about half of his food and decided it was best for them to excuse themselves before the bickering started.

"That's him, Jay, that's Harold Davenport. He can't sit down and have a decent meal because he's always running off to do work. What are you doing so much work for, anyway? Our house is paid for, cars are paid for, our daughter has one year of college left to go. There isn't that much work in the world. You need to retire with your old ass," her mother yelled.

Jay chuckled at Patricia's antics.

"See, what I go through, Mr. Santiago? See, what I deal with? My husband has no time for me or anything else besides his damn real estate business. This was supposed to be a nice dinner and a chance for us to get to know you better. He even barges out on that. I think I should leave him, what do you say?"

"Mama," Carmen began.

"I heard everything you said, Patricia," her father said, holding his plate. "You know I have a business to take care of. Have you seen all those requests on my desk? Now, you're talking about leaving me. Where would you go? Please, Patricia, I say very little about this idea of yours to open a new clothing store. Not to mention you want to open it up in Texas. That is halfway across the country. You have a lot on your plate, too."

"Let's go," Carmen said to Jay, getting up from the table.

"No, don't let him ruin our dinner. Harold, if you want to go in your office and continue staring at applications and whatever architectural bullshit you look at, go right ahead. We'll sit here and enjoy dinner without you."

"Don't you see we have company? Why are you acting like this?"

"I'm sick and tired of not having my husband around."

Patricia got up from the table and rushed into the kitchen. Carmen followed behind her with her own plate so she could calm her mother down.

Once Carmen had disappeared in the kitchen, Jay looked at Harold in disgust. "Y'all have some issues."

"You know nothing about my family."

"True. I got the whole scoop on you, though."

"Your father would be ashamed to see you disrespecting me."

"My father would be ashamed to see your bitch ass running around with a license that says Harold Davenport. You're a fake, Mr. Pagua." Jay stood up from the table and grabbed his plate.

"I would rather be a fake than die at the hands of one of my own men."

Jay's face tightened. He had never found the man who shot his father and Lotus' words were the closest he had ever come to knowing who could have done it. "I will kill you." Jay felt his temper flare and his hand automatically touched the gun in his waistband. He then watched as the kitchen door flung open and Carmen came out. He took his hand off the gun, but he knew she had seen the red in his face.

"What's going on?" Carmen asked, seeing Jay's expression.

"Nothing, Mr. Santiago was leaving."

Carmen looked at her father and then at Jay. She knew something had gone down between them, but she missed overhearing what was said. "Okay, I'll walk you out," she said to Jay, grabbing his arm.

Carmen hated the fact that dinner had been ruined with her parents' arguing, but there was not much she could do to control them. She wanted to talk to Jay about it, but she quickly learned his mind was elsewhere.

"I want you tonight," he whispered, pulling her towards him. "You can be butt naked or clothed; all I care about is that you're there."

Carmen looked behind her at her house. There was tension between her parents, and she didn't want to be a witness to any more of it. If she spent the night with Jay, it would take her out of the middle since her father already accused her of being on her mother's side.

"Do I need to remind you of what I feel like?"

Carmen giggled only because he couldn't give her the reminder outside. If anything, they would have to be behind closed doors for him to demonstrate. If he had enough condoms, they both were good. He could demonstrate as much as he wanted to. "Give me a second or two. I need to get a few things."

"I'll be in the car, Peaches."

Carmen winked at him, hearing her nickname and went inside the house. Her father was in the foyer, and she wasn't quite ready to tell him she was going to be spending the night with Jay. It wouldn't sit well with him since he met him only a few short hours ago.

Instead of telling him where she was going, she simply ran up the steps until he called her name. Carmen froze, aware her father was going to question why she had run from him.

"Peaches, can we talk for a second?"

Carmen wasn't ready for the discussion. She had covered her ears when he tried to talk about the birds and the bees, and she would do it again. "Can it wait until in the morning?"

Harold let out a loud sigh. "Carmen, I want to say I'm sorry. I want to formally apologize for anything I've done in my past or that I might do in the future. I want to simply say I'm sorry."

Carmen stared at her father, trying to figure out what he was talking about. She could ponder on his apology all day long, but his words still didn't make sense. *Maybe he has something up his sleeve. Maybe he's the one considering divorce.* To Carmen, it really didn't matter who was considering it. She only knew it was coming.

***

Carmen had snuck out her parents' house with a change of clothes for church in the morning. She figured she would leave Jay's house in enough time to get to Sunday school so her parents would be less harsh on her for spending the night with him. If anything, she wasn't ready to admit to them that she had lost her virginity. If she was careful, she could make it down the aisle without them ever knowing.

Although she was now in Jay's bed, they were only cuddling. He was busy talking about his parents and had even started comparing them to hers.

"My father was always at my mom's beck and call. He did everything for her. She never had to work or worry about a bill. Shit, my father bought her diamonds every single day."

"Sounds romantic," Carmen commented, not wanting to talk about their parents anymore. She placed her hand on his chest, feeling his rock hard abs. When he had time to work out, she didn't know, but he kept himself in shape. As for her, her stomach was flat, but it was smooth without definition. Jay didn't hesitate to grab her hand and stick it in his boxers. Carmen knew what he wanted, and she was about to give it to him until his phone rung. She was shocked when he answered, but she figured the call was important.

For Jay, any call from Carlos at one o'clock in the morning was important. When his friend told him Shakeem was awake, Jay sat up in bed. He knew it was only a matter of time before he ordered a hit. "Keep your eye on him," he told Carlos. "Make sure you know his every move. I want to know the second he's released." Once Carlos agreed to the plan, Jay hung up the phone. He placed his cell on the end table and directed his attention back to Carmen. She let out a soft cough as a hint she wanted to know what was going on, but Jay didn't buy it. "I'm not telling you shit, Carm."

She pouted for a bit, but he didn't let up. He was serious about keeping her out his business and it showed. Now aware she wasn't getting anything out of him, he pulled his boxers down, exposing his manhood. Though it was only going to be her second time, he wanted to try something different. He mounted her on top of him, sliding his body in between her legs. He then directed himself inside of her and guided her on how to please him. She caught on quick, riding him the entire time until they both passed out from orgasmic bliss.

Chapter Fourteen

June

For the rest of the spring semester, Carmen tried her best to manage her classes and her relationship with Jay. As their relationship grew, so did the amount of time they spent together. Although Jay had refused to tell her about his conversation with Carlos, Carmen eventually learned of his plan to take out Shakeem. When Pierre's right-hand fell back in a coma, after only being awake for one day, Carmen was grateful. The last thing she wanted was for Jay or anyone in his crew to catch a murder charge. She had enough to deal with and didn't need any added stress.

During the last week of exams in April, Carmen was really going through it. Things hadn't improved with her parents but had only gotten worse. Her mother moved in with one of her sorority sisters in Manhattan and had neglected her store. It left Carmen to run things while Tiara acted as assistant manager. She was responsible for all the store's finances and from going through the store's financial reports; she learned that Flame was damn near bankrupt. Carmen wanted to inform her parents, but they both appeared to be nonexistent.

Three weeks into the summer, nothing had changed in her life. Her mother still had not come back to work, even though business was slowing down drastically. Although they talked on a regular basis, her mother still didn't want to come home. Carmen had thought about permanently moving in with Jay, but she had never mentioned it to him. She knew her father wouldn't notice, because he didn't even see her when she was at home. She was used to him ignoring her because he was putting all his energy in his work.

Even now, as she sat in Jay's living room, Carmen wondered if there was anything she could do to get her parents to talk. She had to come up with a solution because her mother's sorority sister had already called, frustrated, with her mother being in her house.

"I need her to get out the house, go back to work or something," Soror Byers had said when Carmen last spoke to her. "She hasn't even been in church."

Carmen closed her eyes, knowing that neither one of her parents had been in worship. She only attended with Jay, who would drop a big check in the plate for them both. With her money now wrapped up in Flame, Carmen could barely afford to give anyone anything.

Carmen stretched out on the couch, knowing Jay wouldn't be back until later that night. She figured she would continue browsing through the house, especially the library, which she had stumbled upon a week ago.

The library wasn't a huge room and didn't even contain books she wanted to read. Bookshelves lined the walls while a large oak table served as a desk in the middle of the room. Carmen started with the first shelf, reading each book's spine until she grew bored of hearing the titles. At the bottom of the bookshelves were several cabinets, which caught her eye. She opened the first one to see several suitcases. Her first thought was that she would find money or some important documents pertaining to his father's business.

Carmen knew she was being nosy, but she also believed that rummaging through Jay's house would solve her problem of boredom. She didn't hesitate to open one of the suitcases and discovered several clippings of news stories related to unsolved murders. Most of the newspaper clippings involved local drug dealers or mobsters in Brookstone. She figured Jay kept them because of his involvement or simply because he knew the person.

Carmen closed the suitcase, picking up another one, and opened it. This one was filled with a collection of photographs. Carmen picked up each one, examining the photos and set the pics to the side. Hector Santiago had kept record of every single person who worked for him. If a person was deceased, their photo was attached to a death certificate.

Carmen continued to sort through the pictures until a folder become visible. She picked it up and noticed it was different than the others. Many of the folders were manila while this one was black. She tossed the pictures in the suitcase while holding the black folder in her hands. About to open it, she stopped and listened to see if Jay had come in. Only the ceiling fan sounded above her. She flipped it open to reveal a typed document regarding a man named Lotus Pagua.

Carmen could tell from the information presented that the man served as Hector's main connect to the Bahamas. Lotus was born in Nassau, stood at six feet four inches tall, and at the time the document was written, was a little over a hundred and ninety pounds. He had a clean record, except for a few traffic tickets he had gotten in the Bahamas. Included with the documents was a black and white copy of Lotus' driver's license.

Carmen stared at it and slowly felt her mouth open as she recognized the man in the picture. Her mind began racing as she thought back to her father's first meeting with Jay. She remembered how her father stared at him like he was in total shock. Jay had even come to their house, after taking her virginity, to supposedly apologize to her father. She then thought about all her father's business trips throughout the years. Carmen flipped the copy of the license over to see another page. It was a letter addressed to Hector Santiago.

Carmen was impressed by her father's writing, but it formed hatred in her heart towards him. He had stated in the letter that he was going nowhere. Her father was one of the men who resigned from the Santiago cartel before Hector had been murdered. Her father mentioned in the letter that he was not leaving due to the bad blood that had occurred between the cartel and the Bahamians, but because he was tired of the constant running. He was ready to settle down the right way and raise his family right. Her father slightly reprimanded Hector for the way he had raised his own son. Lotus declared that his child would know nothing of the cartel or the pain it had brought to the families of Brookstone. Her father made a promise to Hector that he was always his right-hand man before severing his ties.

Carmen looked up from the letter and turned it over. The next page was the copy of her father's new driver's license and social security card under the name Harold Davenport. The sight of it made Carmen close the folder in shock. Her father had been a part of the Santiago cartel. *No wonder Daddy has such good business sense. He knows all kinds of ways around the government. I can't believe this. Jay knew all along. He knew from the moment he saw my dad who he was.* Carmen wondered if the only reason Jay was with her was to get revenge on her father. Somewhat unsure, she knew she had to get in contact with her dad. He was going to have to explain everything to her. Carmen took a deep breath and picked up the folder to put it back in the suitcase. When she turned on her heel, she ran into Jay. She hadn't even heard him come in.

"You find what you were looking for?"

Jay jerked the folder out her hands only because he didn't know what she had found. When he saw Lotus' old driver's license, he became more at ease. He hadn't reneged on his deal with her father, but Carmen's nosy spirit had led her to the truth. "Well, the secret is out."

"So, when were you going to tell me about my father?"

"I wasn't," he said, honestly. "I made a deal with him. If I kept his secret, I could keep dating you."

Carmen couldn't believe her ears. "You blackmailed him?"

Jay didn't answer but placed the folder back into the suitcase that was sticking out the cabinet. He figured she had pulled the folder from there. "I didn't know who your father was until the first time we had sex. I didn't even recognize him. I only had a bad feeling about him. The minute I confronted him about the matter, he demanded I leave you alone. I wasn't going to do that. I did what I had to do."

Carmen stormed out the room confused at whom to be mad at. Should she be mad at the father who had harbored a terrible secret from her or the man she loved who only wanted to stay with her? She heard Jay's footsteps behind her as she headed towards the living room to get her tote.

"You should be proud of your father. He got out the game early."

"My father is a murderer, con artist, and a member of a drug cartel."

"He was those things. He's a successful real estate agent now."

Carmen ignored him, grabbing her tote. "I'll be back later. I need to see my dad."

Jay blocked her path. He knew Carmen was upset, but confronting Lotus wasn't exactly the best idea at the time. Her parents were separated, and it could be the one thing to drive them to a divorce. If anything, Carmen needed to wait and allow Lotus to tell her. "Do you know what this is going to do to your mother when she finds out?"

"I can't concentrate on that right now. I need to talk to him." Carmen pushed him out her way, moving past him. She didn't want any of his advice especially when he had blackmailed her father. If anything, he needed to be supporting her. He knew from day one of his father's criminal enterprise while it took twenty-one years for her to learn of hers. Now that she had, it was time for answers. The only way to get 'em was to ask.

***

Carmen had plenty of time to think as she waited on the steps for her father to show. Three hours had passed, six missed phone calls from Jay were displayed on her phone, and she still hadn't seen her father. Where he was, she didn't know. His secretary claimed he had already left the office and he wasn't at the city's local country club. If anything, he was driving around, trying to stay away from an empty house. At the thought, Carmen peered at the walls that surrounded her, wondering if it was bought with drug money. Although her father had ended his ties with the cartel, he still had all his earnings, which he put into his business and possibly their home.

At the sound of locks turning, Carmen wiped her face so her tears wouldn't be displayed. The door opened shortly after, displaying her father's lofty frame.

"Hey, Peaches," he said, solemnly.

Carmen could hear the stress in her father's voice. She knew the separation was weighing heavily on him and the distance between them didn't help. Everything seemed to be taking a toll on him and she was only going to add to it. "Lotus," she mumbled.

Harold looked at her hard unsure if he heard right. "What did you call me?" Harold waited impatiently for Carmen to repeat herself. The second she did, he knew his ears hadn't played tricks on him. "That son of a bitch," he yelled.

Carmen swallowed before telling him that Jay hadn't spilled his secret. "I was snooping in Jay's library and found Hector's folder on you. He had copies of your drivers' licenses, even the letter you wrote him severing your ties to the cartel. I know everything."

Harold held his head in his hands, backing up against the front door. "I tried to protect you. I didn't want you to know. You wouldn't understand. It's something that shouldn't even be talked about. I try not to remember."

"Why did you get involved with him?"

"The same reason everyone got involved with him. We came from poor backgrounds, and he showed us money signs. I was seeking a way to the states. He was my main connect in Puerto Rico. When he moved to the states, we continued working together. We worked well together. Of course, as time went on, with the more money we made, the more problems we had. It didn't take us long to assemble a crew. Everyone wanted what we had."

"Hector, Domino, and I, were the ringleaders," he continued. "We had people working underneath us. Hector controlled the government, I controlled the real estate, and Domino took over the banks. We had it made. Then, people started getting suspicious. The Triad began investigating Hector. They were paying people to stitch. That was when our problems started. I saw countless nights where Jay walked in on us killing someone for snitching. I didn't want you to go through that, so I pulled out. I vowed I would stand next to Hector for the rest of my life and I did. I simply didn't do it the way he wanted me to. I didn't want my child to turn out like Jay. He's merciless and psychotic. He's mentally sick."

"So you murdered people, too? How do you have the heart to take someone's life?" Carmen stared at her father, realizing he was like Jay in more ways than one. He had described her boyfriend as being mentally sick, but her father had to be as well to pull a trigger.

"I had to protect myself. I did what I had to do. I live with regret every single day of my life. I've stayed awake many nights, wondering, if someone will find out. I could be imprisoned for the rest of my life. I left because of you. I didn't want you to be affected."

"I have this whole other life I never knew about. I have family in the Bahamas who I've never met. You said my grandparents were dead."

Harold shook his head thinking of his parents, who he hadn't spoken to in years. They were ashamed of him. They didn't even know he had changed his life. They didn't know he was married or that he had a daughter. They refused to let any of his siblings even speak his name. He knew they were still living, because he kept in frequent contact with one of his sisters. "I'm sorry," he told her, softly. "There's nothing I can do to change anything I've done."

Tears formed in Carmen's eyes as she stared at her father. "Why don't you talk like Lotus Pagua? Leave this Harold Davenport character behind? If you want to do things right, tell Mama who you are."

"I can't. Our whole marriage will be down the drain."

"Tell me who killed Jay's father then."

Harold shook his head, knowing he wasn't going to reveal that information. He knew he couldn't. The killer was still alive. He knew that was the one secret Jay desperately wanted. Harold also knew if Jay discovered who murdered his father that he would take out the whole family. "I can't tell you that."

"You're still harboring a secret, huh? From this moment on, you mean nothing to me. You should turn yourself in to the police and rot in jail. Shoot, from the looks of it, you probably put a bullet in Hector's head."

Harold grabbed her face, shutting her mouth closed.

Carmen was startled. Her father had never gotten violent with her. He held her mouth closed tightly with his hand and pushed her away, ashamed of what he'd done.

"Hector Santiago was my best friend. The day he died, I wanted to go with him. I can't change anything, Carmen. I will always be Lotus Pagua. I will always be the man who changed his name to Harold Davenport. The book has been written and sealed. There are certain things in life we can't go back and change. I left the cartel for you, and only you."

Carmen felt a stream of hot tears slide down her face. She wanted to believe her father, but she was too confused to make sense of any of it. "How can I know who I am, if I don't know who you are?" Carmen watched as her father shrugged his shoulders. He muttered he was going to tell her mother before picking up his briefcase and going up the steps. She wanted to follow him, yet she knew the conversation was over. Not wasting another second, she turned the doorknob and left the house.

Chapter Fifteen

When Carmen left her house, she needed a safe place to run to. Since Jay was partly to blame for her anger, she didn't return to his mansion. In her opinion, the best place to go was to the Westside where Rakim lived. Lucky for her, she was able to catch him at a time when his brother wasn't there or Carlos. Once again, she was in his room, however, this time, she was crying on his shoulder.

To make matters worse, her father had called while she was there, saying her mother refused to take his calls. It was now her responsibility to get her mother to come to the house. Carmen had done it, and her mother was expected to show up later that evening for an impromptu meeting. Her mother didn't sound suspicious of anything and even apologized for not being around like she should've been. Carmen accepted the apology although she still cried in Rakim's arms after the call.

"Everything is going to be all right," Rakim whispered in her ear. "I promise you, Carm. Let your parents do most of the talking. You only need to be the mediator like you've always been."

Carmen nodded her head in agreement. She was going to say more yet Rakim was pulling away from her. She moved away as well, looking up, to see where he was going.

"I have a few drops to make," he explained. "Jay is on me about his money, and I have to deliver. I can't stay any more than fifteen minutes."

Carmen knew she didn't want him to leave. At the same time, she knew Rakim owed Jay a lot of money. He had been so busy pledging; he had forgotten about his job as a hustler. The worst part of it all, he still wasn't an official member of the fraternity. According to Rakim, their pledge process was still going on strong. "I'll go now. I don't need to hold you up." Carmen stood up from his bed and headed towards him for one last hug. He held her closer than normal, and Carmen couldn't help, but to rest her head once again on his shoulder. Over the last few months, Rakim had become one of her closest friends although he had been somewhat distant throughout his pledge process.

"Come here," she heard him say.

When Carmen peered at him, she didn't expect to see his face moving closer to hers. It was, though, and soon, Rakim's lips softly brushed against hers. Carmen kissed him, but when she parted her lips, he pulled away. In a split second, she became nervous, and she could tell he had as well. In fact, he even wiped the kiss from his lips as if it would undo the deed.

"I need to walk you out," he said, hurriedly.

Carmen nodded her head, knowing she needed to get out the house. If anyone saw what happened, Rakim's life was over. Jay would be furious if he ever knew she and Rakim had shared a kiss.

Due to the nature of the situation, Carmen didn't even say goodbye. She simply got in her car and drove straight to her house where she found her mother parked in the driveway. Her mother was early, which meant she might be ready to move back in. "Hey," Carmen called to her, getting out the car.

Patricia smiled, seeing her daughter. "Hey, Peaches," she said, opening her car door. "I see, your father's not here, probably at work, huh?" Patricia laughed nervously only because she didn't know why she was there. She knew her daughter was worried about her and had begged her to move back in the house. She figured that was the same reason her husband had called almost ten times that morning.

Carmen gave a sly smile at her mother's comment and pointed towards the front door so they could go inside. Her mother followed behind her, yet Carmen caught her mother looking around their garden to see if everything was still in its proper place. She didn't ask about anything until they were seated at the dining room table.

"Well, I'm here. Can we go ahead and get this show on the road?"

"We're waiting on Daddy," Carmen announced. Those words alone made her mother become slightly disturbed. Carmen knew the possibility of her mother leaving was now great.

"Peaches, I didn't come here to talk to your father. You said you wanted to discuss some things with me. I bet y'all are trying to pull my leg."

"Mama, no one is pulling your leg, your arm, or anything. We want to talk to you about something. I think you owe us that." Carmen knew her mother was feisty. Patricia was sometimes intimidating and known to throw a fit to get what she wanted. If her father didn't hurry up, her mother would leave before he could even reveal his secret.

"I don't owe your father anything, Peaches. He owes me plenty."

Patricia's voice was stern, and she rose from the table, preparing to leave. "I know this has been hard on you, but I couldn't live like this anymore. I would go to work, come home; fix his dinner. He would come in, eat, and before I know it, he's back in that office of his."

"Mom, please—" Carmen paused at the sound of the front door opening. Shortly after, her father walked in the dining room, appearing surprised that her mother was there.

"I was leaving," Patricia voiced. "I bid you both good day."

"Please," Carmen begged. She watched as her mother sighed and pulled her chair back out, sitting down. Carmen sighed as well and looked at her father. He sat down and then nodded her head for her to start.

"Do you remember Hector Santiago?" she began. Carmen waited until her mother said yes before she told her that her father used to work for him. While she thought her mother was going to question his actual job responsibilities, she only glanced at her father and then back at her.

"Can we talk about something I don't know?" Patricia shook her head, wondering if this was what all the hoopla was about. "I've known that since I've met your father. Is this why I'm here?"

"You knew?" her father asked, standing up.

"Of course, I knew. I wasn't the good girl on the block. I dated lots of guys who worked for him. They never admitted Hector was a drug dealer, though. It was only a rumor he was involved in some illegal business. I mean, who really saw him sell a drug or two?"

"Daddy's name isn't Harold, Mama." Carmen wanted to clear that up as well. From the looks of things, her mother probably wouldn't care.

"Well, when my friend showed him to me, she said his name was Lotus. He was some guy who had come to America from the Bahamas. It wasn't until we had a formal introduction that he introduced himself as Harold Davenport. I figured Lotus was a street name."

"I wasn't even legally Harold Davenport when I told you that. Why didn't you say something, Patricia?" her father asked.

"Do you really think I wanted the whole world, including my parents, to know about you? My mother would kill me if she found out you were a drug dealer. You got out of it shortly after Carmen was born. I didn't see why I needed to make a big fuss about it. We had a house, cars, and a brand new baby. I was happy. Besides, at that time, I enjoyed living the life of luxury," her mother explained.

"I guess this conversation was pointless then." Carmen threw her hands in the air. She had been more upset over her father's involvement in the Santiago cartel than her own mother. In fact, her mother had kept it a secret from her as well.

"I guess this is what I was forced to come here to talk about." Patricia looked at her husband confused. She figured he would have known she knew the truth about him. "You haven't been eating well," she said, noticing the thinness in his face. "Obviously, you haven't been getting any good meals lately. Your work can't cook for you."

"You're right, it can't. I haven't been eating well—barely eating at all," her father replied. "I come home late because I know there isn't anyone here waiting on me. Carmen is with her boyfriend. I don't have any company besides a cell phone and a laptop. Besides, the main person I use to talk to left me a long time ago."

Carmen got up from the table, seeing she needed give her parents some time to talk alone. "I think y'all need the house to yourselves. You never know. You might want to use the time to walk around naked while I'm not here," she joked. "I'm kidding. I'll be back later."

Patricia rolled her eyes before questioning her own daughter's behavior. "Have you been walking around naked? You've put on some pounds since I've last seen you. What happened to let's wait for marriage? I know I've talked to you about the importance of staying abstinent. Are you and Jay using protection?"

Carmen tried her best to avoid meeting eyes with her parents. The meeting was never supposed to be about her sex life. If it was up to her, they would think she was a virgin until she walked down the aisle. While she had gone back on her decision to remain abstinent, she hadn't made the promise to anyone, but God. If she really wanted to, she could stop having sex;

however, it would be hard. She was used to getting hers on a regular basis like a paycheck.

"Go ahead, Peaches," her father instructed. "We're not going to hound you anymore. You're a grown woman and I trust that you're protecting yourself. It was bound to happen one day."

Carmen smiled, nervously, and picked up her tote bag. Since her father had granted her dismissal, she didn't need to stick around to be subject to any more questions. He had given her a way out and she was going to run as quickly as she could. Besides, her job was done. She had gotten her parents to sit down and talk, which meant they could finally start working on their problems. Things could potentially be looking up for them, yet she couldn't say the same for Flame.

***

When Carmen walked in Jay's house, she wasn't surprised to see he wasn't there. It took him only an hour or two to show and when he did, she gave him all the necessary updates on her parents. His mind appeared to be elsewhere even when she gave him an update on Rakim. She knew he wanted his money and Rakim was months late on it. Since Jay considered Rakim to be his little brother, he let him slide. However, he told her a long time ago that the extension made him appear weak.

Throughout everything she said, Jay didn't respond. She was standing on the stairwell, which overlooked the living room, so she knew he heard her. He was playing around with his phone, so she knew something was wrong. Somewhat desperate to find out what it was; she headed down the steps.

Jay was sitting on the couch, which was where she sat as well. He was busy texting and had barely even noticed she was beside him. She tried to look over his shoulder; however, he quickly slid the phone in his pocket.

"I'm stressed as fuck right now," he finally said.

Carmen waited for him to elaborate and when he didn't, she touched his temple. "Talk to me. What's going on?"

"I think Carlos is keeping something from me regarding Shakeem. I think he's awake. People in the streets have been telling me stuff. Matter of fact, I think Shakeem is out the hospital. I think Carlos is gonna try and take him out by himself."

"Is that such a bad idea?"

Jay turned to look at her like she shouldn't have asked the question. "Carlos doesn't know how to have a clean murder. He likes to run up and start guttin' 'em. If he takes his time and sets up a plan, he can have a smooth kill without any errors."

Carmen was aware he was concerned about his friend. Nevertheless, she didn't want Jay involved in anyone's murder. If Carlos wanted to take out Shakeem, he needed to let him do it so he could take the fall. Jay's involvement would only put him closer to a cell than she wanted.

"You want to help keep my mind off this?"

Carmen's lips formed a smile, but she shook her head. "We've been going hard for a long time, and I think tonight, we need a break. For one night, let's try and keep our hands and private parts to ourselves."

Jay looked at her, angrily. Here he was, ready to unleash some steam, and Carmen was asking for a break. He didn't need a break, he needed something to release his frustration, and climbing in her kitty box was the trick. "I'm not going to sleep without getting some. I suggest you go ahead and get undressed."

"It isn't going to hurt you to use your hand for one night. Come on, I've given it to you in the past whenever you've asked. This time let's just hold and kiss each other. Let's make it a romantic night. Or better yet, let's talk about this. What would you do if I got pregnant? Any day now one of your little rubbers could break and we both could become parents. Not to mention, there have been a few occasions where we've had sex raw. Luckily, I haven't gotten pregnant."

"I would make you my wife," he replied. "The day you told me you were pregnant; we would go down to the courthouse and file the papers. You know that. How many times have I told you that? Right now, though, I want to fuck, so shut up, and jump on this dick."

Carmen glared at him because of the blatant disrespect in his statement. She knew he was stressed but barking an order for sex wasn't going to get her out her panties. "I'm going home. Grab some lotion and a flick, I'll see you tomorrow." Carmen stood up from the couch and headed up the steps to retrieve a few of her things. She could hear Jay following behind her until they were both in his room. While she was busy gathering her personals, he was stripping down to his boxers.

Unexpectedly, she felt him grab her and throw her on the bed. When he climbed on top of her, both his hands grabbed her shoulders tightly, holding her in place. Instantly, she was reminded of Pierre's attack. "Please don't do this. You know how I feel about this position."

Jay loosened his grip, moving away from her. He allowed her to get up and when she went back to collecting her things, his anger tripled. "I shouldn't have to beg you to sleep with me. You see I'm stressed, why can't you just give it to me this one time? It'll take, what, maybe twenty minutes of your time?"

"Did you even hear anything I said about my parents, Jay?"

"Fuck your parents. When was the last time any one of them called to check on you? Your mother pushed Flame in your hands, knowing the store was going bankrupt. They don't give a fuck about you. You're a grown ass woman with a grown ass boyfriend who needs a grown ass pussy to fall into. I need you to act your age and stop chasing after your parents."

Carmen stared at Jay in disgust. It had been a long time since he had displayed a tantrum and she had forgotten how he was. He had calmed down after the months they had been together. She figured he was getting help. Now, it appeared he had forgotten everything he learned. She knew she was only going to add on to his frustration when she told him to beat his dick. Just like she thought, Jay immediately went in for the kill.

"I'll call another bitch before I do that."

"Is that what you want to do? I'm not stupid, Jay. I know you can have any girl you want. What you need to remember is that those girls out there only want you for your money. They're not going to put up with your bullshit like I do. They'll get you for every dollar you have and the minute you get caught, they will be out the door. So, if you want to call someone else, go right ahead. Matter of fact, you can use my phone."

Jay watched as her phone landed only a few inches away from him. The mere sight of it told him Carmen was serious about not putting out. If she was giving him permission to cheat then the odds of him getting any from her was nonexistent. "Get the fuck out my house, bitch."

Carmen sneered at him before walking out the bedroom. She wasn't quite sure what Jay was trying to pull. She knew he was upset but threatening to cheat on her wasn't the way to go. He could test her if he wanted to, but if he did, Carmen knew their relationship would be over.

***

The following morning, Carmen showed up at Jay's house, hoping to catch another female there. She didn't see an unknown car in his driveway and when he answered the door, he was already dressed like he was headed out. Automatically, Carmen thought he had taken her advice. She could smell breakfast cooking and wasn't surprised to see pots and pans all over the kitchen counters. "Were you done cooking?"

Jay didn't answer. He knew his actions were more important than any words he could say. Therefore, he pulled her phone out his pocket and set it on the counter. When a look of horror appeared on her face, he turned his actions up a notch. "Thank you, for everything."

Carmen looked at her phone and then at him. She knew what he was hinting at, but she didn't think he was serious about it. *He should know right now that if he went and slept with another girl that it is over between us. He shouldn't even be playing this game.* Carmen picked up her phone and checked the call log. Everything was the same. No calls had been made, but he could have easily erased the numbers. "Did you sleep with someone last night?" Carmen feared the reply, but she needed to know. There was no way she was going to offer herself to him if he hadn't been faithful. If anything, they would be breaking up that very morning.

"Maybe," he answered, leaning on the kitchen counter.

"You did it, didn't you? Is she already gone?"

Carmen wasn't going to wait for his response. She didn't even need the confirmation. She simply needed to get away from him. If she didn't, he would only see her crumble, which was what he wanted. She couldn't stop him from seeing it either. The tears were already coming down her face as he yelled at her.

"The minute I need you, you have to go run to your parents. Tricia didn't do that to me. I haven't spoken to her since we broke up. I called her;

she was over here in no time, giving me what I needed. She sucked my dick, too. You never even offered to do that."

"I hate you."

Jay stopped in his tracks when he saw the tears that were flying down Carmen's face. He was lying about the whole thing only because she rejected him when he needed her the most. He had never cheated on her and couldn't even look at another woman, better yet, touch one. Since he was Carmen's first, he knew his words would sting. He would always hurt her more than she could hurt him. When she told him it was over, Jay continued with his plan. He kicked her out, slamming the door in her face and immediately went up to his room.

Inside of his closet, tucked away, was a ten carat promise ring he had picked out for her about a month ago. His plan was to make up with her in a week or so and give her the ring. Like he had forced her to date him, he would also force her to accept the ring and take him back. If Carmen really knew him then she should've known he was all talk. Half of the shit he said he was going to do to her, he never did.

Jay was always a man of his word, but when it came to her, he did stuff to fuck up her head. He knew he could control Carmen mentally if not physically. In a short amount of time, he was going to turn everything around when it came to their relationship. All Carmen had to do was take one peek at the ring and he would have her exactly where he wanted her.

Chapter Sixteen

July

Carmen wasn't too big on keeping a journal, but after the incident with Jay, she had started. She had so many thoughts running through her mind when she left his house she immediately stopped at a drug store and purchased a notebook. If she didn't find some sort of outlet for her anger, she would have set fire to his cars and even burned his clothes. A real *Waiting to Exhale* moment would have occurred.

The journal did the trick and Carmen quickly discovered the therapy that came from writing. Her intention was to keep the breakup a secret, which was easy to do. Only a week went by before she received a phone call from Jay that he wanted to talk. Carmen was quick to say no until she heard him break down on the phone. He kept saying how he couldn't live without her and how much he loved her. Carmen didn't believe he was truly sorry until he told her he was attempting suicide. The second he spoke those words, Carmen rushed to his house. She knew Jay had mental issues, but he had never talked about suicide before. With a house that was filled with weapons, she knew he had the means to do it.

A key to his house was still in her possession and she let herself in. She found him inside of his living room with a white box in his hands. Like the one that contained the diamond earrings he'd given her; he opened the box to display a princess cut diamond ring. She wasn't quite sure what to do with it or if he was hinting at a proposal. All she knew was that he was telling her he loved her and asking for forgiveness. Carmen gave it to him, and she left his house shortly after with the ring on her finger.

Now, she was sitting inside of Justin's, waiting on Tiara to show so they could discuss a new direction for Flame. Though her mother had returned to the store, things still were going downhill. In less than two months, if a change wasn't made, they would be forced to close the store.

"Damn, Carm, it took me so long to find you because you were blinding me. What the fuck is that on your hand?"

Carmen heard Tiara before she even saw her. When her friend slid in the booth, she quickly explained that Jay had given her a promise ring. Her friend gazed at the ring in amazement before kindly pushing Carmen's hand away.

"I wish I could've stuck with Carlos long enough to get one of those. He's been trippin'. He is on this, "I'm the King," type shit. When he comes down from that, he can call me. Other than that, it will be me and my rabbit." Tiara paused only because she wanted to see Carmen's reaction. Her best friend had never confided in her that she was sleeping with Jay though she suspected it. "You wouldn't know anything about a rabbit; you're used to getting the real deal."

Carmen kept her face blank and opened her menu. She wasn't admitting to anything until she necessarily had to. So far, she had done a fairly good job of not coming up pregnant.

"Well, since you're not going to talk about your favorite sex position, can we talk about Monifah and Rakim? They've been dating for months on the low. From what she told me, she and Rakim have been freakin' for a while now. Can you believe it? I didn't even think she noticed him."

Carmen batted her eyes at Tiara's news. *If Rakim was with Monifah, why did he kiss me? That kiss happened a month ago.*

"Did you fuck him, too?"

Carmen's eyes grew large at Tiara's question. "Hell, no, Tee, what kind of girl do you think I am? I haven't done anything with Rakim. I—" Carmen paused only because she was having second thoughts about telling Tiara about the kiss. Though it was rather harmless, it still happened and technically, she had betrayed Monifah by kissing her boyfriend. "It was one kiss," Carmen admitted. "It was like a month ago. I was stressed and it happened. Now, I've learned one of my good friends is dating him."

Tiara wasn't surprised to learn that Carmen and Rakim had shared a moment. She always thought there was a mutual connection between the two. "Carm, I know you love Jay. I also have seen firsthand how well you get along with Rakim. You may not be ready to admit it, but you love him."

"I love the fact that he is there for me. I can talk to Rakim about anything. He has such a bright future ahead of him and I want to be a part of it…as a friend. I don't love him like I love Jay. With Jay, I can't help, but be drawn to him. It's like, he's my soulmate."

"So why do you look upset? You should care less that Rakim and Monifah are fuckin'. Damn, you can't hog all the dicks."

Carmen had officially lost her appetite. She didn't want to eat or even think of food. All she wanted to do was get Rakim on the phone. While she couldn't bail out on her meeting with Tiara, she could take the evening off from work to meet up with him. Since Tiara was busy looking at the menu, Carmen texted Rakim to see if he could meet her outside of the diner in two hours. When she received confirmation he could, she breathed a sigh of relief. She was going to get to the bottom of his relationship and force him to answer any questions she had. *Yeah, I'm heated he has a girlfriend. He could've told me something.*

***

For ten minutes, Rakim stood outside the diner waiting on Carmen. He wasn't quite sure what was keeping her, and his time was precious. Everyone was talking about the large sum of money he owed Jay and he needed to be using every hour he wasn't pledging to make a sale. If Carmen didn't show in the next five minutes, he was calling. If she didn't pick up, he was leaving.

Right when the thought left his mind, he noticed a Lexus coming in the parking lot. He could see Carmen behind the steering wheel, and he ran to meet her unsure if they were grabbing a bite to eat or simply talking in the car. When he got inside, he instantly felt her negative vibe. Carmen didn't greet him, nor did she look his way.

"Why didn't you tell me you were dating Monifah?"

Rakim looked at her shocked, yet he still answered her question. "We made a mutual decision to keep it on the low. I respected the relationship enough to stick to the decision that was made."

Carmen narrowed her eyes while at the same time, turning to face him so he could see her anger. "I'm not some random friend of yours, Rakim. It's me, Carmen, remember? I'm the girl you said you would ride or die for. You know everything about my relationship with Jay. You're the only one who knows I've slept with him. You know he cheated on me."

Rakim sat back in his seat because of all the hostility Carmen was showing. "I would still ride or die for you, Carm. This thing with Monifah is much deeper than what we have. She's my girlfriend. You're my friend. We made a mutual decision together."

"So, why did you kiss me? We never talked about it. Why did you kiss me? Did you tell her about it? Does she know you did it?"

Rakim wasn't one to show anger, yet Carmen was bringing him to that point. He thought they had put the kiss behind them since it was obvious nothing was going to become of it. "What the fuck is your problem? You're talking to me like I'm out here chasing you or some shit. Did I kiss you? Yes. Do I have feelings for you? Yes. I'm not going to sit here and go tit for tat. You chose Jay, remember? I slipped up when I kissed you and I'm sorry. I put us both in an awkward position. However, I'm not gonna discuss this any further with you. I'm with Monifah, you're with Jay, and that's it."

Silence filled the car as Carmen allowed Rakim's words to marinate. She knew he was right. She did love Jay and although her boyfriend had cheated on her, she wasn't going to end the relationship to be with Rakim.

"Do you want me to choose, Carm? Is that it? Do you want me to choose between you and Monifah? If I did, would I have a chance?"

Carmen unlocked the car doors so Rakim could know he could get out. "No," she told him, "you don't need to choose. You've already made your decision. I've made mine as well." Carmen held up her hand so he could see the ten carat ring on her finger. She could tell that the ring took Rakim to a different place because he immediately got out the car. He didn't say anything to her, and she watched as he went inside the diner. Where their friendship was headed, she didn't know. For the time being, it appeared as if it was going to be nonexistent.

***

Carmen walked inside Jay's bedroom just in time to see him counting a slew of money. The entire bed was covered in large and small bills. Very much intrigued by how much money he had, Carmen climbed on top of it, lying down. She expected for Jay to tell her to move yet he didn't. He simply kept counting his money, separating it into huge stacks.

"I spoke to your father today."

Those were the last words Carmen expected to hear. The first thing out his mouth, she waited for him to elaborate as he wrapped a rubberband around a large stack of money. He then dropped the money down on the floor where it landed with a thud. It was then Carmen realized there was a suitcase on the floor.

"I need a warehouse and he agreed to give it to me."

"So that is what the money is for? You're going to pay for the building in cash?" Carmen picked up a hundred dollar bill and stared at the picture of Benjamin Franklin. If she had a thousand of those, she knew where she could put it. Flame desperately needed a new fall collection and if she had her mother's permission, she would invest thousands into her very first line of business suits for men.

"This is for one of my business partners in Ohio. I am about to end business with him, and this is a little, "nice working with you," type of gift."

Carmen dropped the bill down on the bed only to pick up a couple of twenties. She didn't know how much Jay was giving his business partner, but she knew she could use some of the dough.

"Your father invited us to dinner tomorrow night. He says it is imperative that we come." Jay paused when he saw how fascinated she was with the money. The sight of her laying on it reminded him he had never told her the truth about Tricia. She still thought he cheated, which is probably why they hadn't been intimate.

"I think they're going to renew their vows," Carmen told him, interrupting his thoughts. "My mom has officially moved back in and they're doing great. You never know, you may have to be the best man to stand in for your father."

Jay looked at her, noticing she was still admiring the money. Aware he had a duffle bag of cash underneath the bed; he pulled it out and dumped the money on top of her. "You look good in green," he said, getting the itch. Her entire body was covered in twenties and fifties, but he knew the image would be much better if she was completely nude. "You want to fuck on the money?"

Carmen pushed the money off her at his question. Although they had made up, she wasn't quite sure about allowing him to have her again. She also didn't know if he had been checked out for any possible STIs or even AIDS.

"You don't have to be scared, Carm. I'm clean," he said, as if he read her mind. He trailed his fingers down her arm and onto her chest. He pulled at her tee until her cleavage was in full view. Then, he proceeded to write his name, penning ownership. Carmen used it to her advantage and pulled him towards her until he was lying directly on top of her. Jay could hear the money being squished underneath their body weight, yet he could care less.

"Do you have a condom?"

"Damn, Carmen, I'm not even hard yet. Can you at least play with it for a little while?"

"Show me you have a condom first."

Jay grunted at her request, but quickly complied, reaching over to open his drawer. He felt around for his box of Magnums and once he had it in his hands, he noticed the box was empty. In the past, they had been using condoms on almost a daily basis, he figured he had forgotten to restock. "I don't have one," he told her, showing her the empty box. "I think we've used them all. I mean, we've done it before without one. I'll pull out before I cum. We'll be fine. I promise."

Carmen didn't want to hear those words. She wanted him to tell her he had protection. While he obviously didn't care, which was evident from the fact he was stripping himself of his clothes, she did. She knew he had been with another woman and the last thing she wanted was to get anything Tricia might have had.

"If I give you a baby, we'll get married. We'll have the marriage license before you even show. I promise."

Carmen didn't speak. Though she didn't want to get pregnant, he kept reassuring her that if she did, he would marry her. Certain he would, Carmen allowed him to penetrate her once again.

Chapter Seventeen

Jay hadn't even walked in Carmen's house before Lotus demanded to show him the pool house. Though he had already seen it, he knew Lotus really wanted to talk to him in private. He kindly obliged while Carmen went in the kitchen to help her mother finish cooking. Once they were on the back patio, Lotus immediately started in on what he wanted to discuss.

"My wife and I are announcing today that we're moving."

Jay noticed how nonchalant Lotus sounded.

"We're moving to Texas. My wife wants to open a second store and we want to get away from Brookstone. You know we're trying to get our marriage back on track."

Jay looked at him, trying to figure out where he came into play. "Are you saying I can't buy the warehouse?"

"No, that's not what I'm saying. What I am saying is that we're moving and selling the house. See, Carmen has a year of college left to go and we would hate to make her transfer to a school in Texas. We know she loves designing clothes, we were kind of hoping that—"

"Basically you want Carmen to officially move in with me so you can sell the house?" Jay watched as Lotus nodded his head. "You don't really want that." Jay knew it was a trap. There was no way Lotus was going to lead his daughter into his lap that easily. "What do you have up your sleeve?"

"Do you think I want to do this? This was my wife's idea. I told her to get Carmen an apartment and raise her pay at the store, or sign Flame over to her. It is time for Carmen to be independent."

"I'm not about to turn down the offer. I'm trying to see what the catch is. Besides, there are a few things you don't know about me."

"Like what?" Harold asked, glaring at Jay. He figured he knew everything there was to know about Hector's son. He was aware of the business sense Jay had. It was of no surprise to him to learn he owned a nightclub.

"I'm a hustler," Jay said, finally admitting he was continuing his father's business. "I'm the ultimate hustler."

"When are you going to let that shit go, Jay? Don't you know all that shit is going to get you is a cold cell? You will be in prison for the rest of your life if you're trying to live up to what we did. My daughter can't live with you. We'll have to work something else out. We'll get her an apartment. Then, when she takes over the store, she'll be on her own. If I had of known you were still doing dirty work—" Harold's voice trailed off. "I was in that cartel for a long time. I stood by your father through a lot of shit. I remember everything that happened when you were little. It was almost like seeing a war every night, wasn't it? You've seen people in every shape or form and—"

"Who killed my father, Lotus?"

Jay had wanted to ask the question for the longest. He knew if he let Lotus talk long enough they would never discuss it. Jay still remembered the night clearly, and he blamed himself for not reaching his parents' bedroom in time to see his father's killer. His mother couldn't even bear to speak the name or give him any kind of information on who it could be. "It had to be done by someone he knew. It had to be someone who was so close to him they knew which bedroom was his."

"Your father's killer is going to come around one day."

"I think it's you. You disappear for a few years; pretend you're out. Then, when he's at his prime, you take him out."

Harold knew those were Jay's thoughts. He didn't get angry with him like he did Carmen when she accused him of murdering Hector. "That's not my style. That never was my style and I never wanted to take your father out. I wanted him to get out. I wanted him to be legit so he wouldn't end up the way he did."

"How do I know you didn't kill my father?"

Harold took a step back. "You really think I killed your father, Jay?"

"You would've had the best motive."

"I left the business eight years before your father was murdered. There were many men who stayed by your father's side until his death. They found out things about his businesses I never knew. They knew his plans and career goals. I reckon you have men like that now working underneath you."

"I have a whole army, but only a few soldiers I keep close. All I need you to do is to give me a name. I can handle the rest."

"Do you really want to start World War III? The man who killed your father has a higher power to answer to. Leave it in God's hands. I know you don't want to spend the rest of your life in prison. It isn't going to bring your father back. I promise you."

"Dinner is ready," Carmen yelled, stepping out on the patio. She walked up to her father, grabbing him by the arm. "Glad to see my two favorite men are getting along. Come on and eat. Mama worked her butt off." Carmen unhooked her arm from her father and headed in the house.

"She's not living with you," Harold stated, following behind Carmen.

Jay snickered and watched as Lotus disappeared in the house. He looked at the pool, trying to figure out what other man was close to his father. Lotus had given him enough clues for him to see that his father was murdered by someone very close to him. Jay thought about Domino Rodriguez, but he knew it wasn't possible. It had to be someone who his father never mentioned.

"Jay," Carmen called. She watched him as he stared in the pool as if he was thinking of jumping in. "Baby, what's wrong?"

"Nothing, I was coming," Jay said, realizing he was in a daze.

"Okay, well, come on. Mama wants you to say grace again. She wants something short and to the point." Carmen stared at the pool as well, admiring the pretty sky blue color of the water. "Let's go, you have to say grace," she said, giving him a slight squeeze.

"I'm good for that." Jay pushed his thoughts aside as he followed behind her. He quickly took his seat and ordered for everyone to bow their heads as he prayed. Once he was finished, Lotus didn't hesitate in starting the discussion as Patricia passed around the food.

"Well, there's no need to cut corners or draw anything out, let's get started," Harold said, picking up the cornbread. "Your mother and I—"

"Carmen, you know your father and I have been trying to work through our problems," Patricia interrupted, eyeing her husband. She knew he was going to be blunt with telling Carmen the news, but her daughter needed to be prepped. "We've decided we need a change of scenery."

"You need a change of scenery?" Carmen questioned.

Patricia knew her daughter was thinking the worst. "Yes, a change of scenery. You also know I want to open a second store. I know money looks funny right now with the way sales have been, but I think opening this second store will be good. Besides, we might generate more revenue if we put forth a younger, fresher, marketing campaign. Not to mention, your father has agreed to help with some of the costs. So—"

"You are officially leaving me to save your store."

"Carmen, we know you want to do this men's line. I figured a good start would be to give you Flame. You can start the collection and change everyone's view of the store. I believe in you, and I think you can do it. It'll be like your inheritance. The land, the building, everything will be in your name. You can then start turning your designs into actual merchandise. You can get the store remodeled to add the men's section and the dressing rooms. If you need extra staff, we're willing to work that out, too. Of course, this all takes time considering the way sales are going."

Carmen dropped her fork on her plate. "It sounds good, really good, but what about this change of scenery for you and Daddy?"

"We're moving to Texas," her father blurted.

Carmen stared at him and then at her mother. "You're moving to Texas? That's across the country, Mama. You're going to give me your store, and then tell me you're moving to Texas?"

Patricia huffed at how Carmen was taking the news. "Baby, it's time for you to be independent. You'll have a job, and you should have enough money saved to get an apartment or you can move in with Jay."

Carmen sat back in her chair trying to figure out the bomb her parents had dropped on her. "I don't have any money saved. All the money I have, I was putting back in the store. I sacrifice my paycheck to keep the doors open. I'm already in the negative."

"Peaches, we want to teach you independence. With this store, you'll be paying your own bills and making sure you have a roof over your head," her father explained. "You'll be responsible for taking Flame back to the top. Lord knows, it might take years to do that."

Carmen turned to Jay. He raised his glass, sipping on his iced tea as if he didn't want any part of the conversation. "So you're abandoning me without any money?"

Patricia sighed. "It's not that, Peaches. Don't look at it like that. You have a clothing store that is going to give you plenty of money. Yes, the store is struggling right now. The money is going to start looking even worse when we start paying out for the store in Texas, but we believe in you. Your designs are great. This is what is going to save Flame. Your father has even contacted some designers to work with you. He knows some great people, Sherri Hill, Kidada Jones, and even Kimora Lee Simmons. They are all willing to meet with you, to discuss your designs and ideas."

"How do you expect me to run your entire store and go to college? I barely did it when you left this time." Carmen felt like her parents had driven a knife through her heart. Slowly, they were turning it, making sure it stuck. *If they were moving, what were they doing with the house? Why couldn't she live there?*

Harold was trying his best to understand Carmen's point of view. "Let's be real about this. You are twenty-one years old. It is time for you to get out the house and live on your own. You can run this store and go to school, too. You only have one year left, and your mother is not going to lead you into this blind. This is what you wanted. You've begged your mother since you were sixteen for her to let you do this men's line. Now, it's your time to shine and you don't even want to take it?"

"I do want it, but not like this. I was going to get my degree first, go to fashion school, then work on the line."

"Baby, listen, this is not going to be easy. We're trying to think of what will be best for you. How are you ever going to learn how to be an adult if your father and I keep taking care of you?" Patricia looked at her daughter wanting her to see their good intention.

"Mama, the store is going downhill and y'all are leaving me here."

"Do you want to transfer?"

"She's not transferring," Jay said, finally speaking up.

Carmen looked at him and saw the concerned look on his face.

"She can live with me. I'll make sure she's taken care of."

"She's not living with you," Harold said, sternly. He had already spoken with Jay on the matter. He didn't know why he had brought it up.

"Well, baby, we did say that could work." Patricia shot her husband a look, reminding him of their past conversations.

"You knew about this?" Carmen turned to Jay as if he was the enemy. If he had kept the secret from her, he would feel her wrath as well.

"I found out five minutes ago. Your father wanted to discuss it with me before he told you."

Carmen folded her arms over her chest. She knew she looked like a spoiled brat, but she didn't care. She wanted the store, and she wanted the men's line, but she wanted her parents there to see it all come alive. Not to mention, she wanted her father's money. With them in Texas, they could never rush to her aid when she needed them. They would have to fly out to see her. "So you're selling the house, too, aren't you?"

"We are," her mother began, "there's a man who is actually starting up his own clothing store right on the same block as Flame. He's moving from Manhattan to Brookstone. He needed a place to stay, and he was interested in the house. He's a bachelor and well-known socialite in Manhattan so the house will be perfect for his lifestyle."

"So you're selling the house to a hoe?"

"Carm, we found a buyer. Besides, you'll be meeting him soon. He's here in the area. He's currently working on the renovations for his own store. By selling the house, we'll have money for the new store in Texas."

"This is too much for one day," Carmen said, realizing she hadn't eaten anything. She noticed that most of the food was still in the pots and bowls because they were too busy conversing to serve themselves.

"Do you want to move in with me?" Jay asked.

"I said no." Harold eyed Jay, angrily.

"She's a grown woman. It's her decision," Jay shot back.

"Harold, we talked about this." Patricia looked back and forth between the two men. "What's wrong with her living with him? She's already spending the night over there like she's a permanent resident."

Harold grunted. "I don't want her there."

Carmen didn't want to hear them fuss over the issue when the decision was majorly hers. "I think it's a good idea. I think Jay and I are ready for it. We've discussed it. We've discussed a lot of things."

"I said no," Harold yelled, hitting his fist on the table.

At the sound of the man's voice, Jay knew he had no choice, but to tell Patricia what was going on. "The reason Lotus doesn't want me—" Harold interrupted him.

"She can stay with you," Harold said, not wanting Patricia to know about the cartel. He looked at Jay and saw his lips form a large smile.

"Great," Patricia added, "now, Carmen, are you going to take the store, or do you want me to give it to Tiara? She's been an excellent assistant these days, don't cha think?"

"Of course, that was never a question," Carmen replied, happily. "I am most definitely taking the store."

"Then, it's settled," Patricia stated. She picked up her fork right when Jay made the announcement that Carmen would be moving in that weekend. The statement only angered her husband who had another outburst. It tickled her because he was the main one trying to send Carmen into the world of independence. She figured he realized Carmen would no longer be under his watchful eye. Patricia planned on telling him that night that the only way Carmen could grow up is if they let her. If they didn't, she would always be a little girl with her hand out for the world.

Act II:
The Bad Girl

Chapter Eighteen

August

At the beginning of August, Carmen started the move from her parents' house to Jay's. While she made the transition known to everyone, only Tiara came to help her pack. It had been ages since she had seen Monifah and her friendship with Rakim was currently on the rocks. They hadn't spoken to each other since their argument and when they did see each other, he was distant.

Fed up with the whole thing, she went by his house unannounced to make amends. When she didn't find him there, she spent her afternoon driving around West Brookstone looking for any sign of him. She was only a few blocks away from Tiara's house when her phone rung. Based off the ringtone, she knew it was Jay since she always had Faith Evans', "I Love You," play when he would call. Before she could say hello, he barked a question at her.

"Have you seen Carlos?"

Carmen stared at her phone to make sure she was speaking to the right person. "I'm the last person you should be asking that," she told him. "I'm on the Westside, though. I'm looking for Rakim."

"I'm looking for his ass, too. I can't even find Malik. I think some shit went down. I got a message from some street cat that Carlos went and bought up a whole lot of ammo and shit. He isn't answering his phone and I have this feeling in my gut he went to take out Shakeem. I told you he was keeping shit from me, Carm. I'm going to crush his skull when I see him. I'm about to fuckin' puke over my whole damn car."

"Jay, calm down, and keep calling him. I'll call Tiara to see if she knows something." Carmen realized she had gone past Tiara's house and cursed under her breath. She couldn't turn around from the number of cars that were passing her. Therefore, she turned on another street that led to a convenience store. Still somewhat in the turn, Carmen slammed on her breaks when a light-skinned man almost ran into her car. "Damn," she screamed as the car jerked. Carmen watched as the man jumped on top of the car and quickly rolled off. Easily recognizable, she stared at Carlos, noticing the red blood stains on his shirt.

"What the fuck are you doing?" she yelled, putting the car in park. Carmen opened the door and got out, watching as Carlos limped towards her. His entire right pants leg was covered in blood and his white Air Force Ones were tinted red. "Damn, Carlos, you're shot."

"Get in the fuckin' car," he yelled. Carlos opened the passenger side door and slid inside. He let the seat back as Carmen got in so he could stretch out his leg.

Carmen didn't know what to say or think. She only knew she needed to get Carlos to a hospital. She also needed to call Jay so he would know his instinct was right. "You shouldn't have been in a gunfight by yourself. Where was Malik?"

"I don't know where the fuck he went. He went ghost when the guns came out. I'm going to tell Jay about his bitch ass, too. We were in his fuckin' car and he left me and Rakim there."

Carmen pressed down hard on her brakes. "Where is Rakim?" she yelled. "He was with you? Where did you leave him?"

"I don't know, back there somewhere."

Carmen did a quick three point turn in the road and headed down the street. She had gone a few blocks up the road when she saw a mom and pop store come in view. "Is this it?" she asked him. Carlos was busy wincing in pain. She opened her glove compartment, knowing a bandana was inside. "Tie your leg up with this. I don't want you bleeding to death." Carmen watched as he proceeded to tie it around the wound. In the meantime, she parked the car outside the convenience store, leaving it running. She didn't know if Rakim was inside, but Carlos hadn't tried to stop her.

As for Carlos, he knew what Carmen was going to find. He just wasn't going to stick around to see it. Still in a lot of pain, he lifted himself into the driver's seat. He backed out the parking space, leaving Carmen inside the store as he took off for East Brookstone.

"Get an ambulance. I can see he's still breathing," a man yelled as Carmen ran in the store. She could see a few people standing in an aisle, but she didn't know who they were looking at. She walked towards them only to find a stream of blood coming from a body in another aisle. As she approached, she saw more. Random cereal boxes were around the corpse and when she gave the person a closer look, she recognized Shakeem. His eyes were wide open and the sight of him made her turn away in disgust.

When she went to the next aisle, she had a clear visual of the person the other onlookers were staring at. It took her only an instant to recognize Rakim who was trying to pull himself up.

"He's trying to move. Is the ambulance coming?" a man yelled.

Carmen pushed him out her way, dropping to Rakim's side. He was still breathing, but she knew he was barely hanging on.

"I'm here, baby, I'm here," she said, pulling his body into her lap. Carmen tried to hold back her tears, seeing the blood on his shirt. Rakim was trying his best to tell her something, but Carmen didn't want him to waste his breath. "Don't talk, save it, you can tell me later. Where is the fuckin' ambulance?" Carmen looked for any sign of a paramedic and then at Rakim. When she lifted her hand off his chest all she saw in her palm was blood.

Carmen started to pray as she cradled Rakim in her arms. She could hear people chattering around her, but she couldn't make out their words. Rakim was holding onto her, and he was tightening his grip every second she held him. "Give me something to stop the bleeding."

The people seem to ignore her. Rakim's eyes were still open, moving back and forth as if he was searching for something. "I need you, don't leave me," she told him, trying to put pressure on his wounds. The blood was coming from all over. "Where is the fuckin' ambulance?"

The people looked at her as if she was crazy, but she didn't care. She looked at Rakim whose eyes were focused on hers. "I love you, Rakim, I always have," she admitted as tears slid down her face. "I love you," she repeated. Carmen could feel his body starting to relax in hers. Automatically, she started applying more pressure to his chest. "Don't leave me," she begged him. "Please, I love you. I want you."

"He's gone," one of the women said behind her.

Carmen looked at him, realizing Rakim was dead. "Wake up, baby, wake up," she said, shaking him. Carmen screamed out in pain as the onlookers tried to move her away from him. "Let me go," she yelled, pushing them away. She held Rakim's body in her arms continuing to cradle him. It wasn't long before she heard the sirens and the door busted open with police and paramedics. "He's gone," she yelled at them. Rakim's body was lifeless in her arms. Carmen felt hands on her once more, but she only pushed them away. Fully aware she had to let him go, she grabbed his face and planted a final kiss on his lips.

***

After leaving the scene of the shootout, Carlos headed straight to Jay's house. To his dismay, the news of the gunfight had beaten him there. He didn't even make it in the house before he started experiencing what he believed to be was his demise. Glass figurines shattered underneath him as Jay threw him onto the coffee table. He could barely move or breathe as a sharp pain ruptured through his back.

"You don't feel any fuckin' pain," Jay yelled, picking Carlos up from the table. He threw him against the wall before pistol-whipping him with his nine. "I told you about trying to run shit. Rakim is dead because of your fuckin' ass. Where is Carmen, Carlos? I heard she was with you."

"I left her at the store. Come on; ease up on me. I did what you wanted. You wanted Shakeem dead. I killed him."

"You didn't follow fuckin' protocol. Running up on him without a fuckin' plan is not protocol. We are the ones that kill, not the ones who get killed." Jay pistol-whipped Carlos again, this time, sending a streak of blood into the air. "Then, you're going to leave my girl in the middle of the fuckin' Westside?" Jay raised his gun to hit Carlos again until he heard someone coming through his front door. He looked towards the foyer to see Carmen coming in the room. Blood covered her clothes, and her hair was matted to her head.

Now concerned about her, he backed away from Carlos. When he reached for her, she pushed him away, but somehow managed to grab his nine.

He watched her as she pointed it at Carlos, and he tried his best to talk her down. "I'm going to handle him, Peaches," Jay said, knowing Carmen didn't know how to use the weapon. "I'm—" Jay was silenced when she turned the gun on him. He held his hands up in defense as he tried to bring her to her senses. "I didn't plan this shit, Carm. It wasn't me."

Carmen turned the gun on Carlos. She knew he was the reason Rakim was dead. Carlos was the one who kept everything regarding Shakeem away from Jay. "You wanted him dead so bad. You don't know how to let things go. You don't know how to let things fuckin' go." Carmen fired the gun into Carlos' other leg. It only grazed him, but it was enough for him to grab at the wound and for Jay to tackle her to the floor. They battled over the gun until he was able to pry it out her hands.

Jay tossed his gun to the other side of the room as he pulled Carmen in his arms. "I promise you. I didn't have anything to do with it," he whispered. He felt a stinging in his heart. It was the same feeling he had when he walked in his parents' bedroom and found his father with half his head off. The feeling took years to go away, and he knew it would be the same when it came to Rakim.

***

Two hours later, Jay was finally able to locate Malik and gave the order to Tiara to bring him to his house. When he saw his friend's face, he knew Malik was struggling with what happened. His hands wouldn't stop shaking and he demanded for all the mirrors in the house to be taken down. He couldn't even look at himself.

Malik hadn't showered or ate since he left the convenience store. When he saw Shakeem's gun come out, he knew they weren't getting out alive. He tried to grab Rakim, but his brother decided to put up a fight. While he wasn't sure how many times Rakim was shot, he knew it was one too many. All the bullets that hit his brother hit him as well. His flesh burned like Rakim's, and his body even fell limp when Rakim took his final breath. That was when he knew he lost his other half. "I'm sorry," he mumbled. "I should've stayed with him."

Carmen stared at the only person in the world who was an exact replica of Rakim. "Stop apologizing," she said, finally speaking. She knew he wasn't to blame for Rakim's death although she wished he had warned Jay about Carlos' plans.

"I pray to God," Malik cried, "that Rakim's soul is with our parents." Malik closed his eyes. "I only want him to know I'm sorry."

Carmen parted her lips to respond yet she was interrupted at the sound of someone coming in the house. She turned around to see Monifah who had been let in by Tiara. Her friend didn't even look at her and Carmen knew it was because of her kiss with Rakim. To make things even more awkward between them, everyone knew Rakim died in her arms.

To keep down the tension, she went in the kitchen, but Monifah only followed her. The situation went from bad to worse when Jay and Tiara joined them as well.

"Nothing matters anymore, Carmen. The anger I had, the hurt, the feeling of being betrayed when Rakim told me he kissed you. None of it matters. I don't care anymore that he was in love with you. Or that he broke up with me because you were pissed about our relationship. Neither one of us can have him now."

Carmen looked at Jay and saw the uneasiness in his face. Monifah had put her business out there, spilling a secret Carmen thought she was taking to the grave. In addition, she never knew Rakim had broken up with her. "I don't want to argue, Mo. I—"

Monifah cut her off as if she didn't care about her apology. "I don't want to argue with you either. I only wanted to come over here and stare you in the face before Rakim's funeral. I loved him, Carmen, and he loved me. You should've accepted it instead of trying to break us apart. Maybe, one day, you'll find that kind of love." Monifah stared at Carmen for a solid five seconds before leaving the kitchen. Shortly after, she left the house, as if she had only come to give that message. If so, Carmen was left with a head full of unanswered questions.

Chapter Nineteen

The atmosphere in Jay's house was one Carmen couldn't bear. With everyone there, Carmen had no choice, but to leave. Though Jay begged her to stay and claimed he wasn't upset over the kiss, Carmen begged to differ. She told him to give her some time while she went to visit her parents. They were already in the process of moving and had several U-Haul trucks parked in the front yard. When she pulled up, she heard her father calling to her before she even saw him.

"I'm right here, Peaches," her father yelled, coming up behind her car. "This has been a workout. Did you—" his tone changed once he took a good look at her face. "What's wrong, baby?"

"Rakim was murdered today," she told him. Her lips started to quiver and before she knew it, she broke right in front of him.

At the sight of her tears, her father rushed to the car, grabbing her into his arms. "Peaches, it's okay," he said, rubbing her shoulders. "Tell me what happened."

Carmen knew she would have to start at the beginning. She had never told her father about Pierre or how Jay had killed him. Now, she felt obligated to tell him. "I met a guy at a party named Pierre. He was a drug dealer in West Brookstone. Pierre found out that Jay and I were a little bit more than friends, and things got ugly. He tried to rape me, and Jay killed him. I was there when it happened. It was the night I came home late. Since Jay killed Pierre, one of his workers, Shakeem, wanted retaliation. He went after Carlos and got messed up bad. Once he was out the hospital, Carlos went at him, and now Rakim is dead."

Harold looked out the window as several different emotions overcame him. Most of the emotions had been suppressed from years living as Harold Davenport, but now Carmen had resurfaced his thirst to kill. She was continuing the story yet all he could think about was how he wished he could've been the one to kill Pierre. "Did Jay authorize the hit?"

"He says he didn't, but he wanted Shakeem dead, too. We both keep looking for someone to blame."

"You know, things like this happened a lot when I was with Hector. He had men stepping out of line all the time. People get bigheaded. They want the same power as the ringleader, but what they don't understand is that everyone has their place. I know Jay is trying to bring back his father's legacy by continuing the cartel. What he doesn't realize, and the signs are there, is that the men stepping out of line now are the men that are going to be giving him trouble in the future."

"Carlos was always trouble from the start," Carmen admitted. She looked at her father when she caught one of the points he made. He admitted to her that he knew all along that Jay was a drug dealer.

"So Carlos was the one who stepped out of line?"

Carmen nodded her head as she separated herself from her father.

"I've always said, what is done in darkness will always come to light." Harold placed a firm kiss on Carmen's forehead. "I know it's tough, Peaches. You'll get through it and so will Jay. If y'all want to come here tonight, feel free. You know our door is always open."

Carmen whispered thank you although she knew they would be staying at home. If anything, they needed to be inviting her parents there since most of their belongings were packed. Carmen figured they would do it one day, but as for now, she and her parents were going their separate ways.

Chapter Twenty

Carmen had spent numerous hours slaving over the design of Rakim's suit. She had taken it upon herself to design it, wanting him to be the first person who ever wore one of her original designs. She had designed the suit only for him and promised herself that no one else would wear it. She had originally made it a dark purple until Malik asked for his brother to be buried in all-white.

Even now, as she looked at the final design, Carmen noted the way she had drawn the cufflinks, how the buttons were aligned on the jacket and even how she had designed the hem of his pants. Unable to measure him in time for the funeral, Malik had agreed to let her use his measurements. They were the exact same size, height, and weight included. When Carmen saw that the suit fit him, she knew it would fit Rakim as well.

Nonetheless, nothing prepared her for seeing Rakim in the suit. His face appeared so angelic, free of scars and blemishes except for his mole. Carmen cried at the sight and if it wasn't for Jay, she wouldn't have moved from his casket.

While Carmen believed Rakim's funeral was the hardest thing to get through, returning to school for her senior year was even harder. During the probate show for Theta Beta Psi Fraternity, a pair of black boots was left in a single spot, informing the campus that Rakim had been pledging their organization. The mere thought of it had Carmen about to cry again until Tiara peeked inside her office.

"I got your realtor on the phone," Tiara voiced.

Although she was having a private moment to herself, Carmen accepted the phone call. Ever since she had taken over Flame, she had discovered more and more about the hole the company was in. Her mother had been manufacturing new items, knowing the budget didn't allow it.

"Hey, Daddy," Carmen said, happily, trying to hide her thoughts.

"Peaches, how are things going?"

"Good," Carmen lied, not sharing her concerns.

"Things are going well here, too. Your mother started hiring her first little employees. I think Texas will be a good fit for Flame. The people here in Dallas are excited about the store's opening."

"That's good." Carmen twisted around in her chair as her father continued talking about his new life in Texas. She could tell her parents were happy and Carmen was glad to see them together. She only wished her own relationship wasn't going down the drain. Since Jay had gotten the warehouse, he never was home. With school and her mom's business in her hands, she barely had time to see him. Nighttime was the only time they were around each other. Jay would come in, they would make love, and then they both would be asleep for the rest of the night. They didn't even have the energy for a conversation.

"Have you met the owner of Production?"

"What is Production and who is the owner?"

"Carmen, we told you about him. Production is the store that is going to be down from Flame. You need to go meet the owner. If you're nice to him, he might let you see your old room again."

Carmen playfully rolled her eyes. "The only thing I want to see is what kind of product he's going to be putting on his shelves. Other than that, we don't need to be friends."

"Come on, Peaches, give him a chance. You two can probably learn something from each other. He is building his store from the ground up. I only want you to talk to him. He needs a friend. Everyone he knows lives in Manhattan."

Carmen rolled her eyes again although she told her father she would meet up with him. To ensure she did, she told him she would call him back in five minutes after she peeked at the store. Since Production was in walking distance, it took her less than a minute to reach.

Upon looking inside, she noticed the amount of construction the store was going through. Contractors and painters were hard at work while a tall, dark-skinned black man was in the middle of the store, pointing at the ceiling and various spots on the wall. He was of medium build and his complexion was the same as her father's, rich, and ebony. *No wonder he likes him so much*, she thought. Carmen watched the guy in action as he directed his workers to several items that needed to be touched up. There were already several solid gold circular lines on the ceiling, which entrapped a huge pink rose that had been painted in the middle.

Artistic and fresh, designs of the sort were absent in her store. There were only a few wall-sized ads, which didn't compare to anything inside of Production. Carmen knew she had to step up her game.

"Do you like what you see?" a voice asked, taking her out her daze. "You've been standing out here for quite a while."

Carmen focused her eyes, seeing the owner standing in front of her. He had a perfect set of white teeth, which stood out against his dark complexion. "I like the rose," she told him. "The pink and gold colors match well together. It would catch anybody's eye."

"My favorite song is "Kiss of a Rose," by Seal. I don't know if you can tell, but the lines around the rose form lips. The rose is in the center," he explained, placing his index finger on her mouth.

Carmen jumped at his touch, leading the man to chuckle. She didn't find the move very humorous, but after staring at his perfect smile, she was able to form one of her own.

"Kane," he told her, introducing himself.

Carmen shook his hand, yet she didn't give him her name. He seemed to notice because he said it for her as if he already knew who she was.

"Carmen Davenport," he guessed. "Your father has been begging me to come over and meet you. He said we needed to get together. If you're free, we can get a bite to eat. What do you say? Do you like Southern food? I haven't been able to find a good soul food restaurant in Brookstone."

Carmen held her hands up because Kane was obviously moving too fast. Her father might have encouraged them to meet, but Kane was practically asking her out on a date. He was too forward, which was distracting her from what she had really come to discuss with him. "Mr. Kane, we will not be going anywhere with each other. The line stops here."

Kane gave her a nervous smile. "I apologize, ma'am. I wasn't trying to come on to you, well, not yet," he joked. "Look, maybe I can stop by tomorrow and look at Flame. Does that sound fair?"

"Very fair," Carmen stated, glad to be almost out his presence. He nodded his head in response before going inside his store. She did the same and the moment she was inside, Tiara was in her face.

"What did your father say about the building?"

Carmen stopped in her tracks because she hadn't even mentioned it. She had forgotten all about a previous conversation she and Tiara had shared. Carmen had confided in Tiara about the store's finances, and they had thought about asking her father for help. He could get them a new, bigger building and help them change the look of Flame. He could also help them turn Carmen's designs into actual merchandise. They were planning on asking him for a shitload of money. "I forgot to even mention it to him. We started talking about Texas, Kane, and I forgot."

"So you finally met Kane?" Tiara asked, following Carmen into her office. "I met him yesterday when he was standing outside with his contractors. I think we're going to be okay with him. He seems to be very down to earth. However, we don't need to be discussing him. We need to be talking to your father. If you're serious about changing Flame's finances; you need to stick to the plan."

Carmen knew Tiara was right. If she wanted to get Flame out the hole and a chain of stores off the ground, she had to stop sulking in her office. She had to start making moves. To show Tiara she was serious, she excused her from her office while she called her father.

He answered on the second ring and Carmen knew it was because he was waiting to hear about her encounter with Kane. Instead of jumping into a discussion about him, she went straight into her new business plan for Flame. "I want to start my own men's line. I also think we need to make Flame a chain. We can use this building as one of the stores, and possibly get a building downtown as headquarters. It would be good if we could manufacture the clothes in the building as well. Do you have a building available in downtown Brookstone?"

"Um, Carmen, you know that costs money, right?"

"Of course, I do. I know Mama took a big chunk of your money for the store in Texas, but I figured you could help me. If we start the New Year fresh, we could possibly save Flame and I can repay all the millions you've spent. What do you say?"

"Carm, we left so you could learn independence, not so you could call us asking for money to fulfill your dreams. You need to go about this the hard way. It's going to take years of hard work."

Carmen let out a deep sigh. "I didn't want to wait that long."

"Do you want to send Flame into bankruptcy?"

"We're already headed there, Daddy. I think changing the look of Flame might increase capital and get the numbers up. My vision for Flame is totally different from the one Mama had."

"You and your Mama are running out the same account right now. You need to find a way to make the store your own. Now, you own that location legally, but if you created a whole new identity for the store then it can drive people your age to come in and shop. Right now, they're used to seeing a forty-five year old woman there every day. Change the look, reap the benefits, and then use the money to purchase another building. It won't happen overnight, but when it does, the wait will be worth it. I promise you, baby. I see the potential."

"Or you can give me the building for free," Carmen suggested.

"You've fell and bumped your head. This is what I'm going to do. I'm going to see what's available. I'll call you back with some figures, and then talk to your mother about it. Once we see what we're working with, then we'll see how much money you're going to need."

"Are you going to give it to me?" Carmen asked, hoping she could coax her father into shelving out the money for her store.

"Carmen, one of the reasons we moved was to teach you independence. How in the world are you learning independence if I'm still sending you money? I'm not giving you anything. We're going to do this like real businesspeople. You're going to have to do a lot of waiting, praying, and applying for some business grants. This is a lot of money we're talking about. Your mother has been in this business for most of your life. She didn't open another store until now."

"Daddy, this is my dream we're talking about. I've been dreaming of this since I drew my first outfit. I'm going to give you your money back. If you want me to be honest, I'm only asking for a loan. I'll repay you."

"Peaches, this is what I'm going to do. I'm going to see what we have in our listings. I'll look at some small buildings in New York and even New

Jersey. Tomorrow, I will call you with the details of what's available. How does that sound?"

Carmen agreed to the plan only because she didn't have any other options. She had a short amount of time to save Flame and needed a large sum of money. She didn't have a plan on how she was going to get it, but by nightfall, she was determined to have something in the works.

Chapter Twenty-One

Carmen swung by Sapphire only because she wanted to spend some time with Jay. If she stayed home, she wouldn't have seen him or better yet, felt him, until about four o'clock in the morning. He was busy sitting at his desk, counting large stacks, which she knew had come from the front door and the bar. He always had the same guy bring the money to him at a certain hour because the registers would get too full.

At the sight of the money, Carmen thought about asking Jay for a loan. She had never asked him for anything because he never made her. She lived with him scot-free, carried designer bags he purchased, and her collection of diamond jewelry had increased traumatically. She knew if she got a million from him, she wouldn't have to worry about taking money from her father. The idea seemed grand, and Carmen knew she needed to get started on the deal. Although he was stuffing cash into a money counter, she slid into his lap, catching his attention. "I need your help, Mr. Santiago," she blurted, kissing his cheek. Not wanting to keep up the suspense, she started in on her request. "I need some money."

Jay cracked a smile, knowing she was enticed by the large sum of cash in front of him. "What do you need money for, Carm? You have your own store, a rich daddy, and you don't have bills."

"I need it for a building. I want to turn Flame into a chain."

The money that was in Jay's hands ended up on his desk as he took a moment to listen to Carmen's idea. Since Flame was now hers, he knew she would need his support as she ran her own business. "First," he began. "Your father owns Davenport Realty. He can give you a building for free. If not for free then he can put you on a payment plan. He can work the system. I know he can, he did it for me. Do you think he knows what I have in my warehouse?"

"I've already went to him," Carmen stressed. "He said no. Well, he said he would look at some things and get back to me. *However*, he isn't paying for a building, and he isn't going to loan me money."

"How much money are we talking?"

Carmen looked at him carefully so she could see his reaction when she said the word a million. If he narrowed his eyes then she would know he was turning her down as well. "I think I'm going to need a million dollars for everything I want to do. That should cover manufacturing the men's line, headquarters, marketing, and—"

"You want me to give you a million dollars?"

His tone was very sarcastic, which meant the answer was no.

"I'm not giving you a million dollars. Now, I'll give you ten or twenty thousand, but a million? I love you, baby, but you're not about to hustle a million dollars out of me. Besides, I have faith in you. You need to turn Flame around before I make an investment into a struggling store. All you need to do is apply for grants and loans. You have a good track record, Flame is regularly audited, and there aren't any back taxes. You can get your business plan together and apply for some things. We both can start looking. It can be like our little Bonnie and Clyde project."

"You don't understand, Jay. I need 'right now' money. Flame is going bankrupt in like five minutes. I really can't even afford to run the store. I'm sacrificing my paycheck so Tiara can have one. We're working our butts off because I had to let two of our sales associates go. I'm in the hole."

Jay could hear her frustration. "I know you're stressed, but I'm not giving you a million dollars. If you want to take the twenty thousand, cool, I'll write the check and sign it to love. You don't even have to pay me back. Now, in terms of this million, that shit isn't going down."

"So can I hustle it for you?"

The words were out her mouth before she could stop herself. Carmen knew hustling wasn't for her. She didn't know anything about selling drugs or being part of a cartel. She was already a witness to Rakim's demise, and the lifestyle wasn't one she wanted to experience.

"You are on some bullshit, Carm. Get the fuck up." Jay pushed her out his lap. "You're fuckin' insane if you think I'm going to give you weight to sell."

"How am I going to get this money, Jay?"

"The way you know how, and it isn't by driving to different states selling crack or ecstasy. You're smarter than that, Carm. You might have Pagua blood running through your veins, but you're not a hustler."

"So are you going to give me the money?"

"Hell fuckin' no," Jay yelled, taking his cash out the money counter. "I'm not giving you shit now." Jay slid a rubberband around the cash and dropped it in a suitcase on the floor.

"I need a fuckin' drink," Carmen muttered.

Jay watched her as she left his office, shaking his head in the process. He never thought in a million years she would ask to be down with his crew. She had proven she was spoiled and was looking for everything to be handed to her. Jay realized he would have to give her tough love like her father and force her into independence. He would give her a month or two to try and work something out, and if she failed, then he might reconsider giving her the money. *It could work in my favor*, he thought. He could easily exchange the money for her hand in marriage. Marrying her would mean he could start working on his future. Secretly, he had already started. He awaited the day Carmen didn't get her period. Like his father needed him to continue his legacy, Jay needed a son to continue his.

***

Carlos looked at Carmen up and down, having heard her whole conversation with Jay. He knew Carmen didn't trust him, but he also knew women were weak when they wanted something. Carlos knew he could help her get the money. She had a legit background, a fly car, and a smile that even got him hard. He knew she would be the tightest thing on the block if she was slinging. Carlos always wanted his own crew and Carmen could be the first person who was delivering money to him. It would be hard keeping Jay from finding out, but he was always up for a challenge.

"I can help you get the money," he said as she headed for the steps.

Carmen turned to look at him and smirked.

"I'm serious; I can help you get the money." Carlos walked towards her, making sure he was away from Jay's door. "I can teach you how to sell, how to shoot. You can have the money in about two months' time." Carlos looked down the hall and saw that Jay's door was still closed.

Carmen rolled her eyes, walking off, but he grabbed her arm.

"I can help you. I know how to run this drug shit. When I get these next kilos, I'll give you some of the work. If you can sell it, I'll give you a cut. You can call it a favor for a friend. You can stop once you've met your goal."

"Thanks for letting me know you were being nosy. Jay would shoot you dead if he knew you were trying to put me on. Tell me, Carlos, how are you going to be making money if I'm getting a cut of your work?"

Carlos chuckled. "Damn, Carmen, you're already smooth. I already have money, baby. Just like you, I was born with a silver spoon in my mouth. My father always kept a million or two in an account for me. See, unlike these other motherfuckers, I can afford to give you a cut of my work. The average dealer on the street can't work the system like that. Shit, they *wouldn't* work the system like that. See, I'm a greedy motherfucker when it comes to power. I can do the same shit Jay is doing, probably even better. All I need to start me off is a team. I mean, your man isn't trying to help you get this paper. He told your ass no. He was clear about that."

Carmen didn't trust Carlos further than she could throw him. She also knew hustling wasn't for her. Though his deal was enticing, she knew she would be in over her head if she accepted it.

"You want to be like your mother, opening up your second store when you're almost fifty? What are you going to do if things with Jay don't work out? You don't have shit. You can't even afford to put a dollar in church. Every Sunday, Jay writes a check for you and him."

Everything Carlos was saying was right. Carmen was flat broke without a dime to her name. If she and Jay broke up, she would be homeless, probably jobless, and would have to sell her stuff to have a deposit for an apartment and first month's rent. If it came down to it, she would have to sell her Lexus for a Honda Accord. "Damn, Carlos, what do you want me to do?" she asked him, giving in. "You know I need this money."

"I want you to fuck me."

Carmen grinded her teeth as she walked closer to him. She was less than an inch away from his face when she said, "I would rather suffer from cancer than sleep with you. Enjoy the fantasy in your head."

"I'm trying to help you, Carm. Everyone else is turning their back on you. How long has Jay known about Flame? I know you've shown him the figures. Your own father even knows that it's a matter of weeks or days before you start packing the store up. You have the drive to save the store; you simply need a helping hand. Don't think I haven't been watching you. I see you out there. I know what you're capable of doing, especially in the business world. When it comes to the bedroom, thanks to Jay, I know what you can do there, too."

Carmen wrinkled her face. Her sexual nature was supposed to stay behind closed doors. Due to Jay's locker room tales, Carlos was demanding she sleep with him in exchange for money. Carmen honestly believed that over time, she could write that part out the deal if she accepted the offer. It wasn't like Carlos was going to make her sleep with him before she had the money. By the time she had the cash, he would've probably forgotten about that part. "I need this money in two months."

"You'll have it. You can start tomorrow. When you get off from work, come straight to my apartment." Carlos turned around, heading downstairs to the dance floor. "Oh, by the way," he said, catching her attention, "you're probably going to be up all night."

Chapter Twenty-Two

Carmen straightened the display tables, trying to keep her mind off the deal she made with Carlos. She knew she had gone against Jay's wishes and even those of her father. He had tried to protect her from the cartel, but she had chosen to walk hand in hand with it. She could still back out, although she already agreed to the plan.

Carmen rested her hands on the table, staring at a stack of shirts until a shadow came over her. Nervously, she turned around, meeting eyes with Kane.

"In heavy thought?" he asked, placing his hand on hers.

Carmen looked at his hand and tried to crack a smile. She could tell Kane found her attractive. She knew one day she would have to tell him she was involved. "I have a lot on my mind right now."

"Am I making you nervous?"

Carmen was getting ready to answer until Tiara stepped in between them with a cordless phone. She quickly announced her father was on the line, which meant she could get an update on the future headquarters of Flame. Not to mention, be saved from answering Kane's question. "Excuse me," she told him, "I need to take this."

Carmen snatched the phone from Tiara and walked hurriedly to her office, closing the door behind her. "Daddy," she answered, praying the news was good.

"Hey, Peaches, I called to tell you about what my agents found. The cheapest building I have and that you would probably want is $500,000. I know that's not what you want to hear, but that's the best we can do."

Carmen's heart sunk only because she knew that was half of the money she was asking for. She wouldn't have enough to cover the building, renovations, and salaries or put out her men's line. Still, she had to trust that Carlos would give her enough in cuts to make her dream happen. "Okay, Daddy, can you hold the building for me?"

"Now, I may have some wiggle room in that area. I'll pull some strings and get it out our listings so no one can buy it. Do you like that?"

"I love it." Carmen felt some sort of relief although the building wasn't officially hers. She had made a start, which was more progress than she was currently making. At the sound of her father's goodbye, Carmen opened her office door to find Tiara and Kane standing on the other side. It was obvious they had been eavesdropping from the way they jumped when she opened it. "Can I help you?" she asked them.

"I'll take this," Tiara said, sliding the phone out Carmen's hands. "I'll let you two be. Work calls."

Carmen turned to Kane so he could see she was waiting for his reply. All he gave her was a smile before telling her to have a good day. Not quite sure what was up his sleeve, Carmen went in her office so she could dance with no one watching. Already, things were looking up.

***

After work, Carmen went home to shower before heading over to Carlos' apartment. Once she was there, she thought they were going to sit down for Hustling 101. Instead, he grabbed his car keys and told her it was time for the streets. From the second they were inside his car, Carlos was talking a mile a minute, giving her a rundown of Jay's operation, and advising her on where she would fit in. He seemed adamant about putting her in their city's financial district, which Carmen had already visited. Jay had told her about the area very early in their relationship. She felt comfortable selling to the stockbrokers and CEOs.

"The Wall Street crackheads are going to love a girl like you," Carlos told her, "the sales in the East are going to pop."

Currently parked on a corner in West Brookstone, Carlos completed a quick sale before continuing the discussion. "I never thought I would be schooling you on the drug game, Carm. Shit, I told Jay he needed to leave your ass alone, because you could bring down the whole cartel. On the real, you might be what we need. We should've been hanging out."

"Do you really think a friendship with me is going to work?" Carmen asked. "Maybe, we should get money and stop trying to be friends. I know you hate me, and you know I hate you."

"Shit, I use to run your name in the mud."

"You hated me because I was trying to look out for you. You were mad because I told Jay that Pierre had a hit on you. So, what, you didn't want to know? You wanted him to run up on you like you did Shakeem and leave you dead like Rakim? Come on, Carlos; let's be for real for a moment."

"There was no hope for Rakim. He took every single last one of those bullets except one. It was my fault he was there in the first place."

Carmen met eyes with Carlos and for the first time in months, she saw sincerity. She almost thought she could trust him. Too busy figuring him out, she nearly missed what he was telling her.

"When you're downtown, never let anyone know what you have unless they're part of our clientele. If someone you don't know, asks for something, you don't have it," Carlos said, starting to school her again. "It could be a Triad agent or some other undercover cop trying to pull a fast one on you. We know our clientele is legit. We have so much dirt on them they won't ever try and snitch. I'm talking politicians, lawyers, doctors, real big timers."

Carlos started up the car to start the trip to his apartment. He couldn't keep Carmen out long otherwise Jay would start asking questions.

"I'm getting you a new car. Whenever you hustle, don't drive your Lexus. You can park it in my apartment complex. I want you to look like a professional, too. Keep all your money in a good spot until I ask for it. Once you turn it in, I'll give you your cut. I'll also give you more work. I got plenty of money for bricks so Jay shouldn't suspect a thing."

Carmen stared at him as he spoke, wondering if she was in over her head. There was a lot she had to learn, and she wasn't even sure how she was going to learn it. All she knew was that she was rolling with one of the street's best teachers.

Chapter Twenty-Three

September

It didn't take Carmen long to catch onto the drug game. Once she caught on, she had it in the palm of her hand. It was easy for her to coax men into buying the product that Carlos had given her. Some of them even paid extra if she gave them a little bit more attention. There wasn't anything sexual going on, but Carmen knew how to strut her stuff for an extra thousand dollars. Most of the men were young white males, working as stockbrokers while others were lawyers, doctors, or entrepreneurs. Carmen was shocked at how many men in her father's working class bracket were on drugs. They hid it well, but Carmen knew they had veins the size of live wires underneath their Ralph Lauren suit jackets.

She woke up early, every morning, hitting spots all over New York. When it came time for her first cut, she had already made a little over forty thousand dollars. Most of the money wasn't even from even selling drugs, but from simply conning men out their money. By the second time cuts came around, she had a total of a hundred thousand dollars hidden in her new Bentley. Carlos had quickly seen how successful she was and started giving her more to sell. She was lucky not to have any problems, but Carmen knew if any man wanted to test her then she could do what needed to be done.

She tried not to let herself get caught up in the business, but it was hard to do. From day one, she was living a double life. She went to work after making her rounds and then after work, she would hit up a few spots in West Brookstone. She would then head home before Jay got there. By the third time cuts came up, Carmen had acquired a new set of clients. She was working almost double time. Her product was getting more expensive because she had less of it to go around. By raising her prices, Carlos started giving her an extra eight thousand dollars. Any time she ran out, Carmen realized she had more time to herself. She could go to work early or have a small date with Jay, which helped conceal her new lifestyle.

That morning, Carmen was headed to a brokerage firm where she had five clients who contacted her on the regular. Only two had requested her presence and her first visit was to Mr. Toussaint. An older white gentleman with a bad drug habit, he had been feenin' for a hit since last night. Carmen always came to his office with a briefcase in her hand so she wouldn't raise suspicions. A known visitor, even his secretary waved at her when she walked on his floor.

"He's expecting you," the lady told her with a smile.

Carmen nodded at the woman and headed to his office. Mr. Toussaint had gotten her number from Carlos. He was a heroin addict and was about to go bankrupt trying to keep up with his habit.

"You're late," he yelled at her once she was inside his office.

Carmen held out her hand for her money. All she wanted to do was toss him the heroin so she could be on her merry way.

"You got more than you had last time," he asked her, calming down.

"Depends on how much you're willing to pay. You know my type of heroin is hard to come by." Carmen sat on the man's desk, enticing him a bit. He had started buying her product in bulk, hoping to conceal his lifestyle. His plan didn't work because the more drugs he had, the more he shot up.

"A thousand for everything you have."

"It's going to be a whole lot more than that. I have another stop to make meaning someone might be going cold turkey. Wait until you see how many goodie bags I have. Plus, I got pills this time. You're saying you want it all," she told him, opening the briefcase. "This is worth more than a G."

"Two thousand for everything," he yelled.

Carmen smiled, jumping off his desk. He had said the amount she wanted to hear. "Done," she replied and held out her hand. She watched him as he maneuvered behind his desk, opening a drawer. He pulled out two bankrolls, sliding them to her. Happily, Carmen grabbed them, counting, and inspecting the money. Once she saw the funds were legit; she slid the money in the briefcase. Mr. Toussaint hurriedly went inside the bathroom to shoot up. He didn't even bother to hide the drugs. "Two thousand in less than ten minutes," she said to herself.

Carmen quickly left Mr. Toussaint's office, opening the door only slightly so his receptionist couldn't peer in. She then left the building, heading outside. Since Mr. Toussaint had purchased everything she had, she pulled out her cell phone and broke the news to her other client. She could tell the man was angry, but she promised him it would be worth his while. In the middle of call, she was surprised to hear a beep, which was followed by Jay's name flashing on the screen. She clicked over quickly, not wanting to keep him waiting. "Hello," she answered as she got in her car.

"Why did you run out the house like that this morning?"

"I had to get to work, baby," Carmen answered.

"Are you at work now?"

"Jay, where else am I going to be?"

"That's what I was trying to figure out because I'm standing right here in the middle of your fuckin' store and I don't see your ass anywhere."

Carmen didn't get frustrated or show any sign she was lying. She knew how to play this game. "I'm at work. I stepped out for a moment to go to the bank. I'll be back in a couple of minutes." Carmen listened as his tone changed. He even apologized to her.

"I'm sorry, Carm. We've both been busy, but sometimes I like to wake up and know that you're next to me. I want to see you sometimes."

Carmen agreed with him, starting her car. She drove out the parking lot, aware she needed to swing by Carlos' apartment to change cars and clothes. When Jay told her goodbye, she replied in kind and hung up the phone. It was a close call, but she had played it off well. Not in the clear, Carmen made sure she moved quick in case Jay decided to stick around her store.

When she reached the apartment complex, Carmen quickly grabbed her purse and the change of clothes she kept in the trunk. She could never go in Flame with a business suit because people would know she was up to something. She always changed clothes inside her Lexus. Her windows were freshly tinted so she headed towards a dead end street to change. The money she had made from selling drugs had been hid underneath the floorboard of the Bentley, which was where she put her earnings until she could deposit it. The rest was hidden in the driver's seat. Carmen had learned where to hide her money, knowing she couldn't hide it at Jay's house or in her checking account. She figured she would start making small deposits in a couple of weeks.

Once dressed, Carmen headed to her store, arriving in time before business picked up. Jay was nowhere in sight, but she knew that didn't mean she was off the hook. It meant he would pop up later because he had a feeling she was up to something.

Carmen immediately started going through the morning's shipment. Her mother had designed a slew of new dresses, which she now had to market and sell.

"I want to see you taking off that one."

Carmen turned around, seeing Carlos. He was wearing a gray pinstriped suit with a light pink tie that matched his handkerchief and pinky ring. The suit, being well-fitted, looked custom-made. "It's not like you to come here in your work clothes."

"Today was a special occasion. I have some news for you."

Carmen looked around the store. Most of the associates were busy with customers. "Do we need to talk in private?" She looked him up and down once more, wanting to know what was going on.

"I don't think so, what are you doing tonight? You can come over to my place, and I can give you this proposition over, let's say dinner?"

Carmen automatically put up a red flag. "We've never ate dinner together. What are you up to?" Carmen hoped Carlos wasn't trying to take their business relationship in a different direction. She remembered the other part of their deal and she still wasn't about to fulfill it.

"Nah, nah, it's nothing like that. I thought it would be good for two business partners to get together and discuss business."

Carmen calmed down, seeing the evening was going to be innocent. "I'll let you know. I have Jay on my trail right now."

"Okay, I'll take that. Let me know something by six."

Carmen told him she would. She watched him as he left, wishing he hadn't of showed up at her store. She wanted to keep both of her lives separate and he wasn't making it easy. She told herself that once she got the rest of her money, she was done with the whole thing.

Chapter Twenty-Four

When it hit lunchtime, Carmen decided to pick up a few things from the grocery store versus eating at one of the eateries downtown. She figured she would make a hoagie and throw the leftovers in the fridge. On her way to the meat department, she noticed Kane was there as well. Since she had seen him, Carmen thought it was only fair to speak to him. She followed him to the meat department, which worked in her favor because it was where she was headed. "I guess it's a small world."

Carmen smiled as she caught Kane's attention. His mouth widened, displaying the perfect set of teeth she always looked forward to seeing.

"It is a small world. I haven't seen you in a while. Let me look at you. Well, everything is still in place," he said, jokingly. "How is everything going? I see the store is jumping."

"It's coming along," Carmen replied. Flame had picked up in sales, which was partly due to a new ad campaign she was able to put together. "So, how are things with Production?"

"Good, I hit a few bumps in the road, but it's coming along." Kane paused for a quick second before asking, "What are you getting ready to do?"

"Well, I—" Kane interrupted her before she could tell him her plans.

"How about joining me for lunch at your old place?"

Carmen looked at him as if he read her mind. She desperately wanted to see her old house again, even her old room. She didn't quite know how to ask so she was glad he made the offer.

"Look, Carm, I know it was difficult for you to see your parents give it up. Why don't you join me there for lunch? We can talk business, and you can see what I've done with the place."

"I would really love that," Carmen told him. She looked at the basket she was carrying to see if there was anything in there to help with lunch. "I guess there's no use in getting any of this," she said, picking up the deli meat and cheese.

"Well, it could go with this." Kane pointed at the items that were in his basket. A bag of chips and cookies were inside, which would go perfectly with her items.

"It can." Carmen got excited, seeing how everything was falling in place. However, as quickly as her joy had come, it disappeared. Instantly, Carmen felt a stab of guilt. Not only was she selling drugs behind Jay's back, but she was about to have lunch with another man. The whole thing was innocent, but she knew it could easily turn into something else. She started to question her actions even when they got in line to pay for their groceries. Kane grabbed her basket out her hands, paying for both of their things. When he pulled out his wallet, she caught him checking her out. "What is it?"

"Nothing," he said, pulling out a twenty.

Carmen knew he had given the wrong answer. He had been staring at her for a reason. She was going to ask him about it, which she did once they were standing at his car. When she saw he drove a Toyota Corolla, Carmen realized he was on a totally different level than Jay. Most men she knew weren't riding around in anything less than a Jaguar or Mercedes Benz. "Why did you stare at me like that back there?" she asked him as he dropped the groceries in his backseat.

"All I did was look at you, Carm. Did I offend you?"

"You didn't look at me, Kane. You–"

"I think you're beautiful," Kane replied.

Inside, Carmen was smiling, but on the outside, her mouth appeared crooked. His comment gave her another instant reminder she had to tell him she was taken. Somehow, she only managed to mutter thanks before telling him she was going to her car. She followed him to her old house and was surprised to find everything still intact. The grass had been freshly cut and the flowers her mother had planted were still there.

She felt awkward not pulling out a key and waited as Kane came to the doorway with the groceries. Once the door was open, she stepped inside, seeing the bare walls. She looked towards the dining room and saw it was empty as well. The foyer looked so spacious since there was not one single object on the walls or in the hallway. "So what have you done to the place?" Carmen asked. She walked further in the foyer and saw that the house looked relatively empty. "You've done nothing," she muttered. She turned around, seeing Kane who was laying a white sheet down on the floor. "What's that for?"

"It's for our picnic."

Carmen looked at it and then at him.

"I know what you're thinking. Look, I didn't come from a wealthy family. Buying this house was a dream come true. I know you're probably use to luxury, since you're riding in a Lexus and all, but I can show you a good time without a table and chairs."

Carmen walked to where he was. "Maybe it's time to try something different." Carmen sat down Indian-styled, showing him she was comfortable. "Where's the picnic basket?"

Kane's face broke into an even brighter smile. "I'm going to get it," he said, heading in the direction of the kitchen. He returned with an actual picnic basket where he had stuffed everything they needed inside. Once he was on the floor with her, he pulled out plates; a bag of hoagie rolls, mayonnaise, and a Tupperware container filled with lettuce, slices of tomato and chopped onions.

"So did you have this planned or do you do this for your girl?"

Carmen grabbed a paper plate from him, fixing her plate as she waited for him to answer. He gave her a simple reply, saying he had only done it for a few before asking if she was dating. "I have a boyfriend," she told him. "We've been dating for almost eight months." Carmen expected to see a sign of disappointment, but it never came. Therefore, she decided to continue the conversation. "Do you want kids?"

"I want lots of kids. Matter of fact, I want ten."

Carmen looked at him like he was crazy as he slid mayo on both sides of his bread. "Your wife is going to be busy," she joked. "I want kids, too. I think I want a son first, though." Carmen watched him as he fixed his sandwich. When he looked at her, she quickly turned away.

"You were staring now."

"I was looking," she corrected.

"You were staring."

Carmen decided not to argue with him. "Okay, I was staring. It's your fault, you have a pretty smile." She grabbed the bag of chips from him and dumped some on her plate. "You have a nice complexion, too. You know, I gotta tell my mother about this. I've never had a picnic inside an empty house. This is definitely a first."

The more she thought about it, Carmen realized she hadn't done anything that romantic. Jay never did little things like that. He always bought her stuff, but she had plenty of shoes, clothes, and jewelry.

Carmen told herself not to compare her relationship to the picnic. To keep her mind off the differences, she picked up her sandwich and bit inside.

As time went on, Kane struck up a conversation about the ideas he had for his business. They gave each other advice and Kane even talked about his past girlfriends and how he had grown closer to God. The discussion made Carmen almost resentful for what she was doing. *Key word is almost*, she thought. The future of Flame was in her hands, which meant she had no choice, but to hustle. From the way things were going, she was too close to her goal to turn back now.

Chapter Twenty-Five

"To us," Carlos toasted, tapping Carmen's glass of Chardonnay.

Carmen raised the glass to her lips, keeping her eye on Carlos as she sipped. She didn't have a clue why they were toasting, but she did it anyway. She knew in the back of her mind that this could be the night when Carlos asked her to fulfill the other part of their deal.

"Why don't you sit down so I can bring dinner to you?"

"Why don't you tell me what this is about? We can skip dinner."

"Don't rush me," Carlos snapped, heading in the kitchen. He picked up two plates, which he brought to the table, setting one in front of her. "Bon appetite," he said in a French accent.

Carmen stared at her plate in amazement. "Baked chicken, asparagus, red potatoes, dang, Carlos, you did it up." Carmen took a whiff of the food and was pleased with the aroma. Ready to dig in, she bowed her head, quickly blessing her food. Once she was finished, Carlos immediately started in on his new business idea.

"I got a proposition for you," he said, chewing.

"More details," Carmen ordered. "I don't have all night and neither do you. I want to eat, learn about this deal, and go home to Jay."

Carlos looked over Carmen's attitude. "There's these diamonds," he told her, starting in on their new business venture. "White diamonds, real without a scratch, that a drug dealer is bringing up from the Bahamas." Carlos was still wearing his suit from earlier and pulled a photograph out his jacket pocket, which he slid to Carmen.

Carmen picked it up, seeing a thin man with dreads. He had a medium complexion, and a small scar ran down the left side of his face.

"There's a ship leaving out of Florida headed to Nassau. He's going to board while it's in the Bahamas and get off in Florida when it returns. Then, he'll be on his way to Brookstone."

Carmen stared at the picture and then slid it back to Carlos. "Diamonds are a girl's best friend." She went to pick up her fork and noticed that Carlos had slid the picture back to her. "What does this have to do with me?" Carmen could tell he wanted the picture in her possession.

"I want you to steal the diamonds."

Carmen laughed loudly, sticking her fork in her asparagus. "You are nuts, but the food is good," she told him, continuing to eat.

"This isn't a joke, Carm. I got two tickets for you to board the ship at the end of the week. You find him, take the diamonds, make your way back to Florida, and then board a plane for New York."

"Has it dawned on you I might say no?"

"Shit, Carm, I would do it myself if I wasn't catching so much flak from Jay about what I'm doing with his product. You've made us a lot of money. I need to take the heat off me for a while, meaning I need you to stop selling for a few days. I need business to slow down so Jay won't think something's up. However, I know I promised that you would have this money in two months. That's why I'm giving you this assignment. The diamonds are worth about two million. We'll split the money evenly at next week's Diamond Exchange. You'll have all the money I promised you. All that will be left is the final part of our deal. Please believe; I'm looking forward to tasting your kitty cat."

Carmen ignored his last comment. "How am I going to steal these diamonds? How do you expect me to steal diamonds from some man?"

"He's going to have them in a black suitcase. You find him, seduce him, make a smooth kill, and take the diamonds."

"Oh wow, thou shall not steal, thou shall not kill, and thou shall not lie. We're breaking a lot of commandments," Carmen said, knowing she wasn't going through with the plan. "You need mental help, badly." Carmen stood up from the table, getting ready to leave.

"I'm trying to help you, Carm."

"No, you're not. You are trying to send me to prison for a very long time. I am not about to steal diamonds and kill some man for you, Carlos. You must be out your damn mind."

"It's one million dollars involved. You might not have to kill him, but you gotta get close enough to get the diamonds. If you want me to be honest, you shouldn't be concerned about stealing the diamonds. He stole them from a private collection."

Carmen stared at the man's picture. "How did you come across him? Is he a connect in the Bahamas?"

Carlos loosened the buttons on his suit jacket. "He used to do some work for Pierre a while back when I was down with him. It was only drug-related stuff. I could've cared less about him until I found out he was a jewelry thief. I'm not into diamonds or fancy jewels. That is Jay's thing. He loves diamonds, all kinds, white, pink, red, black, you name it."

"Well, I have good news and bad news. The good news is that you're going to have the diamonds. The bad news is, well, I'm not going to steal them. I bid you good day." Carmen picked up her purse, preparing to leave. When Carlos stood up as well, trying to stop her, she lost her cool. "Why are you so fuckin' money hungry?"

"You think I'm money hungry? It's not the money I want, Carmen, it's the power. Money equals power. I want to get out from underneath Jay's fuckin' ass. I want my own shit. If I do this if I pull off this heist then I'm golden. I promise you, Carm, you will have the money you need for Flame, and I will run this drug shit."

"Did you say if you do this? You're not doing shit, Carlos. My life is on the line."

"I'm setting it up. I can walk you through everything. If I could go, I would, but Jay is on my back."

"You're doing all this for some damn power?" Carmen huffed. She was done with the conversation and ready to go home.

"How is Kane? Do you always go over to his house for lunch?"

Carmen paused in her step at Carlos' words. He walked up to her as a devilish grin flew across his face.

"I always have my eye on you. I don't think Jay would appreciate you having one on one time with another man."

"It was a business lunch. He owns a clothing store next to Flame."

"Jay doesn't know that," Carlos said, walking back to the table. Carmen watched as he brought the photograph over to her.

"It'll be easier for you, if there's something on the line."

"Don't do this," she told him as he handed her the photograph. "I don't want to kill anyone."

"People will do anything if they're getting paid. I know some guys right now who will make up some wild shit about you. Jay has told me all about your sex game and I can recall the stories. It's obvious he taught you well. Anyone can pretend they're fuckin' you. Besides, I already have pictures of you going inside Kane's house."

"You've been following me?"

"I've always followed you. Did you really think I was going to let you sell my stuff and not watch you? I have to protect my worker."

"You know I could tell Jay about your little scheme."

"Then I will tell him you've been selling his drugs. I think Harold, excuse me, Lotus, would love to find out that his daughter has been following in his footsteps."

Carmen swallowed, realizing she was being backed into a corner. Carlos had her exactly where he wanted her. He knew she didn't want to let her father down. This part of her life was something he would never know about. "When does this ship leave?" she whispered, accepting the assignment.

"Thursday, you have two tickets. I want you to take Kane."

"Why would I take him?"

"Well, if you cross me, I can frame you. I have pictures already of y'all together. I'll even have pictures of y'all at the airport."

Carmen could see exactly how far Carlos was willing to go to make sure she carried out his plan. She shook her head; knowing there was no way Kane was going to join her. He was putting a store together and didn't even have time for a vacation. That was the least of her worries, though. Carmen felt a tear slide down her cheek as she thought about the possibility of leading Kane into something that could get them both arrested. "Why are you making me do this?" she said starting to cry. "My whole life is on the line."

"Shit, mine is too, but we both want this money."

Carmen turned away, dropping the picture and faced the door. She could risk her whole life doing this. She knew what could happen to her father's career if the media found out his daughter was a drug dealer. Carmen looked at the photograph as it lay beside her right foot. She picked it up and looked at Carlos.

"Finish dinner," he said, nodding towards the table. "We have lots to discuss before your trip."

Carmen turned over in bed, trying her best not to make eye contact with Jay. Since he was in the shower when she came in, she didn't have to speak. She wasn't surprised when he got in bed without saying a single word. She always made it home before him, but tonight was the first night that things were different.

Carmen held her eyes shut, going over the plan Carlos had conjured up. Today was only Monday and she had until Thursday to find a way to convince Kane to go to the Bahamas with her. She also had to tell Jay she was going out of town. Carmen didn't know where to start on either one. To make her feel even worse, Jay turned over in bed and wrapped his arms around her.

"I've missed you," she heard him whisper in her ear. Carmen continued to fake being asleep. "Wake up," he whispered. Carmen opened her eyes and looked at him.

"We don't talk anymore."

Carmen nodded her head and closed her eyes once more until she felt him nudge her. She reopened her eyes, glaring at him. "Baby, I'm sleepy," she told him with a yawn. Carmen was faking it, but she knew she had to because of her guilty conscience. "What is it?"

"We don't talk anymore."

"I know. You're busy with what you do. I'm busy with what I do."

Carmen closed her eyes and felt him as he pulled the covers back. She opened her eyes, seeing him standing beside her, completely nude. Obviously agitated, he picked up his pillow and headed towards the door. "Baby, stop," she told him, leaning up in bed.

She watched as he opened the door and slammed it closed. Carmen sighed, knowing she didn't have the energy to deal with one of his tantrums. Still, she knew she was to blame for his anger. No longer hesitating, she pulled the covers back and followed him downstairs. He was in the living room, laying on the couch with all his business on display. "Jay, I'm sorry," she said, walking down the steps. "I have a lot on my mind. There are a lot of things I need to talk to you about, but I don't know how."

"Well, talk to me now."

Carmen bit her lip. "I'm going out of town in a few days."

Jay stared at her and then turned over.

"I'm going to the Bahamas," she continued.

Jay closed his eyes to control his anger. He had told her they didn't communicate and now she was telling him it was going to get worse.

"Will you at least say something?"

"I just told your fuckin' ass we don't talk. Now you throw this shit up in my face." Jay remembered he was nude when he felt a slight breeze. He got up to get a blanket and walked past her to the closet.

"It's only for four days," Carmen told him, watching as he opened the closet door. "Jay, you don't have to sleep on the couch."

"Yes, I do," he said, grabbing a blanket. "I'm not about to sleep in an angry bed. I can stay down here and be in peace." Jay walked past her into the living room.

"Whatever, I'm going to bed," he heard her say. He listened as she walked up the steps. He knew she was pissed, but so was he. This chain was taking more of her time than he thought. It made him want to take out his checkbook and write her a check for a million dollars. Then, she would be back to her normal routine.

However, he didn't want to slide a silver spoon in her mouth. He simply wished she was around more. He had come home several nights to find the house empty. He would leave back out only to return early in the morning to see her in bed. He had pretended for the longest he was the one who stayed out late. The truth of the matter was that he wasn't. He had built his empire and now it was time for him to invest his money into something else.

Jay focused his mind on her trip to the Bahamas. He knew it was innocent, but he wondered if Tiara was going with her. If she was, he knew they would get in some devilment. The last thing he wanted was a surprise from her. He had calmed down a lot from being with her, but he knew the old Jay could easily be awakened. A part of him had resurfaced now. Instead of sleeping in the bed with her, he was laying downstairs on the couch.

Fed up with his tantrum, he grabbed his pillow and walked towards the staircase to join her. Since he wasn't there, she had curled up in the middle of the bed. He placed his pillow in its regular spot and laid down on top of her. He knew he was heavy although she didn't complain. He figured she was used to it because of the numerous times he had been on top during sex.

"You want to tell me about the Bahamas?"

"I'm going to sleep, Jay," she answered with an attitude.

"Who are you going with?" he asked, slightly curious. He ran his fingers along her shoulder blade waiting for her to respond. "Who are you going with?" he repeated. Jay felt his temper rise as she ignored him. She was hiding something from him. If she wasn't, then she would have answered his question. Jay knew she hadn't fallen asleep that fast, but he wasn't going to bother her anymore. If she wanted to play games, then she could play games. He was only going to have to catch her in her game.

Chapter Twenty-Six

On Tuesday morning, Tiara officially became suspicious of her best friend when she spent her first hour of work going through the numerous amounts of paperwork on Carmen's desk. Based off the large number of unsigned forms and checks, Carmen had obviously been preoccupied. Although she was glad to be off the floor, catching her friend up on her paperwork was becoming a hassle. She voiced her opinion the second Carmen walked in her office. "What have you been doing back here?" she asked, pointing at all the paperwork that covered the desk.

"I've been working. Did you approve those ads yet?"

"I was hoping you would. It's going to be hanging in *your* store," Tiara grunted, handing over the 8x10s. Carmen took a quick glance before setting the photos on her desk. Somewhat offended, Tiara picked the ads up only to see a folder that contained two tickets for a flight to Florida. In addition, there were two boarding passes for a ship she never heard of. "Going somewhere?" Tiara asked, holding the tickets up.

Carmen looked at her friend, seeing the tickets. "Apparently, I am," she replied. She hadn't found a way out Carlos' plan, which meant she would be making the trip to the Bahamas.

"Are you and Jay going somewhere? It says here y'all are going to the Bahamas. Do you really think you should be taking a trip? I mean, shouldn't we concentrate on sales and how to improve things so we can increase capital and get these ideas rolling?"

"That's what I've been doing," Carmen snapped.

Tiara sensed Carmen's attitude and dropped the tickets on the desk. "Look, Carm, I've been covering your ass a lot. I don't know what you've got going on, but you need to tell me. I feel like I own this store with the amount of work I do. I know you've promoted me to store manager, but your mother gave you this store not me."

Tiara waited for her friend to respond, but Carmen looked as if she had zoned out. "Which ad do you want?" Tiara asked, holding up a photo. "One of these has to go in the store window by Saturday."

Carmen shook her head and watched as Tiara held up another one. This time, she nodded her head. Tiara sighed as she initialed the back of it and slid it in the return envelope.

"You need to get yourself together. Maybe this vacation will be good for you." Tiara looked at Carmen, seeing her friend was still in a daze. "What's wrong with you?" she said, throwing a box of Kleenex at her. It hit Carmen in the chest before falling on the floor.

"I'm tired, girl," Carmen said, closing her eyes. She had gone on a run early that morning and was still stressed about the slight argument she had with Jay. She would hate to go to Bahamas with their relationship on a bad note.

"You didn't go to bed last night? Shit, now that you and Jay are doing the do you probably didn't." Tiara chuckled.

"I'm working for Carlos," Carmen revealed. A huge boulder was lifted off her shoulders as she unveiled her secret.

"What are you doing for Carlos? Are you counting his money?"

"I'm selling drugs for him," Carmen whispered. "Jay wouldn't give me the money to start the chain. My Dad wouldn't give me the money. You saw how long it was going to take on those grant applications. I had to do what I had to do. You know, to make my dream come true."

Tiara's mouth dropped open. "Are you fuckin' crazy?"

"I'm up to almost two hundred thousand dollars. I have some business to take care of in the Bahamas, and then we're set. We can buy the building for headquarters and start the chain. We'll have enough to start manufacturing my first line of men's suits. I promise you; the men's line is going to save Flame."

"Carmen, you will be in prison without a window by then."

"I have to get through this week, Tee. When I get back, Flame will be the main thing I'm concerned about. I promise you. We'll have the chain before graduation."

"Does Jay know about this? Why did I even ask that question? I know he doesn't know. I'm the dumb one. Carlos is basically doing the same thing he did when he decided to work for Pierre. He can't stand being second in command. He always wants to be king."

Carmen agreed with her wholeheartedly. She had told Carlos about himself only hours ago. "You're not going to tell anyone about the trip, are you?"

"Have I ever told any of your secrets?"

"No," Carmen answered.

"Then I won't tell this one." Tiara watched as Carmen grabbed the folder with the tickets and left the office. "Where are you—" Tiara stopped, seeing the door close. Carmen was always the one preaching about right and wrong. Now, the girl was selling drugs. It was as if she had become a new person. Tiara knew Carmen desperately wanted to save Flame, but there had to be an underlying motive for her friend's behavior. *Was she that desperate she would risk her future for some damn chain?* Tiara bit her lip. She didn't know what it was, but Tiara knew she had to keep a close eye on Carmen. She also knew she had to talk to Carlos. He had gone behind her back on this one.

***

Carmen took a deep breath, stepping outside into the cool air. Aware Tiara had been working hard; Carmen decided to reveal her secret so her friend would understand why she hadn't been devoting a hundred and twenty percent to Flame. Once all the money was in her hands that they needed, her drug dealing days were over. It would merely be another story to take to the grave, like the trip to the Bahamas.

"Peaches," she heard a voice say.

Carmen glanced to her left to see Jay walking down the sidewalk. Nowadays, she hardly saw him at her store. He was probably there now because he wanted to make up. Unfortunately, he proved her wrong.

"I got a text from one of my workers, Noc, that you've been cruising in a Bentley all morning. Where did you get that car?"

Carmen felt herself freeze at Jay's fiery tone. She blinked for a second before putting on her best act. "Who in the world is Noc? I wasn't in a Bentley this morning. I was in my Lexus. It is parked right behind the store."

"So are you telling me Noc is lying? Do I need to choke him out because he's out here spreading lies about you?"

"You don't have to do anything. Tell him he was mistaken."

Jay eyed Carmen carefully because he knew Noc was telling the truth. Noc was one of his small-time hustlers that mainly ran the streets of West Brookstone. Jay was trying to move him up, seeing that the guy had somewhat of a promising future in the game. Noc was also trustworthy and at times, put him in the mindset of Rakim. To prove he was right, he called him. "Yo, Noc, Carmen says she hasn't been in a Bentley. Tell him, Carm." Jay held the phone out to her, hitting the button for the speakerphone.

"Look, Noc, we've never met, but I think you may have me mistaken. I wasn't in a Bentley. I drove my Lexus from home to work."

"Nah, I'm not mistaken. I saw you. You were downtown near the bank. I was headed the same way and I saw you when you pulled into Clover Estates, Carlos' apartment complex."

Noc had a voice thick and heavy as molasses that reminded Carmen of Notorious B.I.G. It was obvious Noc had seen her because she was at all the places he said. Now, she simply needed to come up with an excuse of why she was in a Bentley. Her mind worked double time as Jay realized he caught her in a lie.

"What were you doing at Carlos' apartment?" Jay hung up the phone, not needing Noc's services any longer. "You and Carlos aren't cool. His ass is grimy. You know that. I can tell from your face that Noc saw you. Whose Bentley were you in? If you have the balls to be in someone's car, have the balls to tell me who you're fuckin'."

"Why do I have to be fuckin' someone?"

"Why were you at Carlos' apartment then?"

Carmen took a step back because she knew Jay was getting ready to blow a fuse. His face had turned red, and he was barking his words like he was on the verge of attack. "I may have been at Clover Estates, but it doesn't mean I was at his apartment." Carmen didn't think twice about her comment until Jay snatched her up by her shirt.

"Bitch, are you fuckin' someone?" Jay held her shirt tightly, staring her in the eye. He could tell she was shocked he grabbed her, but he was tired of trying to figure her out. She had been coming home late and leaving early for far too long. He was sick of it and whatever game she was trying to pull. "Answer me, bitch," he said, shaking her.

Carmen remained silent, somewhat embarrassed. She was standing in front of her store, in broad daylight, allowing everyone to see the man she had fallen in love with. She knew her customers and probably even her employees were on the verge of calling the police. Then, as quickly as she tried to get the conversation under control, she watched as Jay was pushed into an illegally parked car. Kane had come out of nowhere and now the two were fighting like cats and dogs on someone's Charger. Automatically, Carmen went to rectify the situation. If she didn't stop Kane now, Jay was liable to kill him. "Kane, it's okay," she yelled, grabbing him. She pulled him away from Jay, but her boyfriend only socked Kane in the face once his arms were free. When he tried to get another lick, Carmen grabbed him, using her body as a shield to keep him away from Kane. "Baby, calm down," she blurted, "it's okay."

"Who is he?" Jay yelled, staring her in the face.

"Don't you ever put your hands on her again," Kane retorted.

Jay grabbed the pistol that was in his waistband and pointed it at Kane. The mere sight of it caused one of the onlookers to scream she was calling the police. Jay's adrenaline didn't allow him to hear her, but he heard Carmen when she tried to talk him out of a murder charge. The gun was still in his hand, but he was using his time to study the guy's face. The man was the exact opposite of him. He was a couple of inches shorter, had skin the color of midnight, and a bald head. Whoever he was, if it wasn't for Carmen's soothing voice, he would've been dead or unrecognizable.

"Baby," Carmen was saying, having her story together. "I was in the Bentley. Noc was right. I was in the Bentley because I bought the car as your birthday gift. Sales are picking up for Flame and I wanted to use the money while I had it in case things turned around. Carlos told me I could hide the car at his apartment so you wouldn't suspect anything."

"Birthday?" Jay inquired. He dropped his gun at his side and eventually put it in his waistband although the man was still outside. "Carmen, you didn't—" His voice trailed off as he realized how he had jumped to conclusions. "I'm sorry, baby. I flipped out because you've been acting so weird lately. I was thinking there was someone else."

Carmen grabbed Jay's face, pulling it closer to hers. "I love you. I don't want anyone else. All I see is you."

Without hesitation, Jay pressed his lips down on hers. He kissed her hard, knowing the guy was watching them. When he did finally break away for air, he looked in his direction. "I don't know where you're from but shit like that can get you killed. Stay away from Flame."

"Are you threatening me?" Kane asked, walking towards him.

Jay got ready to charge at him again until he saw a patrol car coming down the street. If he didn't get his emotions under control, he would be leaving inside of it. Thankfully, Carmen talked the guy down and the patrol car passed Flame without stopping.

Not wanting to press his luck, Jay gave Carmen another kiss and apologized once again for ruining his birthday gift. Once she accepted, he took off, heading towards the store's parking lot.

In the meantime, Carmen tried to get herself together. The sales associates had moved away from the window, which gave her time to calm down without an audience.

"What's this?" a voice said, interrupting her thoughts.

Carmen had forgotten all about the folder she had been carrying. She opened her eyes to see Kane holding her tickets to the Bahamas. She snatched it out his hand although she was supposed to be talking him into accompanying her. "I'm going on vacation," she told him.

"You need a vacation," he replied. "Is your boyfriend beating you?"

Carmen looked at him like he was out his mind. She only changed her expression when she remembered this was his first meeting with Jay. Based off what transpired, Jay did appear abusive. "No, he doesn't beat me. He reacted like any normal man would when they think their future wife is cheating on them. We're fine. I cleared everything up. You can be on your merry way and go back to Production."

"I'm not going back to Production. I want to talk some sense into you. That guy is a maniac. You don't need to go to the Bahamas with him."

"I'm not going with him. As of right now, I'm going by myself."

"Your parents aren't going with you?"

"I told you I'm going by myself," Carmen repeated. She raised her voice and now she had new onlookers looking in her direction. "Come here," she told him, grabbing his arm. Carmen pulled him inside her store and eventually inside her office. "Why are you interrogating me?" she asked once they were alone. When his face fell, Carmen knew he was only trying to help. "Look, I don't have anyone to go with me."

Carmen stuffed her hands in her pockets hoping Kane was debating about coming. She needed him to invite himself so she could be one step closer to completing Carlos' plan.

"Look, the painting is almost finished. I'll go with you."

"You can't go with me. My boyfriend is one step away from killing you. If he finds out you're going, you're dead on contact."

"I don't care about your boyfriend. I can deal with him."

Carmen gave him a smile only because he had fallen in her trap. With the plan now in motion, she opened the folder and handed him a plane ticket and boarding pass. He took it from her, sliding it in his pocket.

"I want you to take care of yourself. That relationship doesn't look healthy."

"It is healthy," she reiterated. "We had a disagreement, one that happened to be public. We're fine. We love each other."

Kane seemed to believe her because he muttered goodbye and left her office. She watched him as he left the store, noticing that everyone's eyes were still on her. Still somewhat embarrassed, she closed her door, not bothering to come out until she no longer had spectators.

Chapter Twenty-Seven

When Thursday came, Carmen showed up at the airport twenty minutes early so she could make it out New York without talking to Jay. While she had told him about the trip, they never discussed the details. To keep from lying to him, all she did was leave a note at the house, saying she boarded a plane for Florida. Her plan seemed to be working because she was able to leave without speaking to him and was now waiting for Kane at the airport.

Ten minutes later, he arrived, pulling out his boarding pass for the ship. "Did you read the fine print on this thing?" he asked her. Carmen knew she hadn't and rightfully told him so. "This isn't some little cruise, Carmen. This is a private boat trip to the Bahamas. If you know anything about jewelry, then you would know that the big time CEOs of some of the country's biggest jewelry companies are going to be on this boat. It's a cruise in celebration of the Diamond Exchange conference."

"So what are you saying?" Carmen needed to know what he was getting at since he was obviously suspicious of the cruise.

"I'm not saying anything other than you have to have some real dough to get tickets like this. Tiara told me about the financial situation with your store. Flame may be headed towards bankruptcy, but it looks to me like you're swimming in dough."

"I see you did your research."

"Flight 345A is now boarding," a woman said over the loudspeaker.

Carmen stood up, holding her bag, and looked at Kane. "That's us," she said, taking a breath.

"Can we say a prayer before we get on the plane?"

"Of course," Carmen replied, sitting down. She watched as Kane grabbed her hands, leading them in prayer. Once he was finished, he grabbed her bag, leading the way to the airplane. Carlos had booked them an evening flight and Carmen was lucky to snag a seat next to the window. Her eyes automatically went to the night sky, and it appeared Kane's eyes had followed, too.

"Do you think we'll get a shooting star? Have you ever seen one?"

"Only in the movies," Carmen said, turning to look at him. She noticed that Kane's eyes were closing, and it was evident Production had taken a toll on him. She figured he had been at the store for most of the day before coming to the airport.

"Are you staring or looking?" he asked, opening his eyes.

Carmen laughed, uncontrollably, because he had caught her. "I was staring this time," she told him. "You caught me yet again."

"Can I stare at you?"

Carmen told him yes but went back on her word and turned towards the window. Kane took notice, letting her know he couldn't stare if he couldn't see her face. Her only reply was for him to use his imagination. "Okay," he began. "I see a young woman who's stuck between a rock and a hard place. She's searching for something but doesn't know exactly what it is. She has dreams and aspirations but is struggling to reach them. With every step she takes forward, it's like two steps backward. She's looking for love, but what she's getting has her confused. She's looking for real, unconditional love. Although she has her struggles, she still shines. I see a woman who is like the stars outside. She is shining as bright as she can with hope that someone sees her, except this woman is far better than them. She's a diamond."

Carmen turned to face him, more speechless than she ever been. No one had ever said anything like that about her. She took her eyes off him, hearing the stewardess giving instructions on what to do during emergencies.

"You know I'm attracted to you," Kane said, placing his hand on her leg. "I know you have a boyfriend. I'm not trying to come between you two, but there is an underlying reason why I came on this trip. I want to get to know you better. The real you, not this Lexus driving, store owning tough woman. I want to know the vulnerable side of you, the crappy side, the 'I don't have my hair done' side," he continued with a chuckle. "I'm not even supposed to be feeling this way, but I am."

"Why?" Carmen asked, "Is it because of my boyfriend?"

Kane shook his head. He closed his eyes and Carmen couldn't help, but stare at him. He was out like a light, yet she didn't take her eyes off him. Instead, she stared at him until her own eyes became heavy and were forced shut. *Dear God,* she prayed, *am I falling for Kane?*

***

Carmen was barely off the plane when she received her first phone call from Carlos. She already knew what he wanted so she gave him the rundown before he could ask. "Perfect timing," she greeted, not bothering to say hello. "We're in Florida now. We're getting a hotel for the night, and we gotta be at the port at noon. How are things on your end?"

"We had a slight change in plans," Carlos announced. He listened as Carmen started a tantrum on the phone and he quickly calmed her down. "Shit, Carmen, stop cursing, it's nothing that can't be fixed. The conference was canceled in Manhattan. They moved the location to Texas. It's not a problem; I've already gotten your plane tickets. All you need to do is head to the airport once you get back from the Bahamas."

"Have you forgotten that I have Kane with me? What am I supposed to tell him? You're just stringing him along," Carmen yelled into the phone.

"It's in Dallas, Carm. If you remember, that's where your parents are. Besides, I'll be meeting you there. You'll bring the diamonds to my hotel room, which is near the location of the conference. I need you to make up something to get away from Kane and your parents. We'll make the sale, get the money, and I promise you, this dick will be worth the wait."

"Let's skip that part, why don't we?" Carmen said, peeking into the airport. She saw Kane headed towards a table with a meal tray. In the meantime, she heard Carlos as he made a slick comment before he hung up the phone. Cursing under her breath, she stuffed her phone in her purse and headed to the table where Kane was. He had bought her a salad, which he pointed at once she sat down.

"Your food is getting cold," he joked.

Carmen giggled and got ready to dig in until she heard her phone ring. She had to answer it. She pulled it from her purse as Jay was calling her. Without a doubt, she knew he caught wind that she left New York. "Excuse me," she told Kane, accepting the call. When he nodded his head at her, she greeted Jay whose temper she could feel even in Florida. "I love you, baby," she said, trying to lighten the blow.

"You know I'm fuckin' pissed. Are you okay?"

"I am," she responded. "Everything has been perfect."

"I don't like this, Peaches. Your phone isn't going to work out there. How am I supposed to get in contact with you? I should've made someone go with you. You were so secretive about this trip. I'm worried about you, Carm. You're doing stuff you've never done before. We've never had these issues. What is going on?"

"Nothing, baby, I promise you. When I get home, I'm going to make it up to you. We're actually going to go on our own vacation."

"Yeah, yeah, yeah, if you say so." Jay didn't believe for one second they would be going on a trip together. Carmen was saying anything she could to get him off the phone so she could continue whatever devilment she was in. While he didn't have proof of what she was doing, his plan was to continue snooping until he did. "I love you, Peaches. Be safe out there."

"I love you, too, Jay."

Carmen hung up the phone and started to eat her salad. A minute or so later, she heard Kane's voice.

"He doesn't know I'm here, does he?"

She quickly told him no.

"Carm, you know I'm feeling you. For you to keep this from your boyfriend then you must be feeling me, too. What are you trying to protect me from?" Kane took Carmen's fork out her hand because he wanted her full attention. He needed her to explain why she was being secretive.

"You couldn't bear the story. Believe me."

"Okay, well, I'll tell it. Rich club owner finds immense joy in putting his hands on his girlfriend. The owner of Production tries to save her and now, the club owner wants him dead."

Carmen rolled her eyes. "Are you judging him?"

"The Bible says judge not that ye be not judged."

Carmen smirked and closed the lid to her salad, losing her appetite. She was upset at his comment, yet she had to understand where Kane was coming from. "Can I trust you?" she asked him.

"You can trust me with your heart."

Carmen looked around the airport only because she had never spoken openly about Jay to anyone. She knew she was taking a chance by telling Kane about him, but she felt like she could trust him. "I'm indebted to him," she told him. "I was about to get raped and killed by a drug dealer who was already on his bad side. He saved me. It is because of that; I will always love him."

"He protected you from the start."

Carmen wiped her face as she saw an image of Jay in her mind. "I'm not the best girlfriend right now, but I love him. God knows I do."

Kane placed his hand on hers. "I will protect you, too."

***

When Carmen saw her hotel room, she knew Carlos had set her up. There was only one king-sized bed in the room, which meant she and Kane were going to be awfully close. Though Kane had tried to get another room, none were available. Therefore, Carmen had to deal with the situation. Still rather uncomfortable, she watched as Kane laid down in the bed. He was completely shirtless, allowing her to see that he possessed the same rock hard abs as her boyfriend.

His image alone made Carmen question if she should undress. She had expected to be in a bed alone and the only thing she had to wear was a tank top and boy shorts. She figured she could get away with it once he had gone to sleep, but his eyes weren't closing. Since he was obviously waiting for her to join him, Carmen changed her clothes and got in bed. She tried to go to sleep yet the image of the man she had to steal the diamonds from was frozen in her mind. As a result, she tossed and turned until she felt Kane's arms around her.

"I'm here if you want to talk."

Carmen told him she was fine only because she couldn't tell him about her plans. She tried to ease her nerves, yet it was pointless when she felt Kane's hands in her hair. His affection was now a distraction since he was obviously trying to play on her weakness.

"I couldn't help myself," he whispered. Kane moved closer to her so she could feel his growing manhood. He even wrapped his arms around her, pulling her into him. "Am I making you uncomfortable?"

Carmen knew she should've told him yes, but it wasn't the truth. His arms calmed her. If she could, for only one night, she wanted to pretend that

Kane was her boyfriend. Without Jay there to comfort her, Kane was the next best thing. Therefore, she turned over in the bed and rested her head on his chest. "I feel protected."

***

Back in Brookstone, Carlos walked in Jay's office at Sapphire for an impromptu meeting. Most of the men on Jay's payroll were there and he couldn't help but stare at each of them. They all viewed Jay as a king or nothing less than a god. It was the exact same way he wanted to be viewed. Once his heist was completed, and he was a million dollars richer, he was going to start his reign. In the end, Jay would come to him for work instead of the other way around.

"This is the day when I find out how many men I can trust," Jay began. "I'm embarking on something new, and I need to know right now whose down for me. I have something in the works that could bring us a lot of money. I need to know that its death before dishonor."

Carlos scrunched up his face because he didn't know what Jay was getting at. His friend had never told him about any new endeavors.

"I've been working on something big. Noc, Jose, Malik, and Consuelo, these are the men you will answer to if you choose to participate in my project. Cuts come up in two days. After that, this drug dealing shit is over. It is no more."

Carlos' jaw tightened as he glanced at each of the men whose name Jay had called. None of them had put in time like he had. None of them were there for Jay like he was. Carlos could feel the steam rising from his shoulders at not being acknowledged.

"Do you see this?" he heard Jay say, the discussion not yet over. "This is our new investment. This is what's coming up for us from the Bahamas. In a couple of days, we will have two million dollars' worth of diamonds. These diamonds will become rings, necklaces, and bracelets, that will be sold at my new jewelry store, Iceland. How many of y'all are ready to leave this drug shit behind?"

Carlos stared at the diamond in Jay's hand. *Diamonds, Bahamas, coming from the Bahamas*, he thought. It didn't take him long to figure out what he'd done. The man who he thought was originally working for Pierre was working for Jay. Without even knowing it, Carlos learned he was doing more dirt than he thought. He smiled at the revelation because he was getting more revenge on Jay than he originally intended. Not only did he get the pleasure of tasting every ounce of Carmen, he also had her stealing from her own boyfriend. Jay's entire future was now in both of their hands.

"Each of you will learn a trade. You will learn how to take care of the diamond, how to make its value increase, and how to turn it into a piece of jewelry. Some of you will be responsible for playing Catwoman. You steal from those that steal. Some of you will help in the construction of the store," Jay was saying. "Are you down?"

Carlos watched as many of the guys nodded their heads.

"I want my money in two days. Whatever product you have left comes back to me. You're dismissed."

Carlos stood there as the guys left Jay's office. When most of the room was bare, Carlos realized a private meeting was set to take place.

"I need to talk to them for a minute. Can you step outside?"

Carlos looked at the four men who Jay had acknowledged earlier. He then looked at Jay. "Are you serious?"

"I said I need to talk to them for a minute," Jay repeated.

Carlos grilled him, angrily. He did as he asked, walking out the office, but he made sure to slam the door. Once it was closed, he gave Jay a small taste of what was to come. "I can't wait to fuck your bitch," he muttered.

Chapter Twenty-Eight

Carmen's eyes opened, adjusting to the sunlight that was peering in the room through the balcony. She didn't see Kane in the bed and listened to see if he was in the shower. When she didn't hear him, she pulled the covers back and walked around the room. She spotted him outside on the balcony in a bathrobe with his cell phone glued to his ear. He was upset about something, and she could tell he was dropping f-bombs left and right. When his conversation ended, he slammed his phone on the table beside him. It was obvious he needed privacy, so she sorted through her luggage to find an outfit to wear.

"Good morning," Kane greeted, appearing to be in a better mood.

Carmen repeated the words to him as she pulled out a camisole.

"I ordered breakfast. It should be up in a few minutes," he said, walking over to her. "I hope I didn't wake you. This store has me bugging. It's like, for everything to be done right, I have to do it myself." Kane threw his hands up in frustration only to apologize. "We don't need to talk about this. We're on vacation; we're supposed to be having fun." Kane ran his hands through her hair like he'd done the night before. "Do you think we're moving too fast?"

Carmen dropped the pants she was holding into her lap. "Kane, nothing happened last night. Yes, I slept in your arms, but that was it. Now, I can't hide that I'm attracted to you, but I also have a boyfriend who I'm very much in love with. If it helps, I can make sure we have separate rooms on the ship. I don't want anyone to get hurt."

Kane parted his lips because he felt almost like he'd been rejected. Before he could speak, the doorbell sounded, which meant room service had come to deliver breakfast. Instead of finishing the conversation, he went to the door, allowing the bellhop to roll in the breakfast table. "Thanks," he told the guy, tipping him. Carmen was quick to rush to the food, taking off the lids to see what he ordered. The scent of steaming hot grits, scrambled cheese eggs, and sausage filled the room, almost making Kane want to eat versus continuing the discussion.

"What do you want from me?" she asked him.

Kane had to think long and hard about his answer. The truth was, he knew what he wanted, yet he feared what came with it. He had met somebody who had caught his attention and something in his heart told him he couldn't let her go. "I know I want you. It's just hard to want something that isn't yours. What is even harder is to want something that doesn't want you."

"You don't have any idea whose girl you're messing with, do you?" Carmen peered at him. She was ready to reveal even more to him so he would understand the amount of danger he was in. "My boyfriend is the head of a drug cartel. He would kill you on the spot if he knew you were even here with me. He has people working for him all over the country. If anyone sees me with you, they will call him. You could be dead in a minute or less." Carmen gave him a few seconds to let her words digest.

"I'll take my chances. Can I have you or not?"

Carmen narrowed her eyes at him. Kane was being fearless, but she knew his stance could change once he had a real taste of Jay. Carmen also knew that this was the same guy who had gone toe to toe with Jay at her store. The incident made her remember that she had forgotten to clean out the Bentley. Her clothes were still in the trunk as well as heroin. In addition, she had also left her spare keys in a jewelry box at home. She knew Jay wasn't the type to snoop. She figured he would wait until his birthday to even see the Bentley.

"Can I have you?" Kane asked again.

Carmen didn't respond, continuing to fix her plate. The silence seemed to bother Kane because he pulled her plate from her hands. Before she knew it, his lips were on hers and his tongue was sliding in her mouth. He took her by surprise, but so did his kiss. It was powerful and Carmen was sucked into it, kissing him with the same amount of passion. They took in each other for several minutes before Carmen was able to let him go.

***

While Carmen was busy living her second life in Florida, Tiara was standing outside of Carlos' apartment, desperate for information. She was concerned about her best friend and the only way to help her was to go to the source. When he opened the door for her, she pushed her way inside and immediately started grilling him. "What do you have Carmen doing?"

Carlos sat on his couch, playing it cool. "Tee, you don't I roll with Carmen like that. I can't stand that bitch."

"So she isn't hustling for you? Are you saying my best friend lied to me?" Tiara's eyes widened with every word she spoke. She could tell she had hit a sore spot because Carlos jumped from the couch, nearing her like she had discovered his long lost secret.

"You need to mind your fuckin' business. How many times do I have to tell you to keep your nose out my shit? I'm not with you anymore. You don't have to keep running over here about what I'm doing. I thought you had a new dick you were sucking on."

"You know I'm not doing that anymore," Tiara ranted. "I haven't been with anyone since you and I shouldn't have given you any. What are you doing to Carmen? She's a good girl. Are you blackmailing her?"

Carlos sat on his couch, digging in his pockets for a cigarette. "I offered Carmen a job. She needed money and I gave it to her. No one else was trying to help her. Her parents turned their back on her. Jay refused to give her one red cent. She had to take the deal." Carlos couldn't find what he was looking for and gave up the search. "Like I said, though, this isn't any of your business. Therefore, you can get out my house."

Tiara watched him as he rose from the couch. He went to the front door, opened it, and while his back was turned, she pulled out a nine millimeter pistol. She cocked it only to get his attention.

"Bitch, are you fuckin' crazy?" he yelled, slamming his door closed. "What the fuck are you going to do what that shit?"

Tiara pointed the gun at him and then directed him to the couch. Once he was in his seat, she demanded he tell her everything. Carmen had started only part of the story and she knew there was more than what was previously stated.

"I already told you everything, Tee. I told you Carmen needed money for Flame. You already know that shit because you work for her."

"There's a fuckin' catch, Carlos, what is the catch? You're not going to let her hustle for you for free. What do you want from her?"

Tiara pressed the barrel of the gun up against Carlos' forehead. The cold hard steel forced him to talk yet it was his words that made her back away. His words cut her to the core more than their failed relationship.

"I get to fuck her," he told her. "Yeah, Tee, I want to fuck Carmen. Do you think I like sitting here watching Jay walk around like he's a fuckin' god? He thinks he can't be touched. I can have exactly what he has. I can have his house, his cars, and guess what? I can even have his girl."

"She's my best friend, Carlos. Why would you do that to me?"

Tears started streaming down Tiara's face. In a few days, Carmen was going to sleep with her ex-boyfriend. Carmen knew how she felt about Carlos. *Why would she even agree to something like that?* Tiara had bent over backwards for her, making sure the store stayed straight while Carmen lived a double life. Now, Tiara saw firsthand how her best friend repaid her.

Carlos sighed as he saw the hurt on Tiara's face. "There's more to the deal," he told her. "I got word that a drug dealer acquired about two million dollars' worth of diamonds. He's coming up from the Bahamas with them and is on his way to New York. Turns out, he's one of Jay's employees. Jay's newest idea is to open some damn jewelry store and leave this drug shit behind. I gave Carmen the assignment of stealing the diamonds. That is why she went on a trip."

Tiara's eyes grew big. "You're planning on sleeping with her, and you have her stealing from her boyfriend? You are shady and disgusting. When Jay finds out, he's going to kill you."

"Bitch, you aren't telling him," Carlos yelled. He moved quick, reaching his hand underneath the seat of the couch for his own gun. Still, Tiara moved faster than he did. She had the gun at his temple in no time.

"You're right. I'm not telling him, but he's going to find out. You may have taken my heart. You may have drawn a wall between me and Carmen, but you won't mess with Jay anymore. I hope he slits your throat." Tiara kept the gun pointed at him as she walked backwards towards the door. Once she saw she was free to leave, she opened the door and ran out the apartment.

Carmen would've been petrified if she had known Tiara was aware of the deal between her and Carlos. Since her best friend had met with Carlos without her knowledge, all she could think of was her kiss with Kane. After what transpired in the hotel room, Carmen tried to wipe Kane's kiss away, yet the deed was done. She had officially cheated on her boyfriend and now her heart had been cut with guilt.

When they were settling into their cabin, Carmen questioned if she should tell Kane the truth. He honestly believed he had a chance with her and believed she was going to end things with Jay. If she was being honest with herself, Carmen had to admit the thought had crossed her mind. Kane reminded her of her past, which was something she had longed for since she had fallen headfirst into a life of crime. To get even closer to her old self, she constantly asked Kane questions about his life and family.

"My parents aren't like yours," he told her. "I didn't grow up rich. We were middle class. My parents are originally from the South. My father worked at a plant all his life until he retired, and my mother was a nurse. I have a sister, too. She lives in Rochester. She's a nurse like my mother, married with three kids."

Even now, Carmen still wanted to do more digging. It was like nothing he ever said was enough. Earlier that evening, they had gone in the ship's theater to watch *Black Dahlia*, and Carmen learned that Kane loved mystery and crime films. He talked throughout the entire movie, and accidentally gave away the ending. It surprised Carmen that such a simple, fun moment could remind her that she and Jay had never actually went to the movies together. They only watched movies at home. The more she reflected on it, she and Jay hardly ever went out on dates.

Carmen longed to hear of a normal life, one that didn't involve drugs, criminals, or unsolved murders. Kane seemed to give that to her so easily, it made her want to know more about him. "What's your real name?" she asked. "You still haven't told me your age."

"You don't think Kane is my real name?"

They were lying on the bed, Carmen's head rested once again on his chest. "Yeah, I think Kane is your real name, but I think there's more to it," she replied. "So tell me, what is your full name?"

"Kane is my real name and I'm twenty-eight."

Carmen leaned up at his response. "Why are you keeping secrets?"

"We all have secrets, Carmen. You have them, too."

Carmen nodded her head in agreement and decided to drop the issue. Silence filled the room and eventually Kane slid from underneath her. He told her he was taking a shower and Carmen watched him as he disappeared into the bathroom. Her eyes were halfway closed when he came back out, but she saw him when he took off the towel, standing completely nude in the room. She couldn't see his package although she desperately wanted a peek. The chance was lost when he slid on a pair of black boxers and grey sweatpants, covering himself. "I missed seeing the goods," she joked.

Kane turned around at the sound of her voice. "I have to leave something to the imagination. I can't give you everything." He walked over to her, pulling the covers back so they could get underneath. Like the night before, Carmen turned away from him as she said her prayers.

I know I'm not living right Lord, Carmen prayed. *I'm not sure what to make of my life right now. I promise, once this is over, I am through with this. Just bear with me, Lord.* Carmen ended her prayer as a tear slid down her cheek. The image of the Bahamian drug dealer was still in her mind, serving as a reminder that tomorrow she had to murder someone. As if the image wasn't enough, she felt Kane's fingers as he wiped away her tears.

"I will protect you," he told her.

At the sound of his words, Carmen slid closer to him and laid her head on his chest. While he wasn't protecting her yet, Carmen believed it was coming.

Chapter Twenty-Nine

Unbeknownst to Carmen, Saturday morning, Tiara was sitting outside of Flame, not even wanting to go inside. There she was, busting her ass, day, and night, trying to keep the store afloat. In the meantime, Carmen was having fun in the sun, was about to steal a shitload of diamonds and was preparing to fuck her ex-boyfriend. Tiara kept going over in her mind how Carmen could have accepted a deal like that. *Is she that selfish? Is she only looking out for herself? If Carmen gets what she wants, where does that leave me? I'm doing all the work, but she'll reap the reward.*

Tiara looked at her glove compartment, remembering her pistol that was inside. *How could she possibly contemplate killing her best friend?* Tiara knew she wasn't crazy. She was only hurt. She knew she could always tell Jay, however, that would make her a snitch. In addition, it could possibly get Carmen killed. There was no point in her running her mouth.

Deep down, Tiara knew what she needed to do. The devil wanted her to quit and let Flame falter while God was telling her to simply confront Carmen and move on. Tiara knew she had to save her, but she didn't know how. Carmen was always the one telling her what to do and how to clean up her mistakes. Tiara never thought she would be cleaning up hers.

Perhaps, she should wait it out. Carmen hadn't slept with Carlos yet, which meant there was a chance she could come to her senses. For now, she had a job to do, and she couldn't do it in her car. She headed inside of Flame and went straight for Carmen's office. When she opened the door, she stopped in her tracks when she saw Jay sitting in Carmen's chair. He was dressed in a suit and tie, which was totally different from his normal attire. Automatically, she put her guard up. "H-H-Hi," she stuttered, coming in the room. She closed the door behind her only because she knew the conversation was going to be private.

Jay didn't respond, getting up from the seat. His lack of response made her nervous. She didn't move an inch. She simply waited for him to ask about Carmen's whereabouts.

"Have you spoken to Carmen?"

"No," Tiara replied. "I thought maybe you would have an update." She watched as Jay's eyes glanced around the office as if he was looking for a clue. She figured he didn't find one when he spoke again.

"Did Carlos tell you about the jewelry store? I'm naming it Iceland."

"Yeah, he mentioned it. Congratulations."

Jay stared at Tiara, looking for any sign she was keeping a secret. He could tell he was making her nervous because her answers were somewhat short while she would usually talk his head off. He figured if was open with her, she would give him the information he needed. "I'm worried about Carmen. She's been acting weird lately and this sudden trip to Bahamas was like the breaking point. I know you're her best friend, Tee. She confides in you. I know she has told you about our problems. You know I'm not perfect. I've done a lot of things that could make anyone question my love for her. Still, I want you to know I love her. I love her to the point that I'm leaving all this shit behind." Jay reached in his pocket and pulled out a red box. He opened it and allowed Tiara to see the nineteen-carat diamond ring inside. "I want to propose."

Tiara wanted to break down crying. Not because of the beauty of the ring, but because of the heartbreak that was coming for Jay. He was in love with Carmen while she was on the verge of sleeping with his best friend. "It's beautiful," she mustered out. "She's going to love it."

"I hope she's ready for it," Jay said, turning to look out the window. He couldn't see Production, yet he still looked for any sign of Kane. "Do you know where I can find the guy who owns the store next door?"

Tiara shook her head. "I haven't seen him in a few days."

Jay continued staring out the window as if he was going to see some sign of him. "Maybe another day then," he replied. He gave Tiara a quick smile only because he knew she could tell he was up to no good. "Let me know if you see him, okay?"

Tiara gave him only a half-smile in return. When he announced he was leaving, she held her breath until he was out the door. Then, she exhaled. Not quite off the hook, she looked out the window, waiting for his car to drive by. Once she saw the Rolls Royce, something told her Kane was in the Bahamas with Carmen. If he was, it only meant one thing—bad news.

***

For the past three hours, the ship had been docked at a Bahamian port, giving Carmen and Kane the chance to explore the island. Their plan was to walk the streets of Nassau, do a little bit of shopping, all before heading back to the ship for dinner. In addition, there was a special concert that night featuring R&B singer, Lloyd.

It was the perfect day out and as much as Carmen tried to hide the fact she was nervous; it was getting harder to do as time went on. Every single time she saw a man with dreadlocks, she thought about the Bahamian drug dealer. Carmen didn't know how she was going to find him, but she figured they were destined to run into each other. Carlos had told her she was going to have to entice him and the red tube dress she found appeared to be the perfect little number.

"I like," she heard Kane say behind her. Carmen turned to look at him as he took the dress out her hands. "Wear this tonight, please?" he begged. "It's beautiful up against your skin."

"Thanks," she told him. "Did you find something you like?"

Carmen watched as he nodded his head and pointed towards another shop across the street.

"I want to go in there. Those clothes are more me."

Carmen looked in the direction in which he was pointing. The style did look more him. She told him to go ahead. "I'm going to try on these dresses. I'll come over once I'm done," she promised. Carmen watched as he left before staring at the red dress she was holding. She knew she could do some enticing in it, but she didn't know how much without Kane noticing.

If I get through tonight then I'm set. I'm perfectly set.

Carmen found an attendant and asked her for a key to one of the dressing rooms. Once she got it, she stepped inside, locking the door, and immediately sat down. She rested her head on the wall thinking she might be having an anxiety attack. She could feel herself starting to get sick and eventually broke into a sweat. She cupped her mouth, but she could still feel something coming up. She tried swallowing, but it only made it worse. She grabbed the dresses with her one free hand and hung them up on a hook. She didn't know if she should call for help because she was going insane or what. She took her hand from her mouth only to feel her lunch rising in her throat. To keep from puking, she covered her mouth, opening the door to the dressing room. She raced to the back of the store not even knowing where the bathroom was. Luckily, she headed in the right direction. With her one free hand, she pushed open the bathroom door and ran in a stall, collapsing in front of the toilet as she vomited.

"Ma'am, are you okay?" a sales associate said, rushing in.

Carmen looked at her, wiping her mouth. She could feel even more vomit on the rise. Instead of answering her, she vomited again.

"Ma'am, stay right there," the sales associate screamed.

Carmen thought of Kane and how no one would know to look for him. No one even knew who they were. No one could tell him she was sick. The sales associate had propped the door open, and Carmen realized she was in a bathroom with only two stalls. Customers peered in on her, wondering what was going on. She closed her eyes, but the vomiting wouldn't stop. Carmen knew she was depressed, but she didn't expect to be throwing up.

"What's going on?" she heard a voice say.

Carmen felt somebody's hands on her, bringing her to her feet. She knew all eyes were on her and she wanted the onlookers to go away.

"Carmen," a voice called to her. She recognized it to be Kane.

"Baby, are you okay?" he asked her, wiping her mouth with a towel.

One of the sales associates remembered he was with her while another one had seen him go across the street to the men's shop. Carmen listened as they talked about it around her.

"I think she's fine. Can I have a bottle of water or something?" Kane asked, looking at the people beside him. "Are you okay?" Kane asked, taking a bottle of water from one of the women who was looking on.

Carmen grabbed the bottle from him and took a few swigs. "Can we go back to the boat? I don't think I should stay on the island."

"Yeah, we can," he said, grabbing her hand.

Carmen took a few more swigs before he led her out the store. "I want those dresses," she told him, remembering her deal with Carlos.

Kane looked at her, quizzically. "Okay, we'll get the dresses," he said, handing Carmen the towel. "In case you gotta vomit again, keep this over your mouth. The last thing you want is to be puking in the street."

Carmen looked at the people who were staring at her. She turned away seeing she was the center of attention. Carmen cupped her mouth again, seeing a familiar face. Standing only a few yards away from her was the Bahamian drug dealer. He was dressed in a black shirt with grey pants while his dreadlocks were held back by a rubber band, the same style in his picture. Carmen watched as the guy cracked a smile only to turn around and head in the direction of the dock where the ship was. Carmen stared at him as he walked, until the sound of Kane's voice interrupted her thoughts.

"You need to sit down, let's get back to the boat," he said, after paying for her clothes.

Carmen nodded her head in agreement and looked at the store. She could see the associates already cleaning up the area where she vomited.

"Don't worry about it. Let's go," Kane said, grabbing her hand.

Carmen followed him to the ship embarrassed at how sick she had gotten. Once they were in the cabin, she laid down trying to calm her nerves.

"Do you want to go see the doctor?"

Carmen shook her head, closing her eyes. She felt a blanket slide over her body, which was followed by Kane lying beside her. The feel of his body against hers reminded her of the Bahamian drug dealer. Since he already noticed her, it would be a little bit easier to get his attention the second time around. However, Carmen didn't need to be concerned about him. She needed to figure out what was going on inside her body.

"You need to talk to me," Kane said in her ear. "You were fine earlier then all of a sudden you're throwing up on the floor."

"I got a lot on my mind. I'm stressed right now."

"Is this what's wrong?" he asked, pointing at himself.

Carmen turned over so she was staring him in the face. "It's one of the things. I love being here with you, but I don't know how this is going to work when I get home. I don't want to lose either of you."

Kane's eyes closed at her words. Carmen wondered what he was thinking. Although she hadn't slept with him, lying in his arms every night was getting to her. She was falling hard and fast. He had so much faith in God, was kind, caring, brilliant, and respectful, that he was wrapping her around his finger and didn't even know it. Carmen knew she wanted to be open with him. She contemplated telling him her secrets. She figured that being open with him would ease her nerves and maybe even settle her stomach. "Can I tell you something?" Carmen paused, thinking about all her early morning rises and trips across New York. "I used to sell drugs. I needed money to save Flame, to start my chain, and to create a men's line. I sold drugs for Jay's friend, Carlos. He offered me a deal. He said if I sold drugs for him, he would give me a cut of the money I made. All I had to do was sleep with him. I accepted it and it has me stressed out. For a while, everything was okay, and I was making it. Now, I want out."

"Are you getting out? Do you plan on selling drugs again?"

Carmen shook her head. "I'm done with that phase of my life. I wanted to tell you because I wanted you to know. I'm not perfect and I wasn't always like this. I've simply made a few wrong choices in life."

"We all have. I know you're a good girl. I'm not going to judge you. If you remain truthful to your words, then I'm fine with everything."

Kane pulled her closer to him so she would know he was by her side. "I have a feeling in the pit of my stomach that things are only going to turn sour. Your father once told me that whatever is done in darkness will come to light. He said that to teach me to stay legit with my business. You know I don't have a lot of money. I'm barely making ends meet with the house and the store, but I have God on my side. Your boyfriend is going to find out one day what has been going on behind his back. It can be ten years from now or ten minutes. Do you really love him?"

"I do love him. He's the only man I've ever loved. Although I love him, I'm questioning right now if he's my soulmate. Once upon a time, I knew the answer."

"Do you think I'm your soulmate?"

Carmen took her time answering the question. "I honestly believe you were put on this Earth for us to meet. Maybe, we are soulmates. To be honest, I also believe Jay was put on this Earth for the same reason. I don't want to choose between you two. I don't even think I could. If I chose you, it wouldn't be a real win. I will never let go of Jay. I'm indebted to him."

Kane understood perfectly what she was telling him. He had a chance with her, but somewhere, Jay would always be lurking. He would never rid himself of him. He was there to stay more than he was.

Chapter Thirty

Jay was busy studying Carmen's engagement ring when he noticed someone walking in his warehouse. The person's attire was totally different than what he was used to seeing and almost matched his own. When he realized he was staring at Carlos, he looked at his best friend from head to toe. Carlos' suit was all black, which he had accentuated with a pink tie. The outfit alone told him Carlos was up to no good. Just his luck, the two people closest to him were both acting strange.

"Why are you staring at me so damn hard?" Carlos barked.

"Did you sell all my shit?" Jay shot back.

"I've been selling it, haven't I?" Carlos knew Jay was asking the question because he was headed out the drug game. While he hadn't yet checked Carmen's car, he was certain she didn't have a lot stashed inside. If she did, he would sell it himself and keep the money for his hard work. "I don't understand why you're so fuckin' concerned about what I'm doing. I've already paid you for my work. Those bricks are mine. You may be leaving the drug game, but I don't have to. I can do this shit on my own."

Jay stood up so he was standing over Carlos. Sometimes his best friend got beside himself and he would have to pull rank. "Sit the fuck down." Carlos wasn't quick to follow his order. "If you want in on this diamond shit then I suggest you sit the fuck down."

Carlos did as he was told but jumped right back up. "I'm not even on your fuckin' team. You went ahead and chose the men you wanted. Why are you trying to put me in this shit now?"

"I hired Enosis to steal the diamonds. He boarded a ship in the Bahamas and is bringing the diamonds back here. I think he is boarding the same boat that Carmen is on."

Carlos wiped his face only because he knew Jay's words rung truth. Enosis and Carmen were on the same boat. They were supposed to be. Nevertheless, he couldn't let Jay know they were. If he was only speculating, he and Carmen both were in the clear. "What do you want me to do?"

"I know you have contacts. I want you to check it out. Let me know what you find. Besides, I've heard the rumors about you. Are you trying to run your own cartel? You're not thinking about staying in this shit?"

Carlos wanted to punch Jay in his face. His best friend honestly thought he was supposed to follow his lead again. "I'm not supposed to go out there and make moves on my own? Do I always have to stay under your ass? You went and gave these other dudes a piece of the pie without me. Without even saying it, you told them I can't be trusted. They know I'm second in command, but you didn't even call my name at the meeting. I wasn't one of your Fantastic Four. Now, my paper is stacking. Hell yeah, I'm staying in this shit. I don't have to be a part of the Santiago cartel. I like the Rodriguez cartel better. I was schooled by my father like you were schooled by yours. I know how to run this shit."

Both anger and frustration were crystal clear on Carlos' face. It allowed Jay to see how much hatred his friend had for him. "I've known you since the first grade. Why are you acting like this? Why do I have to give you a title? Why can't you be loyal and rock with me? You knew you were going to be in on this shit. You couldn't wait for your position?"

"Stop playin' fuckin' games with me, Jay. You did that shit on purpose. Ever since Rakim got killed, you blamed me for that shit. You stabbed me in my motherfuckin' back. He meant more to you than I did." Carlos paused as he caught his breath. "Nah, nah, it wasn't Rakim, it wasn't Rakim at all, it was that bitch, it was Carmen. Carmen blames me for Rakim's death. You love her pussy so got damn much; your ass is sprung."

"Carmen and I are getting engaged," Jay announced.

"You're fuckin' playin' yourself. That bitch doesn't want you."

Carlos marched out the warehouse, his words lingering in Jay's ears. Carlos' comment made him even more suspicious of Carmen. Carlos knew he was the only man she had been with. If there was someone else, he would've known. Since he didn't, he had to find evidence to support Carlos' claim. The second he got home; he was going through her things. Something in her closet or drawers would tell him what she was up to.

By dinnertime, Carmen was back in full swing. She and Kane both went to the dining hall although he was currently searching for a bartender to locate one of their specialty wines. In the meantime, she was sitting at the table alone, waiting for him to come back.

"Excuse me, miss. This was sent from the gentleman over there."

Carmen sat her fork on her plate and took the note from the waiter's hand. She looked in the direction where the waiter was pointing and locked eyes with the Bahamian drug dealer. Then, she glanced at the note.

I know who you are. Maybe, not why you're here, but I know who you are. I'll keep your secret if you'd like. I'm in Cabin 45B.

Carmen looked at him. His eyes were still locked on hers. She wondered if Carlos had set her up. *How did he know who she was?* Carmen grabbed her purse, searching for an ink pen.

How do we know each other and at what cost are we keeping secrets?

Carmen folded the note and motioned for the waiter to retrieve it. Once the waiter had it, she looked around the room for any sign of Kane. She didn't spot him and wondered if he was still in the dining hall. Still, not seeing him, she watched as the waiter returned.

"Here you are, ma'am," the waiter said, returning with the note.

You're Jay Santiago's girlfriend. I work for him. Meet me in my cabin tonight when you're done with your date. I'll be waiting.

Carmen looked in his direction. He was still staring at her. She read the note again. This time, she noticed he signed his name. "Enosis," she said out loud.

"What?" a voice said in response.

Carmen looked up to see Kane standing over her. "That guy's name is Enosis," she said, closing the note. She slid it underneath her plate, hoping he hadn't noticed she was reading something. "He's Bahamian. The waiter and I were talking about names. He said his name was Enosis," Carmen lied.

"Oh, well, they didn't have any of the wine I was looking for."

Carmen ignored his comment, allowing her eyes to fall on Enosis. He gave her a smile and Carmen turned away, not wanting Kane to notice. She knew she would have to wait until Kane fell asleep to sneak out to see him.

They would be headed to Florida in the morning so tonight would be the last night they spent on board the ship. Throughout it all, she had to steal the diamonds and find a way to get Kane to come to Texas with her. Instead of trying to trick him, Carmen decided to be forthcoming and ask him. "I want to go to Texas to see my parents. Would you mind spending a night there?"

Carmen continued talking, not giving him the chance to say no. "See, I kind of went ahead and reserved tickets. I wanted us to stay together for a few more days. We could stay at my parents' house and then leave the next evening or the following morning. I only need you to say yes."

"It sounds like a plan." Kane raised his glass to hers.

Carmen completed the toast, smiling at how easy it was to convince him to come. He had been accommodating ever since the day they met. It was as if he made it his duty to cater to her.

"You want to dance?" he asked her.

"Dance, there isn't a place to dance around here," Carmen voiced, looking around the room. She felt Kane's hands on her chin as he tilted her head a little to the right. Carmen gasped as Lloyd took the stage, his band starting in on the opening riffs of, "Valentine."

"Will you dance with me?" Kane asked, standing up.

Carmen looked at him and then at Lloyd. Still in absolute shock, she wasn't quite sure how she managed to get out her seat. She did, though, and in no time, she was on the dance floor with Kane. For the first time in months, all Carmen felt was pure bliss.

Chapter Thirty-One

Carmen opened her eyes to see Kane sleeping peacefully. His arm was draped over her waist, and she didn't want to move it for fear she would wake him. Tonight was the last night on the boat, the very night she would have to steal the diamonds from Enosis. Every second counted; therefore, she reached down, picked up Kane's arm, and moved it beside him. While he hadn't moved an inch, she had to make sure he stayed that way as she peeled the covers back. Every few seconds, she would peek at him to make sure he was in the same position. So far, so good, but she knew things could change in the blink of an eye.

If only you didn't have to come.

Carmen quickly grabbed her red tube dress, slipping it on as she searched the room for her shoes. In the process, she noticed the clock read 2:55.

In record time, she spotted her shoes peeking out from underneath the bed. She slid them on, tying the laces around her legs and headed to the vanity for her key card. She grabbed it and paused only in her step to take a final look at Kane. He was dead to the world. She kept moving, leaving the cabin on a search for Enosis' room. He said he stayed in Cabin 45B, meaning he was somewhat in the middle of the boat.

Carmen walked down the hallway, checking each room number as well as her breath and hair. She hadn't even looked in a mirror, but thankfully she stumbled upon a small convenience store that was still open on the boat. She walked inside, grabbing a tube of mouthwash and a comb. "Where's the nearest bathroom?" she asked, startling the cashier.

"There's one in here," the lady said, pointing down a hallway. Carmen gave her the key card so the items could be charged to the room and then headed to the bathroom. She looked at herself, seeing the sleep that was still in her eyes and quickly dashed a few drops of water on her face. She gargled with the mouthwash and combed the kinks out her hair, making it appear as if it had been styled for him. Carmen didn't know what Enosis was expecting or what his intentions were. She simply had to be ready for whatever ball he threw her way.

"This is it, girl. This is what you've been waiting for," she said out loud. "There's no turning back now." Carmen turned on the faucet, allowing the water to wash down the mouthwash she spit out. She took one final look in the mirror before walking out the door.

She couldn't think about Kane, Jay, or her parents at this time. She had to focus her mind on getting the diamonds and getting rid of Enosis. He claimed he worked for Jay, which meant she had to put on a good act and clean up her mess well. She knew she would have to kill him, because she couldn't let word get back to Jay that she was with Kane. The only way she wanted him to find out was if she told him. Not a part of her plan, she stopped in front of Enosis' room and knocked on the door. He appeared in a matter of seconds as if he been waiting for her.

Enosis was thin, but muscular with a light complexion and dark brown dreads that were always held back with a rubberband. "I guess it's time to talk business," he told her, looking her up and down.

Carmen gave him a seductive smile in return. Her eyes traced his body, noting the white wifebeater and black cargo pants he wore. His feet were shoeless, and he only allowed her enough room to slip past him. Without any luggage in sight, Carmen questioned the whereabouts of the diamonds Carlos claimed he would have. "Why am I here?"

He chuckled at her and scratched his chin. "Let's see, why are you here? It seems to me like you're doing a little bit of cheating." Enosis slid his finger down the base of her neck until it reached the tip of her dress. Then, as if he was testing her, he stuck his hand directly in the middle of her cleavage. On instinct, Carmen grabbed his hand, placing it at his side.

"I know who you are. You work for my boyfriend. You sell drugs for him," Carmen stated. She remembered that Carlos told her that Enosis used to work for Pierre. Since Pierre was dead, she figured he crossed over and was now working for Jay.

"I don't sell drugs for your boyfriend, Carmen."

"Okay, well, you worked for Pierre."

"I don't know where you heard that from, but I never worked for anyone named Pierre," he said, laughing. "I work for Jay."

Carmen watched as he walked past her, sitting on the bed. She knew her confusion showed in her expression. "You don't work for Pierre? Who are you then?"

"I have never heard of Pierre," Enosis replied. "This isn't about me, though. This is about you, and how I'm going to keep your secret."

"No, this is about you," Carmen stated, walking towards him. "I want to know who you are, and I want to know right now. Who are you?"

"Enosis Constueza," he said, looking at her surprised. "I was born in Nassau. I met your boyfriend through a drug lord by the name of Konstro. Your boyfriend was looking for some new product, and I got the job of acquiring it for him. Now, on to the subject at hand. All I want is to keep your secret, a little kiss here, a little kiss there. Your boyfriend isn't going to wake up and try to find you, is he?"

Carmen cracked a sarcastic smile and tightened her lips together. She knew exactly what Enosis wanted. Sex was always a man's weakness. Certain she could have Enosis passed out in less than eight minutes; she shook her head. "He is sleeping like a baby," she told him, speaking of Kane.

"Then let the games begin. Don't be shy."

Carmen watched as he grabbed her waist, pulling her closer to him. His hands automatically went to her backside, grabbing both of her cheeks with firm grips. It disturbed her to have him touch her and her initial reaction was to push him away. While her hands were on his shoulders, she moved it up towards his neck. Carlos had taught her how to strangle, but she couldn't give Enosis the idea yet that she was sent to kill him. She had to make him think she was trying to protect her secret.

"Why are you cheating on him, anyway? He isn't pleasing you?"

"He has always pleased me," Carmen told him, massaging his neck.

"I can please you better," he said, slowly, lying down on the bed. He pushed Carmen's body down with him, allowing his lips to touch hers. Carmen had to admit the guy could kiss, but she wasn't there to make out. She didn't know how far she would have to go with him, but she knew time was up when he pulled down her tube dress.

"You know what I'm here for," she said, pulling away from him.

"What?" he asked as the dress fell at her ankles.

Carmen allowed him a few more minutes of playtime before she continued with the plan. When she felt him unzipping his pants, she knew it was time. "The diamonds," she whispered. She felt his body jump at the mention of the word and in one svelte move, she grabbed his neck. She applied pressure, but not too much, so he could tell her where the diamonds were. He grabbed her arms to pull her off him, but Carmen knew her strength. She gripped his neck tighter to slow him down. "Do you really think I came all the way here to fuck some man other than Jay? Please," she told him, applying more pressure. "Where are the fuckin' diamonds?"

She watched as Enosis struggled to breathe and eventually raised his finger pointing to the closet. "This is a no-win situation." Carmen applied more pressure to his neck until she knew for sure he was going into unconsciousness. Minutes later, he was dead. The hard part was over, yet she still had to find the diamonds.

In a flash, she picked up her dress, slipping it on. She then pulled the covers back, undressing Enosis, and placing him inside the bed. The scene still wasn't good enough. She threw his clothes around to make it seems as if he died in his sleep. For finishing touches, she closed his eyes, which were still open.

He had pointed to the closet, so Carmen went there next to search for the black briefcase. The door was nearly ajar, and the briefcase was exactly where he said it would be. She pulled it out, quickly opening it and stared at seven small black bags inside. Almost every bag she opened contained only white diamonds. When she got to the last one, she opened it to see a large pink diamond, the only one of its kind. Carmen knew she had to keep that one for herself. She quickly slid the diamond in the bag and into the suitcase. After locking it, she took one final look at Enosis and left the room. Carmen knew she couldn't let the murder get to her. She had a job to do, which was now over. The second Enosis' door was closed, so was her double life.

***

Carmen hid the briefcase inside one of her suitcases and threw her clothes on top. Kane was still asleep but had obviously changed positions since she left. She headed to her side of the bed and pulled the covers back, sliding in beside him. Her movement woke him and his eyes slowly fluttered open.

"Hey," he whispered. "Where were you?"

"I needed some air. I took a walk on the deck," she told him, laying her head on his chest.

"Are you okay?"

Carmen nodded at him and felt his hands caress her back. It wasn't long before Carmen realized he'd fallen asleep. It worked in her favor because her mind went back to the diamonds. She had done well, but she also knew something was up. Enosis worked solely for Jay and was on his way to the states to see him. *If he was on his way to see Jay and was only responsible for getting him new product, why did he have a briefcase full of diamonds? Who else was he on his way to see? Were the diamonds the new product?* Carmen figured Carlos had either tried to screw her over or someone had screwed him over. She tried not to think about it since Carlos was going to call her in the morning.

A couple of hours later, she woke up to the sound of Kane's baritone. "You need to get up," he was saying in her ear. Carmen faked a yawn and closed her eyes.

"We're already at the port. I got your stuff together, but I swear this suitcase is heavier than before. Come on, baby, you have to get up," he said, sitting on the bed. "We have to be out of here in less than two hours. We also need to call your parents and let them know we're coming to Texas."

"I know," Carmen told him, opening her eyes. "You want to hold me one last time before all our privacy is taken away?"

Kane laughed at her question, bringing his face to meet hers. He got ready to kiss her until he heard her cell phone go off.

"Damn," Carmen said, recognizing Carlos' personal ringtone. She jumped out the bed, looking for her phone and found it still attached to the charger. She quickly answered, running inside the bathroom.

"Is that a private call?" Kane yelled.

Carmen ignored him, hearing Carlos asking her if she had the diamonds. "Yeah, I have them," she whispered. "Is everything together on your part? I don't want any games, Carlos. I need that money."

"Damn, Carmen, did you really do that shit? I swear, girl, I'm going to fuck the hell out your ass once I get to Texas. We can talk about that later, though. This is the deal. I'm on my way to Texas right now. I'm staying at a hotel a couple of miles north of where the conference is going to take place. Tomorrow, we need to meet up at the venue. Bring the diamonds the exact way you have them. I have some papers for them that one of my jewelers drew up. We sell them, get the money, and later that evening, we complete the deal. After that, you're free to do what you want."

"I don't know about that part of the plan," Carmen replied.

"We had a deal, Carmen. I don't want to have to pop a bullet in you. Do you want me to tell Jay what you're doing, or do you want to fuck me and get it over with? The choice is yours."

"Carlos, I think I'm falling in love. I think I'm in love with Kane. I need to find a way to tell Jay when I get home that we're over. To be honest, I don't even know. I'm confused."

"Jay is planning on proposing. You throw that shit in his face; you're going to be lying six feet below. Kane will be on top of you in his own casket."

Carmen bit her lip. She hadn't planned on telling Jay about her relationship with Kane. She was simply going to tell him their relationship had run its course. However, Carmen knew she couldn't fully leave Jay alone. He was her first real love and the first and only man she had been with. He was always going to have a soft spot in her heart. "I have the plan, Carlos, I need to go." Carmen hung up the phone and contemplated what she told Carlos. She shouldn't have mentioned that she and Kane had fallen in love.

"Is everything okay?" Kane asked.

"Yeah," Carmen yelled. "I was taking care of business." She opened the door and gave him a wide smile to calm his nerves. It seemed to work because he only told her to get dressed. Carmen did as he asked, turning on the shower. She thought the hard part was over, but it had only begun. The tough chick persona she had been wearing was finally starting to break.

***

Meanwhile, in Dallas, Harold opened his eyes, hearing the phone ring. Aware Patricia wasn't going to answer; he picked up the phone, hitting Talk. He gave the person a quick hello only to hear the phone still ringing. This time, he realized it wasn't the house phone, but his cell phone. Not wanting to miss the call, he grabbed his cell and muttered, "Hello."

"Hey, Daddy," Carmen said, excitedly.

"Peaches, it's been awhile," he said, sitting up in bed. He nudged his wife in case she wanted to have a quick chat with Carmen.

"I know, which is why I'm coming to Texas today," Carmen announced, looking at Kane. "I want to spend some time with y'all. My flight leaves in like forty-five minutes. I should be there by six or seven."

Harold sat straight up. "I don't even know what to say, Peaches. You've really surprised us," he said, nudging Patricia again.

"I'll call you when we land; you can come pick us up from the airport." Carmen winked at Kane only because she was waiting for her father to ask who she was with. He would be in for a surprise when she said Kane.

"Did Jay come with you?" Harold asked, growing somewhat upset. He thought his days of having Jay in his presence were over.

"Kane is with me," she replied.

Harold looked at his wife, seeing she was now wide awake. "Kane, the owner of Production, he's with you?"

"Yeah, we're together, is that okay?" Carmen asked.

"Yeah, I wasn't expecting him, though. I figured he was busy with his store. I guess we'll see you two when you get here."

"You will, we'll see you in a few."

Harold held the phone in his hands as Carmen hung up. He couldn't figure out why Carmen would pick such a day to fly in to see them. She hadn't even flown in when they moved in the house. He turned to look at Patricia to see if she heard the conversation. She had a harsh expression on her face, and he knew she could see through everything.

"She's up to something, Harold," Patricia blurted. "If she wanted to see us, then she wouldn't have called you personally. She knows I don't deal with any mess." Patricia could feel it in her heart her daughter was up to something.

"Let's have a good visit," Harold said, hoping to calm her down.

"Oh, we will, after I get my questions out," Patricia said, lying back down. "She can play you for a fool, but not me."

Chapter Thirty-Two

Carmen leaned her luggage up against the wall as she and Kane waited for her parents to arrive. Now that she had time to spare, she needed to make a phone call to Jay. She excused herself and went to a quieter area, starting to dial his number. She waited as it rung, knowing he was upset with her. When he picked up, she said his name, only to hear silence. "Jay," she said in the phone. She took her cell phone from her ear and saw the timer was still going. "Jay," she repeated. Carmen looked in the direction where she left Kane and saw him on the phone as well. She turned away once Jay's voice sounded.

"I don't even know what the fuck to say to you."

"Baby, look, I know you're upset. You have every right to be. Right now, I'm in Texas visiting my parents. I'll be home sometime on Tuesday. We can talk then," Carmen told him. "We'll talk about everything."

"We are going to talk. I've been worried about you, baby. Why did you do this to me? I couldn't call your cell phone. You didn't even call me with a number where I could reach you."

"I know. I've been having some me time."

"My eyes are all red and shit. I've been stressed as hell."

"I know, and I'm sorry. We'll talk about things when I get home."

Carmen heard silence again until Jay muffled a low okay. She could hear it in his voice he sincerely missed her. She was wrong for how she was treating him. Still, a part of her considered it to be revenge for what he did with Tricia.

Finished with the call, Carmen looked at Kane. In his mind, he thought she was going back to Jay when she got home. She told him she was then she changed her mind. Then, she changed it again, and again, and again. The problem was, she felt like she had life when she was with him. She had never danced with Jay. He also never held her like Kane did. Kane held her like it was his job while Jay did it more out of pleasure. She had spent months with Jay, but she felt like she had spent a lifetime with Kane.

Carmen bit her lip, seeing her parents walking through baggage claim. They spotted Kane first, stopping and hugging him. Carmen walked towards them, seeing they looked the same. Her mother's hair was a couple of inches longer while her father was still bald.

"Well, she looks the same, Patricia," her father said, hugging her.

Only a couple of months had passed since they last seen each other, but to Carmen, it had been forever. She was used to seeing her parents on a regular basis versus once every few months.

"Well, dang, don't be a stranger," she told her mother. Carmen grabbed her mother in her arms and fixed her hair playfully. "Don't want to mess up anything. You always want to stay lookin' fresh."

"Hey, baby," her mother said, softly.

Carmen's smile faded when she realized her mother was trying to read her. It was the exact reason she hadn't called on the house phone. Carmen knew her mother had given her father the third degree on why she was there. She also knew she wasn't going to leave Texas without being on the witness stand. If her mother didn't take her to court that night then it would be tomorrow morning.

"I hope y'all don't mind, but how about attending evening worship service with us?" Harold suggested. "We missed the morning service so we thought we would get our Word in now."

"I don't ever turn down a Word from the Lord," Kane replied.

Carmen knew church was the first place she needed to be. She had a lot of repenting and confessing to do. Carmen quickly agreed and grabbed her luggage so she could head to her parents' car.

"I got that," Kane said, taking it from her.

"Don't be showing off now," her father responded with a chuckle. He grabbed some of the luggage as well, walking ahead with Kane.

"You know I'm surprised to see you. How long are you planning on being in town?" her mother asked.

Carmen swallowed, knowing her mother was starting her interrogation. "I will be here until Tuesday," she answered. Carmen looked at her mother, noticing how muscular she had gotten over the past few months. "You look buff," she said touching her mother's arms.

"Golfing with your father," her mother replied. "If you haven't noticed, I got a nice little tan, too. So, y'all are here on business?"

Carmen looked at her mother, pausing in her steps. "Can this wait until later?"

"I'll let it go for now. When we get home, it's me and you."

Carmen watched as her mother walked in front of her. *I can't hide anything from that woman.* She rolled her eyes at the thought and followed behind her to the car. It was a long ride from the airport to the church, but well worth the wait. Once Carmen was inside her parents' new church home, she started to feel like her old self. She made the decision she was going to work on getting her soul restored with God. She also was going to talk to Jay and tell him their relationship had run its course.

With the decision final, she stared at Kane, believing he was sent to her by God. She had watched how Kane had participated in the service, singing every song, or following along in the songbook if he didn't know the lyrics. He had even spoken to the minister about something he said in his sermon. Kane was the kind of man Carmen used to dream of. Jay, on the other hand, didn't have a special connection with God. He may have believed in Him, but it wasn't quite enough.

Once church service was over, they returned to the house and Carmen settled in one of the guestrooms. She unpacked only a few of her things before heading in the kitchen where she found her mother cutting up fruit for a salad. Meanwhile, her father was outside with Kane, giving him a tour of the backyard.

"You can sit down," her mother ordered, not taking her eye off the apple she was cutting. "We might be a while."

Carmen did as she was told, careful not to speak out of turn.

"Why are you here?" her mother asked.

"I wanted to see y'all," Carmen replied, getting nervous. She could feel her hands starting to shake so she held them together so her mother wouldn't notice.

"A picture wasn't good enough?" her mother said, nastily. "You're not here because you missed us, Carm. Otherwise, you wouldn't have brought Kane with you. Now tell me, why are you here?"

"I'm not trying to be disrespectful, but why can't I come see my parents if I fuckin' want to?" Carmen watched as her mother stood straight up. She had never cursed in front of her.

"Let me tell you one thing, Carmen Denise Davenport. You are about to get yourself cut. I know you're not here because you wanted to see us. If you wanted to see us, the real and sincere part of you would've called in advance, letting us know you were coming. I'm not dumb like your father. I know when you're up to something. I know when you're doing dirt. I told you once before I have been there and done that. You and your father can hide shit from me as much as you want, but I know what you both are up to. I knew who your father was for twenty something years until he finally decided to tell me. So what, you think I didn't know Jay was a hustler? Please, I tried to hint to you that I knew when I noticed he was driving three different cars. I've dated club owners. They don't get rich or drive cars like that because of some damn club."

"Look, Mama," Carmen began.

"I'm not done," her mother interrupted. "I told you what people from West Brookstone are about and you fell right in the trap. I may not know exactly what you're doing here in Texas, but once you're finish taking care of your business, I want you out my house."

"What makes you think I'm doing anything at all?"

"I can look at you and tell. Your actions say it all, Carmen. If you weren't doing anything then you would be defending yourself. Instead, you're sitting here, trying to find out what it is that I know." Patricia paused as she cut up more fruit. "Whatever it is, you better not drag Kane into it. He is a good man; a good Christian man and you don't need to be trying to walk all over him."

"Do you want to know what I'm doing?"

Her mother chuckled, looking at the fruit. "I don't care what you're doing, but if you get locked up then it's on you."

"Why do I have to be doing something illegal?"

"Because you are," her mother said, stopping to look at her.

Carmen swallowed and turned away. She heard the knife as it dropped from her mother's hand on the counter.

"I've been there and done that, Carm. I can see it in your eyes you're doing something you don't have any business doing. I talk to Tiara daily because I want to know what's going on with you. When she tells me you're at work, but barely working, I know your mind is somewhere else. I know how much you want to get Flame back on top. I wanted the same. I did what I did, but I didn't want you to have to do it, too." Patricia paused, trying not to cry. "Carmen, I did things to get money for Flame that I shouldn't have done. I did things I'm not proud of. I'm begging you, Carmen. Whatever it is, please let it go."

"As soon as I get through tomorrow, I will."

"I will kill—" Carmen cut her off.

"Jay has no idea what I'm doing," she admitted. "He doesn't know anything. He would be hurt if he knew what I was up to."

"That worries me even more. Someone else has you in this mess," Patricia griped. "So I guess Kane knows?"

Carmen nodded her head. "He does know, but those days are over, Mama, I promise you. I'm no longer that girl."

"Great, I don't want to have to cut you." Patricia pretended to throw the knife at her and let out a small giggle.

"Mama," Carmen began. She waited until her mother looked at her before she spoke. "I'm in love with Kane."

Patricia mouthed the word wow as she slid the freshly cut fruit in a bowl. "So you're cheating on Jay?"

Carmen nodded her head.

"Wow," her mother repeated. "So I guess y'all want to share the guest bedroom, huh? I already know you're having sex. It would be very disrespectful, but you know your father and I aren't light sleepers. Now, I don't condone you cheating on your boyfriend, but you're a grown woman."

Carmen watched as her mother grabbed a pear and started to slice it. In the meantime, she heard the back door open as her father walked inside with Kane.

"I'm going to have that whole back side over there cleared off for the pool house," he was saying. "I need a place for parties during the holidays." Harold grabbed a piece of fruit from the bowl, which resulted in Patricia slapping his hand.

"Greedy butt," Patricia muttered, moving the bowl.

Carmen chuckled until she felt Kane's hands around her waist. She figured he told her father about them like she told her mother.

"You want to catch a movie?" he whispered in her ear.

Carmen couldn't contain her excitement. Though she had recently seen the *Black Dahlia* on the ship, the experience didn't compare to being inside an actual movie theater. It had been a very long time since she had ever experienced something so normal. Every time she tried to get Jay to see the latest release, he would always find a way to get them to stay at home. With Kane, Carmen realized she wouldn't have that problem. "Yeah," she replied happily. "I would love to go."

"I told Kane he could use one of my cars while y'all were here. He said y'all were in town till Tuesday."

"We are," Carmen confirmed.

"Carmen can drive my other car while she's here," her mother offered, sneaking a piece of the fruit.

"Well, maybe you'll be able to see Flame and my new office before you leave. At least you've seen the church." Harold grabbed a strawberry, causing Patricia to slap his hand once again.

Carmen was about to grab a piece as well until Kane's voice sounded in her ear. "Let's go," he whispered. Carmen got off the stool and winked at her mother as she headed out the kitchen. She didn't know if Kane had something else planned, but she knew she wanted to be alone with him. Until she broke up with Jay, their time together was limited, and she wanted to cherish every moment.

Chapter Thirty-Three

It was early Monday afternoon, yet Carlos' hotel room was barely lit. Once he handed Carmen the check for a million dollars, all she saw was green.

"It looks good, doesn't it?" Carlos asked, admiring every zero. "I bet you never thought this day would come."

Carmen held the check in her hand, rereading the numbers over and over in her head. It was almost too good to be true.

"Everything went perfectly and smoothly. You delivered the diamonds, the conference came, and we got the check." Carlos walked away from her, heading towards the mini bar where a bottle of cognac set. He poured her some in a glass along with one for himself. "Here," he said, facing her. "We need to celebrate."

Carmen shook her head, declining his offer. The last thing she needed was for her parents to smell liquor on her breath. She told them she wanted to browse the city on her own and the lie had worked perfectly. Her father had invited Kane on a tour of his new real estate office while her mother was busy at Flame. It gave her time to attend the conference and get her money from Carlos.

Carmen continued to study the check, remembering the diamonds were worth two million dollars. Her check was written only for a million, which meant she needed to find out the worth of the pink diamond. By keeping it separate from the other diamonds, it didn't affect their payday.

"You sure you don't need this?" Carlos asked, holding up the bottle.

Carmen didn't reply. Her life of drinking alcohol or liquor of any kind was over. She quickly told Carlos no, folding up the check and sliding it in her purse. When she stood up to leave the room, Carlos stopped her, a devilish grin plastered on his face.

"Damn," he said, looking at her. "Come here." Carlos pulled her face towards his, yet Carmen turned away once she saw his lips about to hit hers. "Hey," he snapped. "You got the money, now finish the deal." Carlos grabbed her face again, and when Carmen felt their lips being intertwined, she pushed him away.

"I can't do this," she said, breaking free.

"Do you think I'm fuckin' playin' with you?" Carlos grabbed her arm, pushing her down on the bed. He quickly climbed on top of her, trying to kiss her again. "We had a deal, remember?" He held her against her will, placing kisses over her neck and chest.

Carmen felt a tear slide down her cheek, but she knew he didn't care. She had made a deal with him. She had to do it. She had shaken on it. She couldn't take the money and run. She looked at Carlos, and for a moment, she thought she saw a sympathetic expression on his face. "I don't want to do this," she told him in tears. Immediately, he stopped, moving to the other side of the bed. Carmen watched as he picked up the phone and started dialing numbers. "What are you doing?" she asked him, seeing that some of the numbers looked familiar.

"I'm calling Jay. You don't want to do it then I can't hold up my end of the bargain. I have to tell him everything."

Carmen hit the hold button, causing the phone to hang up. "Carlos, please," she begged. "Something else, but not this," she continued.

"I want this," he said, pushing her arm away from the phone. "It's either this or I call Jay."

Carmen sighed and looked at the phone. She couldn't take that chance. She couldn't take any chances. She looked at Carlos and thought about Kane. He would be devastated to know she slept with Carlos. The experience they shared over the course of the trip was magical. She had even taken her mother's advice the night before. After they knew for sure her parents were sleeping, he snuck in her room so she could sleep in his arms. Before the sun came up, he snuck back in the guest bedroom like they hadn't been together.

Carmen stared at Carlos, seeing Kane, and didn't shy away when he leaned in to kiss her. She knew that was the only way she could get through it. She envisioned Carlos' hands were really Kane's and that he was the one touching and pulling off her clothes. She dreamed it was Kane moaning in her ear as she grinded on him. Then, Kane was the one who sent her mind in a million different places as she climaxed. Like she had done previously, Carmen fell asleep on his chest after it was over. Deep down, she knew it wasn't true. Kane was only a figment of her imagination and Carlos was the real one who had stolen her spirit.

∗∗∗

That evening when Carmen returned home, she found the house completely silent. The only car left in the driveway was her father's car that he'd given Kane to drive while they were in town. Carmen closed the door, setting the spare house key on the table in the foyer. She was glad the house was empty because she didn't want anyone around her. She had cried on her way to the house, ashamed of what she'd done.

She tried to hide the fact she'd been crying in case the house wasn't completely empty. There was a big chance Kane was upstairs while her parents were still out and about. She walked up the steps, using the rail as she went, thinking of Carlos. It sickened her, seeing him on top of her, ramming himself into her like she wanted it. He knew she didn't want him touching her. However, a deal was a deal. Carmen wiped her face and opened the door to her room.

Kane was sitting on the bed with his head in his hands. Carmen had told him she was going sightseeing, but more specifically to the JFK Museum. He appeared bothered and she searched the room for any sign of destruction. "Are you okay?" she asked him. He shook his head and Carmen sat beside him, seeing the computer in the guestroom had been turned on. It was also set on the homepage for CNN.

"Your parents are going out tonight."

"Then, we have the house to ourselves. It is our last night together."

Kane's position didn't change. His head was still between his hands as if he was massaging his temples. "It's a gala for your mother's sorority. She asked me if I thought you had brought any shoes with you that could work with her outfit. She didn't want to buy any."

Carmen tried to piece together what he was saying.

"Y'all wear the same size shoe."

Carmen agreed with him and then she remembered. The red stilettos were in the same luggage as the diamond. Carmen knew he found it. There was no way he hadn't. Carmen stood up, backing away from him.

"I thought you wouldn't mind if she borrowed yours."

Carmen shook her head, not wanting him to continue.

"I got a little bit more than I bargained for. I found this," he said.

Carmen watched as he held the pink diamond in his hand.

"It was funny because we never went to a jewelry store. Then, on the radio this morning, there was a big spectacle because over two million dollars' worth of diamonds were stolen from the Bahamas. A couple of hours later, when I was at your father's firm, one of the agents announced that the Diamond Exchange conference had bought about two million dollars' worth of diamonds from some unnamed representatives of a jewelry company out in Milwaukee. You would think that kind of sale would be all over the news. So, I asked myself, are these two things connected? I mean a robbery in the Bahamas, exactly where we were, and then, a big diamond sale in Texas, exactly where we are."

Carmen swallowed, seeing how he pieced things together.

"So I went online and did a search, trying to pull up the news stories associated with all of this. Come to find out, a man was found strangled to death on the same boat we were on. His name was Enosis Constueza. He was a big time jewelry thief and linked to a Bahamian drug lord named Konstro. I remembered you telling me about a man named Enosis at dinner. You and the waiter had been talking about names."

"Kane," she whimpered.

"You were with me the whole entire time, Carmen. I know you didn't do anything. You do know, however, who did."

"Not the whole time," she admitted, remembering the night she snuck out the room. She wouldn't tell him about the murder, but she would tell him she had taken the diamond. "I stole the pink diamond from Enosis. I knew he had it and I took it."

"We were together the whole time. When did you do this?"

"While you were sleeping," she replied.

Kane tried his best to think back. "You didn't need any fresh air that night. You also didn't go walking on the deck."

Carmen nodded her head in agreement.

"You came to the Bahamas to steal the diamond?"

"It's worth a lot of money. I was trying to keep Flame from going bankrupt. My father wouldn't give me the money, and Jay wouldn't give me anything either. I was desperate."

"Jay doesn't have anything to do with this?"

"He thinks I went to the Bahamas to see some long lost family."

Kane looked at the floor and handed the diamond to her. "I suggest you turn it in. Your sentence will be better than them finding it on you." He picked up his luggage after Carmen had taken it out his hand.

"You're leaving?" she asked him.

"Yeah," he said, picking up his backpack.

"Kane, look, I know I lied to you about the trip. What about us? I mean, does this mean we're through?"

"Carmen, we were through, anyway. This whole thing was going to be over whenever we got back to Brookstone. You kept going back and forth about it, but I already knew what was going to happen."

"I wasn't going to let it. How do you feel about me?" she asked him. "Do you still love me?"

"I was falling in love with you," he corrected, "I guess that does mean I love you. But this, this is not what I came here for."

Carmen stared at him as he walked out the door. "I told you the truth," she said, following him. "What else do you want from me? I made a mistake. Everything is over, though. I finished the deal with Carlos."

Kane stopped in his tracks, turning to face her. "You slept with him?" He dropped his bags, walking up to her.

"I told you that was part of the deal."

"You also said you weren't going to do it. You lied to me. When did you sleep with him? You did it today, didn't you? You slept with him today. You lied about where you were going again. You mean to tell me you were that desperate to save Flame that you sold drugs behind your boyfriend's back, stole a diamond, and slept with his best friend?"

"I am a person who won't stop at anything to get what she wants."

"You're sick, Carmen."

Kane turned away from her and picked up his bags. Carmen could feel herself starting to shake. He couldn't leave her. He was the best thing that had happened to her throughout the entire ordeal. Carmen covered her mouth as tears flooded down her face. She watched as he neared the door, and she could feel herself starting to become sick again.

"Tell your parents the car is at the airport. They can pick it up from there. I'll let you know exactly where I parked it."

"Don't leave me," she begged. She watched as he ignored her and opened the door. Carmen ran towards him, grabbing his arm. "Kane, look, I know I made some mistakes, but I didn't want you here. Just listen to me."

"I've listened to you enough. I gotta go. I need to get home. I need to clear my head," he said, taking his arm out her grasp.

"I was blackmailed, Kane. I didn't want you to come. It was all a part of the plan." Tears streamed down Carmen's face as she reached out for him.

Kane yanked his arm from her grasp. "You got five minutes to tell me what this plan was." Kane dropped his bags down on the floor.

Carmen wiped the tears from her face. "I was desperate to save Flame. I know I could have done things differently, but Carlos offered me a deal."

"You're telling me things I already know, where do I come in?"

Carmen paused trying to get her thoughts together. "He has pictures of us when I went to my, I mean, your house for lunch. He threatened to show them to Jay and make it seem like I was cheating on him."

"So what if he showed him pictures of us? We didn't do anything. All you had to do was tell Jay what happened. You were that scared of losing him? I'm surprised you're not scared of losing him now. You've been in my arms, kissing me every single night since we've been on this trip."

"You don't know how Jay gets when he's upset. He's crazy. I didn't want him to do anything to you. I—" Carmen stopped.

"You're still hiding information," he said, grabbing his bags.

"Kane, I need you to trust me on this one, please. You don't understand how Jay is."

"Oh, I understand perfectly. I saw the way he snatched you up in front of Flame and I told you about him then. You didn't want to listen to me. Right now, I'm leaving. I'll see you tomorrow sometime." Kane walked out the door and headed towards her father's car.

Carmen only ran after him, screaming as she went. "Kane, I love you. I didn't want you to find out like this."

"You don't know what kind of situation you've put me in. It's a very difficult one. I am now that rock in a hard place. I have to make a decision I really don't want to make." Kane got inside the car and started it up. In less than a minute, he was out the driveway, and headed for the airport.

Chapter Thirty-Four

Kane wasn't the only person who had returned to Brookstone. Jay watched as Carlos walked up to his apartment, holding two duffle bags. He had heard Carlos had gone out of town, but he didn't know what for. Jay figured when he went to scope out the Bentley, he would try and see what Carlos was up to. He had taken the liberty of searching for the keys to it, which he found in Carmen's jewelry box. She hadn't hidden the keys well, which made him think she wanted him to see the Bentley ahead of time.

The car was parked a couple of blocks away from Carlos' apartment. When he pulled up beside it, he had to commend Carmen for picking it out. She had made a good choice, which meant she knew his style. Already infatuated with the car, he put the keys to the Bentley on his key ring and planned on putting them back in the jewelry box before Carmen came home. She would never even know he checked out his gift.

He opened the front door, getting inside, and immediately started up the engine. The lights came on, which he dimmed, and he proceeded to check out the car. He opened the glove compartment first, seeing there was nothing there except the car manual, insurance, and registration information. When he let the seat back so he could get comfortable, his fingers slid alongside a zipper. He looked in the mirror at his reflection, growing suspicious. He then unzipped the seat cover. He pushed his hand inside and pulled out a few hundred dollar bills. He reached further into the seat and pulled out more money. *Shit, this must be almost two hundred thousand dollars*, he thought. *Why is Carmen carrying this kind of money around?*

Jay quickly stuffed the money in the seat and zipped the seat cover back. Since he had found the money, he knew there had to be other hiding places in the car. He took the key out the ignition and headed for the trunk.

Jay knew Carmen was trying to find a way to come up with the money for her store, but he hoped she hadn't done something stupid. When he opened the trunk, he noticed it was empty except for a pair of jumper cables. About to close it, he saw something shiny peeking out from underneath the trunk's interior. He reached down, pushing the jumper cables to one side, and lifted the carpeted material up. It moved easily, revealing sets of clothes. He picked up one of the shirts, smelling it. Carmen always wore the fragrance, Coco, which was exactly what the shirt smelled like. He tossed it aside, grabbing a few more items in the trunk.

"Going somewhere?" he asked out loud.

He picked up a pantsuit, which he noticed she hadn't designed. He knew for sure Carmen had been doing something behind his back. He threw the clothes down, picking up the mat and pulling it all the way back. He stared hard at the spare tire, seeing the bags of heroin that had been hidden inside.

"How about letting me hustle it for you?" he remembered Carmen asking. He recognized the bags of heroin. His stamp was still on them, insuring their quality. He dropped the mat on top of the clothes and drugs and then closed the trunk. He then proceeded to get inside his own car. "That bitch," he mumbled. Somehow, someway, she had managed to hustle for him without him knowing it. She was using the Bentley as a cover up. She was probably dealing when Noc saw her and was parking the car at Carlos' apartment. However, it didn't make sense. Carmen was a good girl. She knew nothing about the drug game.

*Carlos...Carlos...*the name sounded in his mind. Carlos had been stacking major paper right around the same time Carmen started her disappearing act. He was always coming to him, purchasing more drugs. Jay knew Carmen was working with Carlos. He had warned her that the game was not for her, but she had gone behind his back. She tried to play him for a fool, but he knew the tables were getting ready to turn. Jay bit his lip, thinking of a plan. Minutes later, his thought process was interrupted when his phone rang.

"Yeah," he yelled in the phone.

"Enosis is dead," Noc announced.

"What do you mean he's dead?"

"They found him on board the ship strangled to death. The diamonds were gone. Early this afternoon, there was a Diamond Exchange conference in Texas. Two million dollars' worth of diamonds was sold there. The pink diamond wasn't sold, though." Noc quickly relayed the message that had traveled through several channels before reaching his ears.

"The diamonds were sold in Texas, huh?" Jay asked, figuring out what was going on. "Let me call you back." Jay hung up the phone and backed out the parking space. He wasn't wasting any time on this one. Most of the time, he planned his attacks, but this one he was doing straight up. He figured Carlos and Carmen had teamed up somehow, went on a Bonnie and Clyde heist, and stole all his diamonds. They thought they had gotten away scot-free, but they were going to be fooled.

Jay parked his car in front of Carlos' apartment building, but sat tight, seeing Carlos coming outside. Jay watched him as he left, remembering the spare key he had sitting in his glove compartment. He didn't know how long Carlos was going to be gone, and he didn't care. He opened the glove compartment, taking out the key. The key was cold inside his hand, almost how his heart was inside. He didn't have a problem getting in the apartment and he locked the door behind him. When it came time for Carlos to come back, he would hear the locks turn before the door opened.

As if on cue, he noticed the two duffle bags on the floor that Carlos had brought in. Jay knew the bags were a point of interest. He turned on a small desk lamp, not wanting too much light, and opened the first bag. There was nothing inside, but clothes and a pair of shoes. Therefore, he pushed it aside and opened the second one.

"This is what I'm looking for," he said, seeing a videotape and a stack of papers. The papers were only details of Carlos' flight, which he could've cared less about. He already knew Carlos had gone to Texas to see Carmen. His eyes landed on a photograph of Carmen who was sitting at a table. She also wasn't alone. She was sitting with Kane, which meant he had gone to the Bahamas with her.

Jay's face tightened, noticing Kane's hand was on hers. He went to the next picture seeing them together again. He threw the pictures aside, seeing a picture of them going in a house. The picture was in black and white, but he knew it was her old house. Kane was the bachelor who bought the old Davenport residence.

Jay scrunched up his face, tearing the picture in half. He then saw a copy of the documents that had been drawn up, citing the diamonds as belonging to a jewelry company in Milwaukee. His anger intensified and he started rocking back and forth as he realized who was responsible for his missing jewels.

Somehow, Carlos had managed to board the ship, kill Enosis, and get to Texas in time for the conference. However, it didn't make sense. Carlos only had a flight to Texas. He was still in Brookstone even after Carmen left. Jay broke in a sweat as he thought about the idea of Carmen stealing from him. He suspected she had and even gazed around the living room for anything that would help him solve the puzzle.

His eyes landed on the videotape. He had tossed it aside, but now it was of value. He picked it up, sticking it inside the VCR, and turned the television on. He turned the volume down before hitting play, almost putting it on mute. He didn't want Carlos to get any warning there was someone inside. He hit play and watched as Carmen and Carlos popped up on the screen. In the first five seconds, he saw Carlos run his fingers down Carmen's face. The remote started to shake in his hand and only grew worse when he saw Carmen's breasts exposed and Carlos' head in between them.

Carmen was the first girl he ever loved. He had told her secrets he had never shared with anyone, but there she was. He watched her as she grinded on top of Carlos. He had never even seen her move like that. He turned the volume up, hearing their lovemaking. He forced himself to continue to watch until he saw them climax.

Carlos had fucked his girlfriend.

Carmen had even laid her head on Carlos' chest like they had been together for a while. Jay's eyes started to water, until he realized he was crying. *Carmen is mine. She is mine. She has always been mine. I should've told her the truth about Tricia. Maybe then, she wouldn't have slept with Carlos.*

Jay stopped the tape when he heard footsteps nearing him. He then saw a shadow move past the window. Jay's veins nearly popped out his arm when he realized Carlos was home. He grinded his teeth, ready to kill him with his bare hands. Carlos had been going behind his back for too long. If he hadn't discovered it, his best friend would've been smiling in his face like it never happened.

Now, the secret was out, and Jay was ready to put him to rest.

He waited, hearing the locks turn, and watched as Carlos opened the door. Jay quickly grabbed him, hitting the light switch, and threw Carlos up against the wall.

"What the fuck are you doing?" Carlos yelled.

"Payback's a bitch, motherfucker." Jay threw a right hook into Carlos' nose. Carlos dropped the bag of Jack in the Box in his hand as he flew into the door. When Jay went to hit him a second time, Carlos caught his fist, preventing him from gauging him in the eye. Jay then used his other hand to pick Carlos up and throw him into a large vase. His body weight broke the vase, shattering the glass into large pieces.

"What the fuck is this about?"

"You fucked my girl."

Before Carlos could respond, he felt Jay's fist punching him.

Jay was on a high, his anger outweighing any thought processes he had. He kept punching him although blood was spewing out his friend's mouth and nose.

"I fucked your girl? I fucked Kane's girl."

Jay punched him again before taking a firm hold on Carlos' neck.

"Kill me," Carlos yelled, spitting blood out his mouth. "Shit, the diamonds are gone. Rakim is gone. You hate my ass, anyway. Kill me."

Carlos drifted in and out of consciousness. When he felt Jay's hands tightening around his neck, he knew he wasn't ready to face his demise. With the last amount of strength he had, he reached for a piece of glass and quickly dug it inside Jay's left cheek. He heard his friend as he screamed from the pain, loosening his grip. Carlos took advantage of Jay's weakness and slid away from him, crawling in the kitchen. As he went, the glass from the vase cut his arms and legs. When he made it to the kitchen, he rested himself against a cabinet. He then looked back at Jay as he pulled the glass from his cheek.

"You walk around here like you are a fuckin' god or some shit. You went and turned everyone against me, talking about how I'm no good. Well, guess what? I am some good. Your girlfriend needed help, and when you turned your back on her, I came to her with open arms. I gave her weight to sell. She was the one stacking paper. She needed money for her store, and I took care of her."

Jay made his way to the kitchen, stumbling a few times.

"All she had to do was fuck me," Carlos continued. Jay was now standing in front of him. His friend grabbed him by the shoulders, raising him to his feet, and then came the sudden blow to his head as it hit the countertop. He blacked out for a minute or two. When he came around, he held out his hands, motioning for Jay to stop. Aware Jay was going to kill him; he wanted to clear his conscience of everything.

"I found out about the diamonds through a man who use to do stuff for me," Carlos whimpered. "I didn't know they were yours. I told Carmen about the stones because she could get the money for her store quicker." Carlos held his chest, unable to breathe, and looked at Jay. Blood was covering the right side of his face. Carlos knew his friend was going to finish him rather quickly, before he bled to death himself. "We would sell the stones at the conference and then split the money. The deal would be over. Everything would be over," Carlos said, feeling like there were a ton of bricks on his chest. He watched as Jay bent down, picking him up again, but Carlos was tired. He couldn't fight him off anymore. Carlos felt he deserved to die and waited for Jay to put more blows to his head.

Jay held Carlos in his hands still feeling the sting of where he stabbed him. Questions fluttered through his mind as he thought about his own father's death. He thought about how so many of his father's men had wronged him. Instead of keeping the cartel going, they had let it fall. They had all stepped out of line like Carlos.

Jay knew he would've done anything for him. He was the only person he trusted for a long time. He stared at him, not wanting to kill him, but he knew he couldn't live with himself if he didn't. "I loved her," he replied. Carlos knew what Carmen meant to him. Still, he robbed him of someone he desperately needed in his life. Carmen made Jay forget about everything he'd done. She made him forget about the monster that lived inside him. It was because of her that he no longer wanted to be a stone cold killer.

Jay thought about his own father's murder. He hadn't really discussed it with Carlos, but he knew he could ask the question before he finished him off. "Wake up," he yelled, shaking him. He shook him repeatedly until Carlos' eyes flew open. "Who killed my father?" Carlos opened his mouth to respond yet he only spat out blood. "Who killed my father?" Jay yelled at him.

"Niggas always stepping out of line," Carlos said, coughing. "It's in the bloodline. It's in my fuckin' bloodline."

Jay looked at the ceiling, figuring out what Carlos was saying. He looked at him and punched him continuously until he knew Carlos was dead. He then grabbed a rag from the sink and held it up to his face. A first aid kit was in his car and once his wound was bandaged, he would be on his way to Domino Rodriguez's house. Like he was the replica of Hector, Carlos was the replica of Domino. This time, Jay planned on getting his revenge for his father's death and Carlos' disloyalty.

Jay snatched the videotape from the VCR and left the apartment. If he could make it out of the complex without any police interruption, his plan was to kill Domino Rodriguez. He didn't even care for an explanation. He knew the answer. Domino, like Carlos, wanted power and knew the only way to get it was to take out the boss.

Jay got inside his car, opening his glove compartment so he could clean off the wound. He bandaged it up and then reached underneath the seat for his glock. Without further ado, he sped to the Rodriguez house.

Chapter Thirty-Five

Jay's house was empty when Carmen returned home Tuesday morning. In addition, the building for Production was also deserted. Even worse, there was an Available sign in the window. She had stopped by the store the second she was back in Brookstone to talk to Kane. Now, she had seen more than what she bargained for. Production was Kane's dream, and she knew he abandoned it after learning what she'd done. Since he was gone, Carmen knew she was a fool for thinking they could have a future. Her place was with Jay, and it was time for her to right all her wrongs.

Carmen waited in their bedroom for Jay to show. She called his cell phone, but he didn't answer. She didn't know where he was, and Carlos wasn't picking up his phone either. Carmen sighed and looked at her luggage that was still packed. The only thing she had taken out of it was the pink diamond, which was underneath the floorboard of their bedroom. Kane told her to turn it in, but if she did, she could possibly be sending herself to prison. The media would have a field day and she would ruin her father's career once the news hit she'd been arrested for theft. She thought of possible alternatives until her phone rung. Tiara was calling her, and Carmen desperately needed her friend.

"Carmen, where are you?" her friend blurted, out of breath.

"I'm at home, where are you? Why do you sound like that?"

"Get out the house. Carmen, you need to leave," Tiara yelled.

"Why, what's going on?" Carmen started to panic wondering if someone had a hit out on Jay. If so, she needed to find her boyfriend fast.

"Carlos is dead. The police found him this morning. Jay knows everything, get out the house. I know he's coming for you," Tiara cried.

Carmen's eyes got big as she wandered into the hallway. Her keys were downstairs. She rushed down the steps but stopped hearing the door open. "I think he's here," she told Tiara. Carmen watched as Jay came in the house. His face was bandaged and there was an image of flame in his eyes. Out of nervousness, Carmen dropped her phone.

"Jay." Carmen backed up the steps, knowing she already looked suspicious. The gleam in Jay's eyes was one she had never seen before. The sight of his face made her turn around and run up the steps. When she did, she felt his hands on her legs, pulling her down. Her face hit the stairs hard as he dragged her down the steps. She could hear Tiara screaming on the phone and then sudden silence. "No," she yelled, as she felt his fist come down hard on her face.

"You fuckin' stole from me," he screamed.

Carmen felt another blow to her face. She grabbed Jay's shirt, trying to push him off her, but he was too strong.

"You fuckin' slut. Those were my diamonds," he yelled in her ear.

Carmen felt his hands at her throat. His tight grip made her feel nauseous although she had already vomited earlier that morning before she left for New York. The queasiness didn't ease until he loosened his grip only so he could slap her in the face. Now that she could breathe, she grabbed the bandage covering his left cheek. Automatically, he yelped, grabbing her legs, and pulling her down the rest of the steps. Carmen moaned loudly as she hit each one until her body hit the hardwood floor.

"I'm sorry," she whispered, feeling the ache in her back, "I didn't know." Her response was only followed by another blow to her face.

"You fuckin' slut. I hate you. I hate you," he yelled.

Carmen blacked out at the numerous punches to her face. She had survived Pierre's attack, thanks to Jay, but now, there was no one there to rescue her from him. Carmen couldn't open her eyes, yet she felt his body collapse on hers as the blows came to an end.

"I loved you," she heard him saying. "I didn't even fuck Tricia. I never cheated on you. I only told you that shit to fuck your head up."

For the first time in several minutes, Carmen opened her eyes to feel blood trickling down her face. Her eyesight was somewhat blurry, but she was able to see the tears that were streaming from his eyes.

"Carlos' father," he said. "I splattered his brains like he did my father. I let his wife wake up to seeing his head blown off." Jay shook his head, repeatedly, as he focused his attention on Carmen. "I love you, Peaches. Why did you do this to me? I don't want to kill you," he whimpered as he tightened his grip around her neck. "I have to, though. No one else can have you. We can be together forever."

Carmen knew there was nothing she could do. She was so much in a daze; she couldn't raise her arms to try and release his grip.

"This is the only way, baby. No one can have you, no one, but me."

Carmen closed her eyes, feeling as if her lungs were getting ready to collapse. His fingers tightened around her neck until she couldn't feel them anymore.

Dear Lord, I repent of my sins.

Chapter Thirty-Six

Tiara studied Carmen's face as her friend laid in the hospital bed unconscious. She had gotten to the house in the nick of time before Jay finished her off. With a bat in her hand, she had snuck up behind him, hitting him twice. While she thought he was going to turn on her, he only ran from the scene. Now, she was staring at her friend who could wake up at any second. Carmen's face was filled with big and purplish bruises while the nurses had cleaned up all the blood caused by cuts from Jay's nails.

"Has she woken up yet?" the nurse asked, peeking in from the hallway.

Tiara shook her head and looked at her hands, which had saved her friend. The doctor claimed that if she hadn't come in time, Jay would've killed her. The thought was heart-wrenching but making the phone call to Carmen's parents was far worse. They were currently on their way to Brookstone from Dallas and Tiara could only imagine what they were thinking. If anything, they were ready to press charges.

"Miss," she heard the nurse say.

Tiara looked at the nurse who was busy pointing at Carmen. At the sight of her friend's eyelids moving, Tiara stood up and went to her bedside. She grabbed Carmen's hand only to feel it move in hers.

"Some of her test results have come back," the nurse said, joining Tiara at Carmen's bed. She had a clipboard in her hand and was updating Carmen's chart. "Can you hear me, Carmen?" the nurse asked. Carmen's eyes were now fully open, and she nodded her head. "Do you know who you are?" Carmen nodded her head again. "Do you know who she is?" The nurse pointed at Tiara.

Carmen's lips parted only slightly. "Tiara Smith," she replied.

The nurse wrote down Carmen's answers on her chart. "I'm going to leave for a few minutes. Page the desk if there are any changes. I want to speak with the doctor."

Tiara nodded her head and stared at Carmen. She watched as her friend started to cry. "It's okay, girl, you're okay," Tiara told her. She squeezed Carmen's hand only so she could know she had her support.

"I'm sorry," Carmen cried. "I am so sorry."

Tiara knew what her friend was talking about. She was apologizing for sleeping with Carlos. Tiara didn't care now that she found out he was dead. "You need to get your rest."

Tiara watched as her friend's gaze turned towards the window. Tiara looked out the window as well and prayed out loud for God to heal Carmen's body, soul, and spirit. She prayed for God to give Jay a change of heart and for mercy on Carlos' soul. In addition, she prayed for forgiveness. After Carmen was admitted to the hospital, she returned to Jay's house, searching through Carmen's stuff. The only thing she needed to find was Carmen's diary. Inside of it, everything was detailed regarding Carmen's life, Carlos' operation, and where her friend hid the money she had acquired from hustling.

Using her time wisely, Tiara took all the money she had found as well as the pink diamond, which Carmen stated was hidden in the bedroom she shared with Jay. She found the keys to the Bentley and took the money from it, too. Then, she snuck to Carlos' place, praying his check from the Diamond Exchange had not been scooped up by the police. Thankfully, it hadn't. She didn't know what was coming, but she had to make sure Carmen was set. She would change everything over to her name to protect her friend. When it came to the pink diamond, she would keep it in her possession until Carmen was well enough to take it.

Not quite sure if Carmen could handle a discussion, Tiara didn't ask her any questions. Glad she hadn't, she listened as Carmen's parents came in the room. "Mr. Davenport," she shrieked. She looked at Carmen who was getting upset all over again.

"Mama," Carmen said, slowly.

Tiara watched as Patricia ran to her daughter's side.

"Tiara, can I speak with you?" Harold asked, standing in the doorway. "It will only take a second, I promise."

Tiara nodded her head and walked in the hallway with him.

"You know what I want to do right now. Look, I still know some people. They can find Jay and have him dead in minutes. All I need to know is—"

Tiara held her hands up, stopping him from talking. "Mr. Davenport, you know better than anybody that killing Jay is not going to solve the problem. Jay is going to kill himself one day. I have everything covered. Trust me on this. I have access and in my possession all of Carmen's money. Right now, we need to be supporting her and nursing her back to health. I can take care of Flame. We will continue business as normal, but you gotta keep your hands off Jay. The police and Triad are already involved because of the diamonds and the Rodriguez murders," Tiara responded, sounding like a professional.

"You better be right about this." Harold pointed his finger at Tiara before going inside Carmen's room.

"It's going to be okay, baby. Your father has a building here with an available apartment. We'll be here for a while," Patricia was saying.

"Hi," the nurse greeted, returning to the room as well. She had even more papers in her hand, which she had come to discuss. "I know this is a really emotional time. I figured since Carmen was awake, she would want to know the test results."

"I do," Carmen said, starting to cough. Her body ached and when she touched her face, it felt almost out of place. She could see her reflection in the mirror, and she had to turn away at the sight.

"You have bruises, but you are a blessed child. There wasn't any major internal damage done. Your head and back are probably sore, but that should be about it. We are going to have to keep you here for about four weeks because of the baby. We need to make sure your baby is making normal progress."

Tiara's eyes became outstretched, and she looked at Carmen.

"Baby," Carmen stammered.

"Miss Davenport, did you not know you were almost two months pregnant?" The nurse pulled out a paper from her stack and handed it to Carmen. "This is your baby," the lady said, showing her pictures of the ultrasound.

Tiara took a step back. The ultrasound must have been completed before she had gotten to the hospital. She didn't even know they had done a pregnancy test.

"This is your baby," the nurse repeated, pointing at a figure.

Tiara watched as Carmen knocked the paper out the nurse's hands.

"Ma'am, I'm sorry. I didn't know you were unaware."

"My daughter is not having a baby by that motherfucker," Patricia yelled. "She's having an abortion."

"Patricia, hold on for a minute. Just hold on," Harold said, pulling his wife out the room.

Tiara looked at Carmen. The nurse had picked up the picture and now had it resting on Carmen's bed. After hearing Patricia's outburst, the nurse had excused herself from the room.

"We're having a baby," Carmen whispered. She laid her hands on her stomach, knowing the baby belonged to Jay. She was certain the child wasn't conceived the night he went in her raw. She wasn't on birth control and had been sexually active almost every day since she'd given him her virginity. She could only assume one of his condoms had broken, which was why she was pregnant. The baby also explained why she had been vomiting. "What am I going to do with a baby, Tiara?"

"Love it," Tiara said, "but girl, do not have an abortion. If this baby is healthy and Jay didn't kill it, keep it. It is a blessing from God."

Carmen stared at her friend and looked at the picture. Inside of her was the offspring of a Santiago. Carmen wanted to curse the name, but she couldn't. She picked up the picture and stared at the baby that was growing inside of her. Jay could come at her from all angles, but she was going to protect her baby. It was the one thing she had, aside from Flame, that was worth fighting for.

Chapter Thirty-Seven

November

Carmen ended up staying six weeks in the hospital. The doctor granted her a discharge after seeing that her baby was making normal progress. It was around this time Carmen noticed her growing baby bump. Once she had squared everything away with Flame, she contacted Malik so she could share the news of her pregnancy with Jay. Although she was never close to Malik in the past, he promised to help her.

From what Malik told her, Jay had hit rock bottom. He was still working on his jewelry store but was staying low because of the warrant that had been issued for his arrest. Jay had been listed as the main suspect in the murders of Domino and Carlos Rodriguez. If convicted, he was to be charged with two counts of first degree murder as well as an attempted murder charge for his assault on her. In addition, Malik told her Jay had asked about her. He refused to give him any major details and didn't tell him about the baby.

Carmen figured Jay was hiding somewhere in his warehouse. She assumed the police were watching it like a hawk; however, whenever she drove by, there weren't any cars nearby. After contacting Malik about it, he informed her the location had moved. Jay was no longer in Brookstone. It was then Carmen announced she was ready to face him. She knew it was dangerous, but he deserved to know firsthand they were going to be parents. Malik had even promised to be there with her in case Jay tried anything. Carmen agreed to it and now was standing in front of Jay's new warehouse.

It was still in New York, but hours away from Brookstone. Malik had given her the passcode to get inside the gate and warned her that cameras were everywhere. Jay would know she was there before she saw him. Carmen became nervous as she approached the front door and even thought of Kane as she raised her fist to knock. She hadn't seen him since they were in Texas and his store had been purchased by a Vietnamese couple who had turned the space into a nail salon. Her parents hadn't heard from him either. His disappearance worried her, yet she couldn't focus on him.

A heavy-set man opened the door, inviting her to come inside. Once he closed the door behind her, Carmen stared at the numerous locks on the door. "This way," he ordered, leading her down a long hallway.

Carmen followed him, looking at the ceiling until the guard's voice caught her attention.

"Go straight down the steps. Gusto will lead you to Mr. Santiago."

Carmen did as he said, walking down the steps until she saw a Hispanic man, holding an Uzi. When she entered the room, she saw men everywhere, examining jewels. Immediately, she searched for Jay, but couldn't spot him.

"This way," Gusto directed.

Carmen followed him, seeing how big the warehouse was. She saw cars, cargo boxes, and another group of men counting money and loading weapons into boxes. Carmen wondered what Jay was planning next.

"Right there," Gusto said, pointing at Jay with his gun.

Carmen stared straight ahead and saw Jay seated on a table. A computer was right next to him where he was watching the cameras. He turned to look at her, allowing her to see the scar, which ran down the left side of his face. About to approach him, she stopped in mid-step when she felt hands on her shoulders.

"Go ahead, he's cool," Malik whispered.

Carmen nodded her head and walked towards Jay. Out the corner of her eye, she saw Malik walking away.

Jay hadn't shaved and his hair had grown out into a mini Afro. He was dressed in a pair of grey sweatpants and a white wifebeater hung tightly to his chest.

Unable to say anything, Carmen stared at him in silence. She remembered when she first met him. His hazel eyes had captured her from the moment she laid eyes on him. She remembered the first night she dreamed about him and the night he killed Pierre. Then, she saw an image of the first time they made love.

Carmen stood there for what felt like forever. She got ready to speak, but the sound of sirens fluttered in her ears. She watched as Jay jumped from the table, grabbing her. He held her tightly to his chest until Carmen heard a loud bang. She turned her head to see half of the warehouse caving in. Men, dressed in all black, rushed in the warehouse from all over. A raid was now in progress, which meant the search for Jay was over.

She looked at him, using her eyes to trace the scar on his face. Before she could speak, he pushed her behind him as if he was trying to protect her. His hands then became filled with an Uzi. He held it out in front of him, pointing at the men who were running towards them. However, he didn't fire.

"Put the gun down, Santiago. You're cornered from all angles," she heard someone yell. Several men ran towards them, encircling them both.

"Put the fuckin' gun down," one of the agents ordered.

Carmen's heart was beating fast. She watched as one of the men put his gun to Jay's head.

"Put the motherfuckin' gun down, bitch." The man cocked the gun, pushing it into Jay's temple.

Carmen watched as the Uzi fell from Jay's hands, hitting the floor with a thud. Another agent rushed up behind him, grabbing Jay's arms, and handcuffing him. Carmen opened her mouth, knowing she had to tell him before they took him away. One agent was even reading Jay his rights.

"I'm pregnant," she told him. She said it loud, making sure he heard her over the madness. "I'm having a baby and it's yours," she continued. "I'm three months." She watched as he turned around, looking at her with a solemn expression on his face.

"Pregnant," he mouthed.

"I'm pregnant, Jay," she repeated.

She pulled her dress tightly to her stomach so he could see her baby bump. She watched as he narrowed his eyes. "Jay, don't," she said, seeing him trying to wiggle out the handcuffs. She watched as he tried to fight the cops using his body as a weapon and they struck him down binding his legs. She knew he was only going to get in even worse trouble if he continued to fight them.

Carmen looked at the agents that surrounded her. She turned around full circle, watching as each one of Jay's men was handcuffed. She searched for Malik but didn't see him. She didn't know where he was or if he had already been handcuffed and taken in. When she looked at Jay, she noticed he was staring at her.

"Take care of my baby," he said to her once they put him on his feet. "You better take care of my fuckin' baby," he yelled.

They held him up in front of her and started repeating his rights to him again since she interrupted them with her news.

"Good job, Mike," she heard one of the agents say.

Carmen looked in the direction the voice had come from. She saw one of the agents take off his mask. He was a white man with a balding hairline and thick mustache. She blinked her eyes and watched as the man he was talking to took off his mask. He was the man who had put his gun to Jay's temple. Carmen felt hands grab her, but her body stood frozen. She watched as the man raised his head to hers. She then felt the cold steel of handcuffs being put on her arms as her rights started being read. Carmen couldn't believe she was being arrested until the man behind her said she was being charged with theft—for stealing the Pink Sunrise diamond. Carmen couldn't move. She felt herself becoming sick as she stared Kane in the face.

"Move them out," the agent said, pulling her out Kane's view.

###

www.ingramcontent.com/pod-product-compliance
Lightning Source LLC
Chambersburg PA
CBHW020729210626
46807CB00016B/506